THE CAPO'S DAUGHTER

J. R. FILLAN

R
BOOKS

This Edition
Rampart Books

ISBN 978-1-915778-87-1

Rampart Paperback

To Lisa, Fae, Tom and Alice

And my thanks to those who kindly read and commented on this book, Lorna Read, Andrew N. Taylor, Lisa Gilfillan and especially to my tireless agent, Leslie Gardiner

THE CAPO'S DAUGHTER

PART I

1

London, 1978

Somewhere overlooking the muddy swell of the river in East London, a man in yellow-tinted, aviator-style glasses and a sheepskin coat approached a pair of chained wooden doors and turned a key in a padlock.

It had rained overnight, and as the heavy chains fell away and the big doors swung open, his patterned socks and brown shoes became spotted with oily water. He peered up and down the disused track and checked his watch.

From far down the river came the blast of a ship's horn, strangely muted now that the merchantmen no longer docked on the island.

The man slid open the cargo door of a white van, checked its contents and slid it shut. Then he opened the driver's door, got in, turned over the engine, checked the fuel gauge and got out. He looked at his watch again and began to curse.

He walked up and down the yard in front of the doors and around the van, waiting for other men to fuck everything up for him.

The Mini Cooper swung into the yard and buried itself

in the darkness of the back of the garage, too quickly for the man to see the occupants, who would of course be Patrick, Desmond, Charlie and Don Garbutt. Malc wasn't with them; he'd be getting into position about now.

They had been a nice little team when they started out and had done two Midland Bank jobs without getting pulled and without anyone squealing.

They all knew their roles, and most of their blags had run like clockwork. Leslie chose the wheels the night before. It was no good telling him you wanted a Daimler or a Jag. You were lucky if he got you an Escort, sometimes opting for a Volvo, which wouldn't look out of place on a school run, or a van that had room for everything.

"You don't need a motor you can't catch; you need one you can't see," he'd told them.

Behind the wheel, Malc was an ace. That heart-stopping bump as the car mounted the pavement right outside the target, then Malc would slam on the anchors, and everyone else would bundle out.

Patrick kept the door while they pulled on their ski masks and charged into the bank.

In the old days, Charlie and Don would be over the counter with their shopping bags before the cashiers knew what had hit them, customers eating carpet as the frightener waved his sawn-off. It wasn't often that Desmond had to blow a hole in the ceiling before they got the message.

Leslie, tapping his watch, calling out, "Let's go, let's go!" had liked to think he ran that team.

Patrick had said, "Let him think what he fucking likes."

Now, even Leslie was having his doubts.

"What time do you call this?"

Four tall men unbent themselves from the confines of the tiny car. Desmond, Patrick, Charlie and that kid who was always hanging around, Peter Wilson.

"And what's he doing here? Where's Don?"

"In hospital. Doreen says his appendix went in the night. So, we're giving Peter his chance."

"Giving him his chance? What do you think this is, *Opportunity Knocks?* We know fuck-all about him."

"He's keen. He's got a shooter, too."

"Has he? What's on your tally card, Peter?"

"I did that post office in Ilford last year. It was on the news."

"What did you take with you?"

"This."

The boy, toothy, nervous, Rod Stewart hair, opened his faux-leather safari jacket.

"Oh, for fuck's sake. How old is that?"

"It's my uncle's. He's got a farm in Essex."

"Then it'll be licensed. It can be traced."

"He never got this one licensed. I know that for a fact."

"You sure? Well, I hope you know how to use it."

"Course."

Charlie, always buzzing before a job, said, "Are we sorted, then?"

"Just a mo. I don't like the equipment. Where's Don's weapon?"

"Must have stashed it somewhere."

"Tell you what, give the gun to Desmond. At least we know what he can do."

Desmond said he wasn't going out with a shooter like that.

"Oh, for fuck's sake. Alright. Everyone in the van, suit up as we go. We're against the clock."

2

Later that day, and eight miles to the west of the Isle of Dogs, a double-decker bus was making slow progress up King's Road. Umbrellas had popped up, and bareheaded walkers were skittering between the cars and taxis, seeking shelter from doorways or a bus signed for Sloane Square.

Juliet Hobson took the stairs two at a time and dumped herself by the window, two rows from the front. She closed her eyes while passengers clomped up the stairs and spread themselves among the vacant seats.

Behind her was the rasp of a striking match, a bright flame in the dark glass, and for a moment, she was enveloped in an exhalation of blue smoke.

The diesel growled; standing passengers lurched as first gear was engaged. The seat gave a slight bounce as someone sat down beside her. She took a deep breath of the smoke-laden air and settled back.

The bus began to make some headway.

Dazzling shop windows slipped by and into her thoughts. Startling furniture, wild fabrics, crazy lights. Did Gerry and Maureen know such places existed? Obviously not, or they wouldn't be so cock-proud of their G-Plan dining table and matching teak-and-glass wall unit, whose only sitting tenants were some bull-fighting figurines from Magaluf, a tray of cocktail glasses and a pristine set of *Reader's Digest* condensed classics.

This street, these houses, there was big money here. Where the fuck did people get it?

It was like that school outing where they'd been bussed out to a stately home. One of the kids had said, "Was the owner dead rich, Miss?" and Mrs Smith had said, "Richer than you can possibly imagine and the money all came from sugar and spice."

Someone else said, "And all things nice, Miss?" and Mrs Smith had paused.

Then she said, "No, not really. They couldn't make this kind of money without using people as slaves. African people."

Mrs Smith had looked at her like she was the only black kid on the bus. She had never forgotten that.

Some party at the rear of the bus was chanting, *God save the Queen, the fascist regime.*

"Any more fares, people, any more for anymore?"

The conductor parted lank, greasy hair to ask her if she wasn't cold in a little skirt like that before dropping her coins into his leather bag, whirring out a ticket for Clapham Junction and swinging down the bus to negotiate with the vocal contingent at the back.

She could not go on like this. She was thinking, living like a magpie in that beige box with two people who couldn't give a monkey's about her and their Colin, whom she avoided like the plague.

Fucking Colin. There was something wrong with him these days. There had always been, but this was different.

He'd stopped tormenting her in the way he used to when they were kids—a vicious pinch under the tea-table or an air gun pellet that smacked her in the cheek by accident, as Colin told his dad. When he hadn't been physically hurting her, he was calling her names in front of his friends, all the obvious, hurtful ones.

Now he only gave her looks which she couldn't read; she waited for it all to start again. As a kid, she'd put up with this just as she put up with the chauvinistic, bigoted crap and worse that she got from Gerry's associates, all because no-one had told her that there was an alternative life that she was entitled to.

Somewhere out there in the darkness was her real father. Down the river, the Albert Bridge was lit up like a Christmas tree.

3

Over his shoulder, Desmond said, "He still with us?"

"I'm not a fucking doctor! Eyes up in his head somewhere."

"Slap him. Bring him round."

"Never mind him, watch the fucking road, Malc!"

The job had been a monumental fuck -up. And now they were getting away nothing to show for it but Charlie's bellyful of lead shot.

"Where now? Give me fucking directions!"

"Left at the end there. Down to the junction. Then sharp right."

"Is he going to be all right?"

"Left! Left! Now step on it."

"I don't fucking know. He's very fucking wet."

"Check his pupils."

"I didn't bring a fucking torch. Charlie, mate! Can you hear me? I think his ticker's still beating."

"Don't you worry, Charlie, we've got you."

"Railway bridge. Slow down."

"Fuck off. Charlie needs sorting."

"Malc..."

"What the fuck was that?"

"The bridge."

"Jesus, Malc, you're not fucking Eddie Kidd. Keep the wheels on the road."

"Are you driving now?"

"This is doing Charlie no fucking good."

"Well, fuck me, it's just a suggestion, but maybe you shouldn't have shot him."

"It's an old shotgun. The trigger..."

"You can tell all that to Jewels. I'm fucked if I will. I don't know. It's like they were waiting for us."

"School crossing. Slow, slow! Nice and easy here."

"It wasn't my fault. Someone knocked into the shooter. I'm sorry, Charlie."

"Old Bill down by the lights. Two candy cars."

"Seen us?"

"Don't think so."

"Take this left. Slowly. Pat, get your fucking head down."

"All right. Slow enough?"

"Head fucking down, Patrick."

"There's blood fucking everywhere. Christ, the seats are sticky with it."

"Shut up, Patrick."

"Can you see anything?

"No. Yes. One of them just turned the corner."

"Are they on to us?"

"Don't know just yet. Don't do anything stupid."

"Can we outrun the bastards?"

"We'll fucking try."

"Hold it. Hold it. He's turned off. After some other fucker."

"Then get us to the London fast. He's not good."

"They'll be waiting for us at the London Hospital as well."

"He needs attention now, Les. It'll have to be King's then. Camberwell."

"Same fucking difference. They'll have all the local A&Es marked. We'll have a chance at Croydon."

"Croydon? That's fucking miles. I don't think he'll make it."

"Course he will. Back roads. Bermondsey. Brixton, Streatham High Road."

"Charlie! Charlie, mate. You're going to be all right, you hear me?"

4

The tall, narrow townhouse with the little square of gravel out front where Gerry parked his car was just across the busy ring-road from Wandsworth Common.

Gerry's Capri was missing, but she could see Maureen in the front-room mirror dabbing her lipstick with a tissue. She had on her new tan coat with its matching bag slung over a shoulder; she would have been disappointed to hear she still looked all of her 46 years.

Juliet slid her key into the Yale, activating an "*Is that you?*" called from within. Maureen had thrown open the living room door before Juliet was halfway up the stairs. The *Crossroads* theme was trilling from the blue-lit, smoky room behind, where she could see the back of Colin's close-cropped skull as he slumped in an armchair, booted legs dangling from the armrest.

Maureen looked flushed. "Mum's not well again," she said, as a car-horn pipped outside. She checked her auburn hair in the hall mirror before fastening the belt of her coat. "That's the minicab. Make Colin something for tea, won't you? He'll live on cereal otherwise. Gerry's out. You won't forget to do the dishes and feed the cat? I'll probably be back late, might even have to stay over; you never know. So don't wait up, either of you."

And she was gone, slamming the door behind her. Outside, tyres crunched on gravel and the car moved off.

On the upstairs landing, she stopped and listened.

Floating up the stairs came the roar of a football crowd and the faint hiss as a ring-pull separated from a beer can. She waited a moment longer, just to be sure that Colin was settled in for the evening. He could get himself something to eat, the lazy cunt.

Shrugging off her coat, Juliet dropped her bag on the floor. The place was as she'd left it. She was fairly sure of that. She'd be more certain if she were allowed a key to her own room, but even Colin didn't get one of those. Locked rooms were fire risks, Gerry said, and according to Maureen, Gerry knew "all there was to bloody know" about fire risks.

Sitting on the bed, she turned on the portable black-and-white TV set. Someone she had never heard of was accepting a big book from Eamonn Andrews. Then, above the noise of the studio audience clapping, came abrasive shouting from the bottom of the stairs.

"Oi, Li-let! Li-Li-Let!"

"What do you want?"

"Nice to get some dinner before kick-off, if it's not too much trouble?"

"Fuck off," she breathed. Didn't she have enough to do around this place without Colin treating her like a bloody servant? Maureen left the housework to her, and she did it all in one go on Sundays, Cinderella with an old upright Hoover and a feather duster.

The ironing alone took the best part of the morning, and all this while Gerry played football on the Common; Maureen lingered over her breakfast dishes and *The News of the World.* Well, that was your life, she thought, if you didn't have parents of your own.

She'd turned up the television's volume to compete with the set downstairs, so Juliet didn't hear the tread of Colin's boots on the thick stair carpet.

The door swung inwards to frame a black Fred Perry polo and a pair of blue 501s hitched with a pair of red braces. Colin's weaselly white face, pupils the colour of toilet cleaner, wore that insufferable sneer.

"Oh, so sorry, *Sis*," he said, stepping into the room and looking about him like this was his first visit. "I didn't know you were *resting*. Christ, what a shithole. Don't you ever tidy up?"

"What do you want?"

"I want my fucking dinner, if it's not too much trouble for your ladyship?"

"Can't you just get it yourself for once? I've had a hard day."

"*You've* had a hard day, Lil-let?"

He sat down next to her, close enough for spittle to fleck her cheek as he said, "*You* try dealing with those cunts down the Social. How would *you* like to wait two hours to be treated like a lump of shit? And where were you? Up west, in your nice, warm shop. You should be grateful, very grateful. Well, you can serve this customer now, I'm hungry. How about getting that little arse of yours off this bed and sorting me some dinner?"

Colin was always obnoxious, but something new in his tone made her wary. She wanted to get away from him, but not at the expense of doing his bidding. She carried on staring at the TV screen, seeing only a grey blur. For a moment, he did nothing. She was unprepared for what he did next. Inching his body closer to hers, old bedsprings whining, he slipped a hand on her thigh and whispered, "Unless you'd rather, you know, stay here with me?"

She pulled off his hand as if this were some minor irritation, not an unprecedented assault. Heart thumping, mind racing, she tried to pretend she hadn't heard what he'd said, hadn't felt his grip tighten on her leg. She started to rise from the bed, but a big hand pushed her back against the wall with L.O.V.E. tattooed between the knuckles.

"What do you want?"

She was trying desperately not to sound shocked and frightened.

"What do I want? What do I *want*?"

He gave her one last push, so violent that her head knocked loudly against the wall, then stood up. He was unsteady, his face a raspberry red.

"Are you deaf or something?"

He tried an awkward laugh.

"I told you what I want, you coffee-coloured bitch. I want my *fucking dinner*."

5

On the Isle of Dogs, Julius Nicholson waited beside a phone box, a shock of red against a black and white world of corrugated iron fencing and rusting cranes.

He lit and smoked a cigarette and facing away from the corruption at his back, he kept watch over the water. When the telephone emitted a muffled jangling, he turned and, heaving open the door, picked up the receiver.

The tinny voice rattled on a bit, then it said, "Looked like a set-up".

Jesus Christ, he thought.

The voice said, "We rolled him out on the forecourt easy as we could and fucked off out of it. Things were too hot." Now, more shrilly: "Jewels, you there? Are you hearing this?"

He grunted.

The voice said, "He's at Croydon. We've told Gillian. She'll be calling the hospital. We'll have the full SP then." The voice waited for him to say something. Stupid fuck. And when he didn't: "It was like they knew we was coming. We stuck to the game plan, I swear. Parked the Tranny opposite Gaskell's bang on time. Malc's in place with a borrowed Granada. We had all the gear, overalls, brushes, painters on a smoke break, yeah? About half past, we clock the Datsun with the guard and the wages girl coming back from the bank. Their security van was still out of action, like I told you it would be. So, Peter's behind Charlie, me and Desmond, and he's got the shooter. One squirt in the sky, and that would have been it. Jewels? You still there?"

"Just."

"So Malc pulls out from where he's parked and cuts off the Datsun at the factory gate. We pile in, Patrick and me on the passenger side, Charlie and Peter, who'd come in Don's place, banging on the driver's door and waving the shooter."

"Where's Desmond?"

"I don't know. Couldn't see him. But the stupid cow won't open the door. Next thing we know, there's blues and twos at the top of the street, steaming our way. Out of fucking nowhere. I don't know what happened next. I think Charlie panicked, knocked into Peter, fucking gun went off. Charlie caught it."

"So?"

"So, we had to abort. Me and Peter grabbed Charlie and shoved him into the Granada."

"The filth?"

"Stopped dead by a demolition lorry backing out the yard across the way, thank fuck."

"Then?"

"Took Charlie to Croydon."

"The van?"

"Ross Brown was waiting for us. He'll have torched it by now. I did the Granada myself. I'm telling you, we was fucking lucky."

"Charlie wasn't. Will he talk?"

"Talk? I won't lie to you, Jewels. Charlie's in a bad way."

"I need to think about this," he said.

We were lucky? One man down and not a penny to show?

They wouldn't have called that lucky in his day. *Looked like a set-up?* If the Old Bill had been tipped off, they'd have blocked both escape routes, not one.

On balance, it didn't *sound* like a stitch-up.

That said, he still couldn't reason away the unsettling feeling that welled in his stomach or the sudden tightness he felt in his chest. Chadwick or Adams with a man in his camp didn't bear thinking about, not after all that had gone on lately.

Dropping the receiver into its cradle, he opened the heavy door as a catapulted missile cracked one of the windows with a resounding smack. The boys who had fired it were already pedalling away, long hair flying behind them like ships' pennants.

The kitchen was just as he'd left it, of course.

Blue-speckled bread spilling from a *Wonderloaf* wrapper, dishes piled in the sink, whisky glasses and heaped ashtrays on the breakfast bar.

Ignoring the sickly odour when he opened the fridge, he took a swig from a carton of milk before carrying it into the living room.

The empty bottles of Johnny Walker and crumpled beer cans were still lined up on the coffee table. He'd meant to do something about them yesterday.

Julius Nicholson took off his jacket, loosened his tie and wondered where to start. He couldn't recall how the mirror behind the little corner bar had broken. He looked broken himself, he thought as he peered into the glass, pallid skin sagging on a blue face that had once been as taut as his frame had been lean, thick hair already streaked with grey.

The rest of the room was just as it was when it all wound

down and people had staggered off to find a bed or to drive home, the silly fucks.

Picking up a couple of LP records, he returned them to their sleeves, then changed his mind and loaded one onto the turntable, hurriedly turning down the volume as the speakers buzzed too brightly with *Be Bop A Lula.* Christ, they must have made a noise that night.

It hadn't even been planned. There were just five of them there to discuss a little business and make a few plans.

Then a bottle of whisky had been magicked. Someone told him it was his birthday, and someone else said why not get the girls over and then every fucker in East London seemed to be there. People who shouldn't be seen together. Faces from Poplar and Hackney. People he hadn't seen since the other side of a five stretch, even. The Sweeney would have had a field day. He was forty-nine. He wasn't fucking retiring.

He'd make a couple of calls, see how Charlie was doing.

"I need to get things straight," he told the line of whisky bottles. "I need to get things straight."

When the voice in his head replied, he stifled a laugh. I know, Kath, I know, he said, I could start with this fucking room. He began to clear away the bottles into the bin bag.

The party had been a dropping of his guard, and he didn't like it.

"The status quo around here is a fragile thing," he'd declared, eliding his words as he stabbed a forefinger at his guests. "Its maintenance being entirely dependent on certain conditions being met. Keep it *quiet,* say the neighbours. Keep what you do *off our patch*, say the plod, and *we'll see*. That's the way of it."

The larch-clad, architect-designed property with integral garage had been bought with scrupulously washed money a seemly time after the noisy Clerkenwell raid, although he'd told Kath it was excess revenue from the betting shops and some houses he'd turned into a honeycomb of flats in Notting Hill.

They had taken the show home, as seen, with all the fixtures and fittings. "It's too posh for us," Kath had whispered when the agent left them to complete the viewing on their own. "Who on the Island has a house like this?"

The phone rang, breaking the silence that had been settling on the place since he'd taken off the record.

"No, no, I don't want to hear it. Shut up. What have I told you. No calls here."

And hung up. Stupid cunts. You couldn't tell them these days. That was the problem: a lack of discretion; they couldn't keep quiet. Thirty years he'd been in the game, and only six months of that inside. *Six months.* And why? Because he was careful. Self-reliant.

Because he never completely trusted any fucker.

He'd trusted Charlie as far as it went, earmarking him as his right-hand man in the not-too-distant future, but a discharged shotgun had changed the game entirely. What a fucking mess.

Now it was the doorbell. He peeked through the front window.

"You shouldn't be here, Leslie," he said. He looked down the street, kids knocking a ball around, and some dogs. "Not now. This is too warm."

Leslie stepped in and closed the door behind him.

"I had to let you know. Charlie's dead."

He bit his lip, nodded, apparently distracted by Leslie's appearance, the loudly checked suit with wide lapels, the fatly knotted tie, the amber-tinted specs.

"All right. Send my whatnots to Gillian. Tell her we'll make the arrangements through another party. Tell her we'll t-take care of her."

He hadn't stuttered in weeks, months, maybe.

"What now?"

"Clean this up, Leslie. All of it. Make sure Browny did the Granada proper, get an eyeball on it yourself, if you can. Then see the others on the QT. Make bloody sure they've got their stories sorted. How's your own?"

"I was at home watching the Hammers-Bristol game with Queenie."

"Score?"

"Two to us. Scorers, Brooking and Robson."

"Queenie's sound?"

"You know she is."

"Alright. Tell the others to lie low. Nobody makes any fuss. Life goes on as normal. And I don't need to tell you that nobody breathes a fucking syllable about any of this. Have you got me, Leslie?"

"You can trust me, Jewels," the other man said, closing the door carefully behind him. Julius watched the orange Escort drive off, his heart jumping like a jackhammer, breath coming short and fast.

He told himself it was okay; he just needed a little time to get things straight, get everything back on the rails, and calm the fuck down.

He dropped heavily into his armchair, knocking bottles onto the carpet as he crashed his scuffed brogues onto the coffee table.

The dizziness was back. *You have angina*, Mr Nicholson, Dr Ahmed had told him. *You cannot carry on the way you have been doing if you have angina.* Alright, you win, he thought. I'll get an appointment, sort this lot out, next week, maybe. Or the following.

And he'd do something about the girl, he decided at last, as his eyes closed.

He awoke to a moment of whirling confusion.

He couldn't make sense of what he was seeing. Had he imagined the party, the blitzed room?

The place was now tidy, everything in its place, *neat as a pin*, as Kath used to say. He half-expected her to walk in the door and ask him if he wanted fish pie for supper.

The standard lamp in the corner had been switched on; dusk was gathering. He sat still, waiting for the penny to drop, for everything to make sense. There was a noise, a door closing quietly. He stood up too quickly, and it was a second or two before he had his bearings again. He listened, but there was nothing, only the muffled yapping of the house next door's Pomeranian. You're hearing things, he told himself. Certain he was right, he was slow to notice the door behind him begin to open. He swung round.

"You," he said.

6

In SW18, the uneasy accommodations that the Hobsons made for each other were being disturbed once more by the girl who was now noisily washing the dishes. Maureen Hobson cut her toast into triangles and returned to her *Daily Mail.*

"I've told you before, so why go on about it? You're like a broken record sometimes."

Wiping her hands on a dish towel, Juliet turned and stood behind Maureen, close enough to read the article monopolising her attention.

"My mother sold cigarettes. In a club? And she died having me? Is that really all you can tell me?"

"Yes, and it would be nice to have a little peace with my breakfast, Julie. And some space."

"You haven't even told me her name, for God's sake."

Maureen dropped her knife with a clatter.

"You mind your language, young lady! Whatever's the matter with you? I've told you, Gerry's the one to speak to, not me. I've no secrets to keep. Now, let that be an end to it."

"Which club did she work at, then? Surely you can tell me that much?"

"Go and get dressed, Julie. You'll be late for work."

But Juliet stayed where she was, breathing down her neck, as Maureen would describe the moment to Gerry.

"I've no idea where the club was, and that's the God's honest truth. It was up west somewhere. Soho, I think. And that's more than I should be saying. Gerry hit the roof when he heard what I'd told you last time."

"I'm 18 years old. I have a right to know. I don't understand. I never have."

"What is there to understand? It's all water under the bridge now. It's not like they were parents to you, not in any real sense. You've always lived here, with us."

"And my dad? What about *his* name? I won't tell Gerry."

"Leave it be, Juliet. It's better for everyone this way, believe you me."

"Is he even still alive?"

Maureen sighed and closed her paper.

"I don't know. What's the matter with you? A roof over your head and all your meals? I knew children in your position..."

"There's more to a family than that. Or so I've heard."

"Is there? You'd count yourself very lucky if you had that much when the war was on. What I can't understand is why this is so important to you all of a sudden?"

Juliet said nothing. You couldn't tell someone like Maureen that their little boy had sexually assaulted you in your bedroom. As you couldn't tell her that Fat Larry, one of Gerry's so-called *clients,* had tried to touch you when you showed him down to his office. Useless, voicing your awful suspicions about what had happened to Fat Larry only last night, because you know that's all they are, suspicions. And no good at all telling her you'd finally had your fill of this stifling and loveless house.

Instead, Juliet said, "Where is my birth certificate?"

"I don't know if we ever had that. If we did, Gerry..."

"I need to know who I am. It's my right."

Gerry's blue jacket was draped over a kitchen chair. Maureen fished in a pocket and extracted a pack of cigarettes. She waved it at Juliet.

"Do you want one... I won't tell Gerry."

"All I want is to know about my parents. Do you know what I dream of every night? What I dreamed about when I was at school? While I was serving customers in that cafe, the ones who treated me like a lump of shit?"

"No, of course I don't. And please, Juliet, do watch your language."

"It's always been the same dream. I dream that one day my dad'll come here and take me away. I still do."

Maureen lit her cigarette, blew out the match and took a deep pull. She looked through the kitchen window out towards the Common, where a man was flying a kite with his little girl.

She said, "I dream my premium bonds will come up, but they never do."

At the King's Road shop where Juliet worked, there were times mid-week when it was empty, but Saturdays were crazy.

Then, the place filled with weekend punks and suburban wannabes up west to buy the latest look and strike a rebellious pose under the pink PINZ sign, which glowed above the blood-red doorway. It didn't hurt that rock stars and curious celebrities took peeks inside, too. It was all money in the bank for Chas Evans, who owned the punk fashion shop and also the small record label that ran out of its back room.

For the next hour of this slow Wednesday afternoon, customers and time-wasters came and eventually went. Juliet dealt with a troublemaker demanding a refund for a shirt he'd obviously trashed on a good night out, surprising herself by telling him that actually, he could fuck right off.

And then they were in the doldrums again. Ammo restocked some rails and warned Juliet about the various dodges of the shoplifting crowd. She listened and didn't tell her she had used smarter ones when she had gone on the rob in the Arndale when she was 12 or 13.

She'd swung the job on account of her turnout, Ammo reckoned. "That, or those amazing green eyes."

At the interview, she'd worn a spangly green lurex dress over yellow tights and a scuffed pair of purple Kickers, crimson plastic earrings dangling beneath braided hair she'd accessorised with turquoise beads. The ensemble owed much to Ammo's own style. Today, the Scots girl's tight, bleach-blonde curls were stuffed under an old red beret stuck with little tin badges. An olive-green army jacket, vintage charity-shop skirt, big, blue-beaded necklace and red-painted Doc Marts completed her get-up.

But even if her own look was right, Juliet sometimes thought, wasn't it also possible that this wilfully contrary venture had hired her just because she was black?

Two men, jarringly out of place in their suits and ties, stood in the doorway as if undecided about coming in.

"Spot the virgin," Ammo said, nodding at three youths who were hovering around a display of bondage wear. All three wore new motorcycle jackets and uniformly rebellious T-shirts.

Juliet said, "All of them. Obviously."

They were coming to know each other's humour and to play off it. Were they friends? Juliet wasn't sure. Maybe there were good reasons why she hadn't been invited back to Ammo's squat, which was just across the river, or so she said.

The squat must be a real shithole; no-one else at PINZ had been invited there, either. Juliet didn't care. *I'm happy here*, she confided to Ammo after work one cool evening. *I didn't know I could be that.*

The two men who now stepped tentatively into the shop didn't look remotely like the usual PINZ clientele.

Ammo gave her a nudge. "D.S.?" she whispered. Juliet had already encountered the Met's drug squad outside the Marquee one night when some supposed dealers were being handled roughly.

She watched the men as they moved uncertainly about the room, aliens in this environment, looking at this and that, mostly not looking at Ammo or herself, although she thought the stockier one stole a quick glance when he felt they weren't being watched.

They were dressed straight as rulers. The tall, stocky one in the well-cut blue suit had a boxer's face going to flab around blue jowls which began under a pair of big Michael Caine specs; he rested his weight on a silver-topped walking stick.

The other man was smaller, baby-faced and some years younger, with long sideburns matching the head of wild red hair, which strayed over the collar of an ill-fitting, fawn two-piece. This younger man browsed, feeling this fabric or picking up that garment while the older man watched.

Juliet could hear the older man muttering, "Funny old place this, funny old place."

The police she'd encountered weren't like that. "*Pervs?*" she whispered to Ammo.

People who didn't like to buy their straps and collars in sex shops were sometimes happier getting their fetish clobber here.

"Uh-uh," Ammo said. "This is something else. Dunno what, though."

The men were conferring in low voices by the door.

And now the shorter man approached the counter, clacking his heels on the black-painted floorboards. He leaned over a little and said to Ammo, "I wonder, Miss, is your guvnor in?"

"He's in a meeting," Ammo said.

Best to be careful when you didn't know what you were dealing with, Juliet thought.

"It's just that we'd rather like to see him."

"If you were to make an appointment?" Ammo suggested.

"Can we ask what this is about?" That was Juliet. Neither of them much liked Chas, but there was something in the man's tone which raised their hackles.

"*My* guvnor." The man jerked a thumb over his shoulder. "Isn't the sort who makes appointments. Not as a rule. You do understand me?"

Ammo stepped back, out of the space the man had invaded.

"Well, can I ask who wants to see him?" she said.

"So, he *is* in there?" He nodded at the door, which was plastered with flyers for bands on the PINZ label.

The other man was watching this interchange, but he glanced sometimes at Juliet.

"Yes, but like I said, he's in a meeting just now. If you leave your number..."

"Oh, I rather think he'll see us now," said the little man in such a decided way that she turned on her heel and went into the back room, smartly followed by the insistent little man.

Juliet waited at the counter.

The stocky one appeared now to be glancing out the shop window, watching the world go by.

When a young girl and a boy, all spots and spikes, pushed open the door, he blocked their way. His broad back was to Juliet, so she could only guess what persuaded the young couple to continue their shopping somewhere else.

"Fucking hell," she breathed.

Another moment, some noises behind the door, and the little man reappeared, signalling to the other.

"Excuse me, my dear," Juliet heard him said as he brushed past her and went into the back room.

Juliet and Ammo listened at the door. A voice was raised, just once.

They could hear Chas now, stripped of the public-school assurance that underlay his affected cockney tones. Some nervous laughter. That was Chas, all right.

Then some more mumbling and minutes later, the voice of the little man said, "Righty-right, all done!" and the door opened.

With one last look and a "Thank you, ladies," from the older man, they left.

Chas slammed shut his door.

When Ammo looked in to see if he wanted her to pop up the road for his cappuccino, he told her to fuck off and get out.

Just when they needed time for conjecture, the shop got busy again. Ammo and Juliet were on the bus before they'd had a chance to talk about the incident. What the hell had *that* all been about?

"I'm fucked if I know. I really am," Ammo said, pulling a crumpled pack of *Silk Cut* from a pocket. "Chas, I suppose. He's had his finger in a few sticky pies. Dodgy recording contracts. Unpaid suppliers. Who knows?"

"They could have been debt collectors?"

"It's not impossible. Fucking Chas. I hope he doesn't get us shut down."

"Or maybe it's his taxes?"

Ammo laughed, loudly enough for the school kids seated in front to turn and stare.

"Aye, well, you never know," she said as she flicked open her Zippo. "But they didn't look like the fucking Inland Revenue to me."

7

"How'd you get in?" Julius Nicholson asked.

The other man shook his head as he peered through the net curtains, hazel eyes following an ancient Thames barge which was tacking its way up the river, red sails cutting through the grey, evening drizzle.

"You had me a key cut. I rather thought you would remember that."

He'd forgotten. Must have been three, maybe four years ago, when Kath still had Dexy, the messy terrier. When he still had Kath. He'd made a pass at her on a soul night at the 100 Club on Oxford Street, having been dragged there by Chisel and his mates. Establishing that she too lived on the Isle of Dogs sealed the deal. No way was she going to put 'Sexy Dexy' in kennels while they went off to Magaluf.

"I couldn't relax on a sunbed, thinking of him banged up in kennels," she'd said.

"What else can we do with him? We can't take him with us."

But Kath remained firm. She wasn't bloody going to Magaluf unless Dexy was properly sorted. Fed twice and exercised three times every day.

"Fuck me," he'd said, laughing. "Even I don't get that kind of treatment."

The dog would need a minder, which made it a matter of trust again. It was always about trust. Who could he trust to do his books, keep their trap shut, and babysit some moody gear? Now it was a matter of who could he trust to look after the dog? Correction, who could he trust in his house? You never knew what some nosy bastard might turn up.

He tried to keep things tidy. Of course, he did.

He stored the ultra-sensitive stuff, the accounts, receipts, little black books and so on down at the lock-up he rented in someone else's name.

But there was still stuff he hadn't been too clever about up in the loft or papers which sometimes turned up misfiled among the vet's bills and receipts for household maintenance.

He'd have a proper sort out, and soon.

Years ago, there would have been no problem. "I'll look after the dog, no sweat," Chisel would have said. "He likes that pedigree stuff, doesn't he? And I'll stick him in the motor and give him a proper run down the Mudchute."

He'd trusted Chisel right up to the time when he stopped trusting him; when he saw him now, it was always on business and only business. There was no chit-chat, no banter, not now. Talk about going back a long way with someone. They had been inseparable since they were kids, partners in crime, his mum had called them.

Well, all good things, he thought...

So that had left Carrot. Carrot did what he was told, and while he was a bit odd in some ways, he was willing; there was no doubt about that.

He couldn't quite remember when Carrot had joined the firm. He'd always been there, it seemed, in the pub, on the edge of conversations, chipping in sometimes but usually just smiling, looking agreeable, waiting to be given something, anything, to do.

By the time they went away again, he'd got him a key cut. It was easier that way.

When they returned from Magaluf, brown as berries, there were no signs he'd been in any of his or Kath's drawers, and the dog looked no worse for the experience.

He wasn't Chisel, though, who would sort stuff before he knew it needed sorting and not even tell him if he didn't need to be hassled by it.

Chisel had been his wingman for longer than he could remember and a schoolmate before that. But that was all history. Fuck all that. Now he trusted Carrot.

Up to a point.

"Did you do all…?" he waved a hand over the tidy room, where the empties and all the other crap had been stacked up, waiting to be cleared away.

"Someone was sick behind the sofa," Carrot said.

"I thought there was a whiff. Kitchen?"

"Sorted. I heard what happened to poor old Charlie. Awful business, awful."

"Yeah."

"Will we be in attendance at the funeral?"

"They'll be watching, seeing who turns up. If they don't know Charlie was one of ours, we don't want to tell them."

"So, private, do, down the pub some other time?"

"Exactly. There'll be a meet at Sol's Snooker to discuss arrangements."

"But what if they have joined the dots? What if any of our crew gets pulled in? I wonder, can we trust them not to spill their guts?"

"They know what happens to people who do," Julius said.

"Not to everyone," Carrot ventured.

"Meaning what?"

"I don't mean anything, Julius. Only I think we need to be prepared for all eventualities. With that in mind, I took a bit of a liberty while you were gone. I hope I did the right thing."

"What sort of liberty?"

"After a noisy job like that, the vandals might be at our gates at any time. So, I had a peek in your desk."

"You did what?"

Carrot took a step backwards.

"Safety precaution, Julius. There was stuff there that wouldn't do anyone any good if the Old Bill searched the place."

"*Was* stuff there?"

"I hope I didn't overstep the mark, but I put a lot of that stuff in a bin-bag along with what I found in a few boxes in the attic, and I ran it down to the lock-up. Not yours, mine. No one knows about my one. It'll be safe there."

"Fuck me. Where's this lock-up?"

"Poplar."

He paused. There was a lot to consider here. He didn't like all of it, either.

Carrot waited nervously, trying a smile, difficult when he could feel Julius' eyes burning into his skull. Finally.

"Well, that's good. You did real good, Chris."

"I just did what needed to be done, Jewels."

"There's something else I want you to do for me."

"Fire away."

"We still keeping that Roger's cunt sweet, down the nick?"

"As and when we need to, yes. Then he gets his little envelope."

"And he's still useful, is he?"

"When it's in his interest to be, yes."

"I want you to go and see him today. Find out what's been stirred up after our little fiasco yesterday. As you say, with Charlie dead, they could be all over us like flies on shit."

"I can do that. He likes a drink on Fridays. I'll see that he gets one."

"Tell him he'll get a large one if he comes up with the goods. And Chris, listen to me. This is big-time sensitive. I want to know how they knew about that raid. If someone is tipping them the wink, then I want to know who that someone is. Are we on the same page?"

"If anyone can find that out, he can, I'm sure. So long as the price is right."

"Never mind the fucking price. Tell him we know where his kids go to school."

Julius watched Carrot shamble off and disappear into the mist that was rolling in from the river, and then he went to check that Carrot hadn't overlooked anything dodgy.

He cursed his leg as he climbed the ladder, which was still let down from the attic.

It took him a moment or two of fumbling in the dark before he could find the cord and light the place up.

Fuck me, he muttered, so much old crap.

His old golf clubs, the *Charles Atlas Bullworker*. Some of Kath's clothes. He wasn't having some fucking tart buying them at Oxfam and turning up down his boozer wearing them.

As marriages go, theirs had been a good one. He missed her and all the love and stability she had brought to what had been a chaotic existence.

Behind the pile of skirts and tops was the plastic sports bag with the Adidas logo, in which he kept the bare essentials he'd need if he had to have it away on his toes at a moment's notice.

Next to that, all neatly folded, were Jimmy's West Ham strip and his favourite boots.

He could still see him in that strip, looking like a trench soldier; he had that much mud on him. And in these cardboard boxes? Jimmy's toys from years ago: look at them all. The *Johnny 7 One Man Army* gun he'd got him for his eighth birthday, his *Corgi* cars and *Action Man* soldiers. He'd kept everything in top nick, and some of them were still boxed. Probably worth something now.

Fucking hell, Jimmy.

He'd been such a good kid, and he had so many new ideas about the business, how to scrub money, where to get the highest return on investments, how to keep people in line without blowing their toes off.

They'd had their differences about some of those innovations, but it showed he was keen.

By twenty, Jimmy was already on his way up in the business, and everyone knew it and treated him with the respect that was his due. Julius had no wish to retire, but when he did, he was looking forward to handing on the whole shooting-match to Jimmy Nicholson.

Then what happened? Jimmy fell in with the wrong people, some tossers in the City, and he'd got a sideline in drugs that grew faster than any business they had touched.

Jewels loathed what he was doing. Kath popping her occasional Dexies was one thing, but heroin and the rest of it?

He had told Jimmy it would have to stop, but then Jimmy showed him the figures and how the totals seemed to multiply magically.

You couldn't really ignore that. So, he told him to separate it from the main business, and he would turn a blind eye.

He never knew that Jimmy had started using himself. Or that his new friends had introduced him to a different lifestyle that made him careless in his activities and careless of himself.

There was a rumour that he had been racing another car, some City boy he had dealings with, when the articulated lorry pulled out of the Nine Elms Cold Store, and he had been too slow or too high to brake his 911 in time.

Jimmy, and then Kath. This empty house. What a fucking world.

8

The night before Juliet interrogated Maureen about her natural parents, an old, silver Mercedes pulled up below her window. The doorbell rang just as *Coronation Street* was about to roll credits.

Juliet let it ring a couple more times, hoping Colin would answer it.

When the ringing became insistent, she got up and stepped into the hallway outside her bedroom. Colin's door was open, his room empty. Maureen was supposed to be seeing her mum, while Gerry should be home by now, but his car wasn't parked outside.

The visitor began to rap forcefully against the wood that separated two panes of mottled glass, through which she recognised with a start, the dark, pear-shaped form of 'Fat Larry' Hughes.

"Oh, God," she thought.

Gerry got a lot of funny visitors, but there was nothing funny about Larry Hughes.

Pulling her bathrobe tight, she switched on the hall light and slowly descended the stairs. The letterbox flapped open, piggy eyes peered through.

"Peekaboo, I see you. What are you playing at? Let's have no more messing around. Let me in or I'll huff, and I'll puff and blow your house down."

She took off the chain, opened the door and almost retched, overcome by the familiar, sickly stink of his cheap aftershave. Drawing back, she asked him what he wanted.

"Well, it's not you, my dusky darling, not this time. Is he in?"

"He'll be back any moment now."

"I'll wait downstairs. I want a word with your Mr Hobson. Two or three, maybe."

"You know where to go, then."

"I want you to show me down."

"I can't; I'm busy."

"You'll show me down those stairs right now, or you'll learn what happens to disobedient young ladies. After you, my pretty."

Fearing a repeat of his last visit when she had distinctly felt the contours of his genitals squeezing past her, she led him towards the narrow staircase that went down to Gerry's office.

This time, the man's mind apparently followed other courses, and he left her unmolested. At the bottom of the stairs, Hughes ducked his head, entered the room, and dropped heavily into one of the old leather armchairs. She turned to go.

"Not so fast, Ebony. Pour me a drink. Large Chivas with a splash."

She found a glass, opened a bottle and tilted it into the glass.

There had been a power cut the last time he visited. Showing him into Gerry's candle-lit office with a small electric torch, she had seen only a dark, misshapen mass and remembered him for his threatening demeanour and repulsive behaviour and little else.

Now, she saw a big man in his mid-forties straining the stitching of a chalk-striped suit whose slightly flared trousers were suspended by Union Jack braces. A silver clip held in place a thickly knotted blue tie which he now pulled loose, before mopping drops of perspiration from his fleshy face with a greying handkerchief. Strands of long, yellow hair were combed over a pink scalp, beneath which a dull red scar stretched from the corner of a lip almost to a gold ear-stud.

Small, black eyes set in deep sockets darted about the room.

When she handed him his drink, he grasped her wrist, squeezed it hard and pulled her towards him before suddenly letting it drop.

"Right, you can fuck off. But before you go, one more thing. I never came here tonight. And if you hear any funny noises, it's just Gerry and me playing games. Understand?"

She nodded.

"Good, you're a pretty girl. Let's keep it that way."

Sitting on her bed with her knees drawn to her chin, she heard Gerry's car crunch across the gravel. The front door opened.

She looked over the banisters, but before she could call out, Gerry was already dropping down the lower stairs to his office.

The conversation two floors below her was muted even in an otherwise empty house. She turned up the volume of her television but kept her eyes on her door and wondered if Gerry was in any danger and then she wondered if she cared.

He'd refused to reveal what was hers to know, the identities of her parents. For someone who was supposed to be a father figure, Gerry was useless.

There was a comedy playing on the television. A documentary followed. She registered neither programme, alert only for the departure of the silver Mercedes.

Turning down the volume, Juliet listened.

The conversation was louder now. That usually meant there was drinking. Often, there was a lot of noise when Gerry's clients came to see him.

A neighbour had complained about the noise only last month. Gerry took him down to his office, where he stayed for about five minutes and then left. There were no more complaints after that, no matter how loud the parties.

The level of noise this evening had been rising and falling, but now she could hear Hughes shouting, then something fell, furniture perhaps.

There followed some other unfathomable sounds, more shouting and then a noise that might have been a stubborn cork pulled from a bottle.

Likely, they had been drinking spirits for more than two hours and now there was champagne. Gerry would know about it in the morning.

In bed, she turned off the light. She might have slept but for some niggling thought that she wouldn't switch off. Turning over, she tried again. She got up and pulled back a curtain. The Mercedes was still there.

Throwing the covers over her head, she pulled her knees to her chin. She was dozing when another car stopped outside. Doors opened, people got out, doors closed.

She sat up.

Men entered the house, spoke in low voices, and then went downstairs.

A few minutes passed, and then she heard heavy footsteps on the stairs again, someone cursing, then the front door opened and after a while, closed softly.

Something told her not to look outside. She heard car doors again, a boot opening and closing.

The engine started, and the car drove away. She listened.

For a moment or two, there was silence. Then she heard Gerry, it must be, messing about in the kitchen cupboards.

She looked outside.

The old Mercedes was still parked where Hughes had left it.

9

"Word is, they'll all be there, every smear of shit from Tottenham to Tower Hamlets."

"Charlie's getting a proper send-off, then."

Julius let go of the breath he had been holding in a long, slow susurration.

"Might have been better kept manageable. But, well, Charlie was popular. What he did for the Island and that. So, we play host."

A voice from the gloom said, "Charlie liked a big do. His wedding, right?"

Everyone except Patrick and Julius was sitting around a low, drinks-freighted table where burning cigarettes danced like fireflies in the gloom, and Julius wobbled a little on his cane as he weighed his words.

"We'll have Benji on the door, and Desmond here has roped in a couple of likely lads from the boxing club to work the floor. All sorted, Desmond?"

"Yeah, sure."

"So, if anything kicks off, we'll be on top of it before it starts."

"We're expecting trouble, Julius?" asked Leslie.

"I don't know. What concerns me is another kind of trouble, if we're not all on our game. So, listen up."

"We are all ears," said Carrot, standing behind Julius, drawing groans from Patrick and Leslie.

Julius said, "Charlie's wake is going to be convivial. Obviously."

They laughed; everyone liked a good piss-up.

"Trouble is, booze and chat make a volatile combination. Like nitric acid and glycerin. Your job, gentlemen, is to soak up that chat but keep schtum. I don't want any of those cunts leaving that pub knowing any more about us than they did when they arrived. So, you sit, and you nod, and you listen. You stay sober, and you say nothing about our business. Not even in jest."

Behind him, a voice said, "Is that clear?"

"Charlie would want us to send him off in style. Not stone-cold sober," remarked Patrick.

The others nodded. These days there were moments when he got them together, he thought someone might turn and tell him to fuck off. When he asked them to jump, they no longer asked, how high?

Carrot filled the silence. "Anyone here have a problem with this?"

Now, he heard a *fuck off*.

"Sit down, Carrot," Julius said.

Standing by the nearest table, Patrick's long, bony face paled under the bright overhead light as he flicked a red ball across the green baize.

"Won't they be playing the same game?" asked Patrick.

"Of course they will. Some lips will be sewn up tighter than a turkey's arse at Christmas. But it's a gathering of the clans. People will be getting lathered. There will be valuable stuff dropped if you listen for it."

"What sort of stuff?"

"You'll know it when you hear it. My unfinished business with some of those gentlemen is no secret. We need to know what they are up to and who wants to see us fucked. There's a decent drink in it for anyone who comes up with something useful."

Julius sat down, signalling the meeting had ended. The others got up and began assembling cues by the two tables. There was some grumbling, but he thought he had made his point.

Resting his eyes for a moment, he heard the clatter of ivory as the first rack was filled, then the clinking of coins being dropped into the jukebox. Leslie broke first, cursing when he left Desmond perfectly lined up.

Julius loosened his tie, sat back heavily in his chair and picked up his scotch. *Brown Sugar* erupted from the jukebox.

"If I could venture an opinion, you might want to watch him."

He hadn't been aware that Carrot had stayed in his seat, which he now shuffled closer to his own.

"All right, which one?" Julius said.

"Leslie," Carrot whispered.

When Julius remained silent, Carrot said, "Thinks he's your main man. Another Chisel, Julius."

"I wish he were another Chisel."

"Be careful what you wish for, my mum says. Mister Chisel was after your job, and well you know it."

"Every fucker's after my job. You seen DC Rogers yet?"

"He's taking a winter break. Lanzarote. Back next week."

"Fuck me. Well, keep on it. If we've sprung a leak, I need to know about it, yesterday."

He watched the players hunched over the two tables in Sol's back room.

If one of this lot had sold out, then who would his money be on? Don Garbutt, with his razored cheek half-hidden by sideburns, would be high on his list. AWOL when Charlie got killed, blown appendix, or so they'd heard. He hadn't been around for a couple of weeks after that, so no one questioned it.

Then there was the human tower-block that was Desmond. He'd been on the firm since Chisel's days, always sound, Julius thought, but Leslie said he was sniffing about.

And what about the horse Carrot was backing? As Leslie lined up a shot, he appeared to be looking down his snooker cue straight into his eyes, like a sniper taking his headshot.

He didn't much like Leslie. Telling Julius that he could trust him, ten times a day.

Well, here's a surprise for you Leslie, he thought. I'm trusting no fucker. In all honesty, it could have been any one of them.

They were a rabble. A shame they were born too late for National Service. And as for choosing one of them as his aide-de-camp, that was a non-starter. Who here could take on that burden? Who the fuck could do what Chisel had done all those years ago?

Funny how he still thought about the old days with Chisel after all this time.

He thought about the girl, too.

Just recently, he'd sent Carrot to make discreet enquiries about her, to see if there was anything he could do for her. Maybe Carrot could find out if she'd be receptive to seeing him. It was about time he did. Kath had been dead a long time, now.

"I just want you to know that I'll be here when you need me," Carrot was saying.

Julius took another slug of scotch and tuned him out, his mind slipping back to that first encounter with Chisel. That would have been 1939, just after the war was supposed to have started. Just before *he* got started.

He remembered the high drama in the school woodworking room. The woodwork teacher had left the boys alone for a few minutes when three of them started on the skinny kid who never got picked for games. Julius expected to see him viciously pinched or kicked; that was usual.

But this time, that didn't happen. Instead, the three boys jumped back, almost knocking each other over. He saw why. The skinny kid was waving a long, nasty-looking chisel and making stabbing motions, like it was a bayonet that he meant to use.

He was still brandishing the tool when the woodwork teacher re-entered the room. Jewels had watched in respectful silence as Chisel—he would call him that ever after—was carted off to be caned. The kid had balls, Julius decided.

He was returned to the here and now by Desmond and Leslie, making a lot of noise and looking like they were about to kill each other. Somehow, Carrot had got himself in the middle of it. For fuck's sake, he said aloud as he rapped his cane on the wooden floor. Stuff like this never happened when Chisel was around.

10

It wasn't that Juliet tried to think about Larry Hughes, it was more that the repellent monster would not leave her alone, trespassing on her thoughts as she tried to sleep, materialising like some awful genie when she did.

At first, she refused to admit the reason for these intrusions. Hughes had assaulted her on the stairs; that was enough. But then there was everything she did not know about that night. Hughes had intimated that he and Gerry had unfinished business and had told her to ignore any funny noises.

There had been a lot of funny noises when Gerry came home. Shouting, crashing, the popping of a cork. Could that have been a gun, firing?

And then those other noises. The car stopping, the sounds of men entering and leaving, the car boot closing. Had Gerry shot Hughes and had his corpse spirited away in the boot of that car?

More questions. Was it possible that Gerry had a gun? And was he capable of killing? She was reminded of how little she knew about him. He was registered as an accountant, but, as she confided to Ammo one lunchtime, "his clients look like residents of the hotel up the road." Meaning, HMP Wandsworth. The thought had already crossed her mind that Gerry did his accounting for criminals.

And yet she had never seen a violent side to him. He hardly ever raised his voice at her, even when she ruined his best suit by putting it in the washing machine. Now, though, she looked at him differently when he ate his meals and smoked his cigarettes and went up and down his office stairs with unlikely-looking clients.

Once she had entertained the thought that Gerry had murdered someone in his basement office, outlandish as it was, she could not get rid of it.

Every time she recalled the events of the night, she became more and more convinced that she was sharing a house with a killer, and quite suddenly, she found herself being wary of the man she had sometimes called daddy. It was another alarm bell, a loud one, telling her to get out of that house.

"You know what, you've changed."

Gerry rarely said anything that might suggest he took an interest in her. He hadn't shown much interest in anything these last couple of weeks, but had fallen into one of his inscrutable, bleak moods that communicated a general irritation with himself and those around him. Without any good reason for doing so, she connected this with whatever had happened that night with Larry Hughes.

She wanted to ask about the Mercedes, which had gone by the time she returned from work. Maybe Hughes had fallen asleep on the basement couch. Maybe not.

She glanced at her beaded braids in Maureen's mirror; Gerry's foxed reflection sat on the edge of the couch wearing his blue blazer and gold tie, smoking a cigarette, and ready for business. He didn't look like a killer, not tonight. He checked his watch.

He'd given no sign that anything of consequence had taken place that night in the basement. Maybe she had let her imagination run away with her. Perhaps she should let it go.

He said, "Not the clobber, you know my position on that. I mean you."

"How do you mean?"

"I don't know; there's a bit more about you these days. You're not on anything, are you?"

She picked up her jacket and found her bag.

"I'm not even on time. Right, I've got my key."

"Where are you going?"

She let herself out the front door, standing aside as a black BMW with opaque windows crunched smoothly into the parking place. So Gerry thought she had changed? For once, he was right. She had changed.

Walking to the bus stop, she recalled the seeds of her metamorphosis, when the punky girl who always sat by the cafe window had thrust an advertising flyer at her one lunchtime. She was on the guest list for that gig, she told her, there was a spare ticket. Did Juliet fancy it?

Juliet was still working at the King's Road cafe-cum-bistro where she had started a few weeks after leaving school. Most of her customers barely registered her existence, but this one, who wasn't much older than she was, liked to chat to her before she ordered her pasta or paid her bill.

When they found themselves on the same bus one evening, they talked like they had known each other for years, not days. The girl's name was Amelia, but her friends called her Ammo.

"What do you think? It'd be a laugh."

She looked at the flyer pressed into her hand. Her face must have said it wasn't her thing.

The girl feigned disappointment. "Oh, I see. So, you're doing something better tonight?"

She could said that she was going home to watch *Blake's 7* on TV, which was the sad truth. Or she could look at the flyer again.

"What would I wear?" she asked.

She meets Ammo in the bar, where they have to wait until the basement venue opens its doors.

Ammo seems to know everyone.

Gathered about their tables are boys in old jackets and skinny knitted ties, drainpipe trousers worn with red and green sneakers, girls in vintage dresses, fishnet stockings or brightly coloured tights, full-on make-up, hair back-combed or spiked, and badges, all those badges.

She is conscious of her own turnout, her hastily subverted school uniform, a slashed, graffitied blouse worn with one of Gerry's striped ties and a handful of Ammo's badges. *Pretty Vacant* says one, *Weekend Fascist*, another. She feels marked out as an interloper, but she is with Ammo, and that seems to count for something.

Downstairs, there are more of what Ammo calls by-the-book punks, bondage gear, bin-bag shirts, razor blade earrings, safety pins, chains, dog-collars.

She has never been with people like this. Never experienced a place where condensation drips from the ceiling. Where heat is generated by the crush of bodies, and excitement zips through the noisy, sardined mass like an electric charge. Ammo is talking—shouting—to a girl at her side.

She turns and grins at Juliet. *This is great, isn't it*? Two big men in suits, bouncers, she thinks, watch her as she responds to Ammo.

Someone at the back heckles the musicians, who are now slouching onto the tiny stage. Amplifiers crackle as a voice calls, "One, two, one two" into a microphone. Three boys stand before the crowd, guitars hung low like gunslingers' pistols, none of them more than 19 years old, for sure. Biker jackets open over bare, hairless chests, they exchange quick, nervous looks, and then the drummer, blonde stubbly head, skinny white breasts scarred with healing cuts, throws himself at his kit.

Simultaneously, the lead singer, dyed black hair matching his stage-paint mascara, leaps as high as he can without concussing himself on the low ceiling, and they are off, the crowd pogoing, the whole room leaping up and down. Juliet was with them, feeling the tight closeness of the people around her, unable to stop herself, becoming one with this surging mass of flesh and transported somewhere new and wild. This cacophonous din isn't music and yet is more music than any other music she has ever heard.

Plastic glasses fly; spittle is spat. A boy, obviously off his head on something, climbs onto the stage and tries to wrest the mic from the singer. The lead guitarist is having none of this and wields his axe like a Viking raider, smacking the kid into the middle of next week. There's barely a break between the songs; one crashes into the next like a pile-up in the fog, as NME will report. It's power-chord magic. No-one is in tune, neither guitar strings nor vocal cords. It's all about the energy, the blind, blistering energy.

The evening unravels in fast time. Before she knows it, the band have thrown down their guitars; the roadie is already looking at all the shit he must clear away into a waiting van, and the gig is done.

Her ears are ringing. There's shuffling and shouting and stairs beneath her feet and then the cold night air. In the dark street, people are bickering about where to go now.

She sees the two big men she had taken for bouncers watching her as she links arms with Ammo and they turn towards the tube.

Working at PINZ, Juliet experienced something new, a feeling that she belonged. Ammo's friends soon became her own. Almost all of them were white, but the way she read it, her difference was not only cool with them, but weirdly exotic. She aligned herself with this new world, raiding the charity shops, renewing her wardrobe and chucking out everything that had defined the Juliet of old.

Known now as 'Julio', she stopped hating herself and her appearance and was surprised at her own newfound confidence. Now when she got home, she met Colin's eye and dared him to start his shit, the name-calling and that nasty new suggestiveness. He'd stared at her bug-eyed when he first saw her wearing her new styles and said something about her looking like 'a fucking parrot', but it had stopped at that.

The first time Gerry saw her in full regalia, he'd said, "Jesus H. Bloody Christ!" and had brought on such a fit of coughing that he stubbed out his cigarette. He struggled to deal with the luridly pink tee shirt with its machine-gunned Betty Boop, the yellow plastic bangles and earrings, the wild hair, the green eyeshadow. "What in God's name do you look like?" he wheezed.

"You should talk," Juliet said.

"What do you mean, *I* should talk?" He sounded not so

much angry as profoundly surprised. She hadn't talked back to Gerry since the early days of her adolescence.

"I'm just saying, it's all a matter of perspective," she said, borrowing an argument of Ammo's. "Some people might see what *you* wear as shocking. It just depends on your viewpoint."

"What I wear?" he said, and she caught him glancing in the mirror, as if he couldn't remember pulling on the diamond-patterned jumper over the old blue shirt with its pointed collar and the beige golfing slacks. She hoped in that instant he reappraised his lank hair, too, which was too long for a man of his age. He went over to the TV set and turned down the volume.

"People will think I'm neglecting you," he said. "Not bringing you up right."

She gave a little laugh.

"You don't care what people think about me."

"Oh, but I do," Gerry had said, "Believe me, I do. For God's sake, Maureen. Haven't you got anything to say about this?"

Maureen, who had been sipping a gin while gazing blankly at *Nationwide,* had a different take on Juliet's transformation. "It's just a phase, Gerry. Kids go through them. They always have. You're not still a teddy boy, are you? Let her alone; she'll grow out of it."

Gerry walked up and down the hearthrug, rubbing his forehead.

"You don't understand," he said. "You just don't understand. Now, listen to me, Juliet, I'm only going to ask you this once. Will you please go upstairs, take that lot off and dress in normal things again?"

"No," she said.

"I bloody thought not. What you don't understand, and

that's the funny thing, is that it's all about you," he said and set himself off coughing again.

"About me? What do you mean?" Juliet asked. But already he was picking up his jacket, pocketing his fags and leaving the house, still coughing. Maureen rolled her eyes, swigged her drink and waved Juliet out of the way of the TV. Juliet had frowned and gone up to her room. How the fuck was anything in this house about her?

11

It was funny, not actually; it was fucking tragic how good news could turn sour so quickly, she thought, as she travelled home alone on the Friday evening. The day had started so well, too. Ammo and she were on a roll, both enjoying the banter between sales, both making the shop and themselves some money. Juliet had banged on some Pistols, and they were caterwauling *I am an antichrist; I am an anarchist!* so loud they thought that Chas Evans had flung open his door to tell them to dial it down. But it wasn't that at all. "You," he said, pointing at Juliet, "a word, if you don't mind?"

She followed him into the back room. "Shut the door," he said, slumping heavily into the *Habitat* recliner by the enormous cheese plant. "Sit down."

Juliet sat herself on the hard chair before the busy desk, which had become a dumping ground for invoices, receipts, coloured vinyl singles, copies of *NME* and *Sounds*, packs of Marlborough cigarettes, unwashed coffee mugs, a typewriter and a red telephone. Under a television in the corner was a video recorder. God knew what that must have set him back.

"I know, I know, you love what I've done with the place," he said

He had taken off the biker jacket, which he always teamed with a pair of Wayfarers; unshaven now in just a grey tee shirt and new Levi's, he wasn't so instantly recognisable as *the Machiavelli of punk,* as the *Guardian* had captioned their photo.

For a moment, he seemed lost in his thoughts. She waited a moment before said, "You wanted to see me?"

His brow furrowed; he sat up; there was business to address.

"I did. Julio, isn't it?"

"Yes,"

"You like working here?"

"Very much."

"Cool. Ammo says you're coming on fine."

"That's nice of her."

"She's a nice girl."

Juliet nodded. Where was this going?

"You think you can do what she does?" he said. His face said he might doubt it. "Around the shop? Stocking, cashing up, overseeing the casuals, the whole shebang?"

"I suppose. Ammo's a great teacher."

"I know. She's great all around."

He offered her a cigarette. She refused, so he lit his own.

"Why are you asking?"

"Why indeed?" The tubular steel of the chair creaked as he leaned further forward.

"This is where it gets difficult. I mean, it's only difficult if you make it difficult. But..."

"I'm sorry, you've lost me."

"Look, this isn't bad news. Not for you. In fact, I'm giving you a raise."

Had she heard that right? She'd only been there a few weeks.

"A rise? That's amazing! Can I ask how much?"

He blew out a big smoke ring.

"Twenty per cent."

"What? I don't understand. This is totally unexpected."

"Life can surprise us all at times. Oh, there's something else, too. Yes, Julio, there is more."

"More?"

"More. This is the difficult bit. I love Ammo dearly, but the thing is, I want you to manage the shop. She'll still get her money, but you'll be in charge."

"No, I can't do that. Why would you want that?"

"I'm going to bring you on, develop you."

"It wouldn't work. I can't be Ammo's boss. That's crazy!"

"I do crazy things, it seems. Look, you can call it a nominal position if you like. I don't care. You two can find whatever way you like to make this work."

"Can I refuse?"

"Absolutely not."

And then she was back at the counter and Ammo was in with Chas and while Juliet screwed up her eyes and stamped on the floorboards and said "Fuck, fuck, fuck!" over and over until Ammo came out again, red-faced and avoiding her eye.

"I'm sorry, Ammo," she said. "I had no idea this was coming, none at all. It doesn't make any sense."

"It sure as shit doesn't," Ammo agreed and went to see about something in the stockroom. For the rest of that long day, neither girl spoke to anyone but customers, who seemed to sense something was missing from the PINZ shop that day and didn't stay long.

12

When Julius Nicholson was eleven years old, his father came home so drunk that he got into his little bed with him. Julius thought he had made a mistake and then found out he hadn't.

Julius had returned to London along with many of the first wave of evacuees and knew it was his mother who had made that possible; the old fuck wouldn't have given a tinker's cuss. Julius didn't care, just so long as he was back where he belonged.

He missed Chisel, Frankie, Sol and the other lads he ran wild with down by the docks, missed the familiar sights and sounds of living on the river, the crowds of men scrambling for a day's work, the great rusting freighters with their steaming funnels, the angular cranes swinging their netted heavy loads.

He'd missed hearing the great blasts from the ships' horns and having that primal feeling that this place belonged to him, and he to this place. What his father did tarnished all of that.

If the old fuck had been an occupational hazard of living at 39 Senegal Street, he was at least a navigable one. He drove his crane for most of the day and would come home only long enough to wash his face and hands, sometimes change his shirt and eat a Spam sandwich before slamming the door behind him and striding off in the direction of the Ship and Star public house.

The war kept him occupied; the ships came in constantly, some ragged and disabled. He was keeping the nation fed, the old fuck boasted. The bombers caught them on the hop. With only barrage balloons in the skies, it was easy to think they weren't coming, or they weren't coming just yet anyway.

The first time it happened was on a warm Saturday afternoon in September, when Julius and Chisel had been mud-larking for coins and saleable scraps on the shores of the river. The planes arrived before the sirens sounded, hundreds of them streaming across the blue sky, more coming out of the clouds.

Someone pointed upwards and said, "That's a bloody..." and then the bombs began falling, ladders of them sailing towards the ground. They watched, mesmerised, until the first ones struck a mile or two away, and then they began to run.

Every night, for months on end, Julius went with his parents and neighbours to the bomb shelter at the end of the road, a cold, dark and malodorous hole where he sat on a plank with his shoes in a muddy puddle.

There was usually candlelight, and sometimes an electric torch played upon the frightened faces sitting across from him. The close calls took away his breath and left his ears ringing. He felt the violent tremors beneath his feet. As often as not, the ack-ack emplacements at both ends of the street made more noise than the grinding of the aircraft or the whistle and crump of the bombs.

Sometimes it all got too close, and the ground shook; it

seemed like great blocks of buildings were exploding between his ears. The sky rained metal debris, which rattled on the corrugated-iron roof arched over them.

People took it in different ways. Some put on a brave face, some whimpered like beaten dogs, and sometimes it took two of the men to prevent the ones who panicked from leaving the shelter. His dad sat with blank eyes and trembled, but he did that anyway, with all that he was drinking now. Julius remembered crouching one night next to a woman in a corner, who was crying and rocking and calling for her mother.

As she leaned forward, he saw the corner of her purse exposed in her coat pocket, the brass twist-fastener catching the candlelight. He slipped the purse from her pocket and slid it under his coat. No one saw what he had done, and later, he found he was richer by 3/6d.

He should have been evacuated again, but Chisel was staying, and once his mother got sick, he was needed at home to care for her. There was no one else to do it. One night the old fuck had sent him out into the thick of it. They had been woken by sirens in the early hours of a Monday morning and arrived at the shelter without half the warm stuff they needed.

The damage had been light in their neighbourhood with most of the bombs falling further down river. A lull had followed, but they hadn't sounded the all-clear. People in the shelter began to talk, one over the other, relieved beyond measure at finding themselves still breathing, still intact after one of the heaviest bombardments yet.

While this was going on, the old fuck had been whispering to Julius, telling him to slip out and fetch him a bottle of navy rum he kept in a cupboard in the kitchen. There had been lulls like this before, when those in need scurried back to their houses to answer the calls of nature, but still, Julius knew these lulls weren't to be trusted.

No 'all clear' probably meant there was a second wave on the way. "I won't do it," he said. "They'll be back soon."

The old fuck had leaned closer. Julius smelled alcohol and felt his father's moustache brushing his ear. "I'll tell them what we do at night," the low voice hissed. "I'll tell them all."

He had slipped out unnoticed by anyone, to find himself on a street he barely knew. Searchlights were tracking across clouds tinted pink by the enormous fires raging below; he could hear the wild crackling of these infernos, smell the burning. Over the road, Corkers' butcher's shop had gone, and Shentall's Grocery, now windowless, sagged like it was about to drop.

Up the street was a gap, maybe three houses wide, where bricks cascaded down into the road, while neighbouring houses were missing windows, doors, parts of roofs and chimneys. An end-of-terrace house had lost a wall, exposing nakedly a bedroom and a dangling flight of stairs.

Bricks and tiles and personal possessions littered the street. An old armchair sat in a corner, the right way up. Julius gaped at a motor-van lying upside-down under a felled telegraph pole. Glass crunched underfoot as he ran up the street towards the house, crossing roads and navigating new obstructions, which frightened and exhilarated him at the same time.

Their house looked as it should, although when he went into the kitchen intent on pocketing the fishpaste sandwiches his mother had set out for them before the sirens started wailing, he found the meal and the teacups buried under plaster dust and bits of the ceiling. Locating the bottle of rum, he hid it under his coat.

He was pulling shut the front door when he heard the

familiar mechanical droning from across the river. The first bombs exploded somewhere in the docks. He began to run. Now, suddenly, there were violent crashes somewhere in front of him. He was running in the direction of the falling bombs.

Glancing up, he saw the silhouettes of aircraft playing in the beams of the searchlights and was nearly deafened as he passed the nearby ack-ack battery. He turned up a side street. It might have been Mafeking Road, but disoriented from the first blast, everywhere now looked strange to him. Ahead and lighting up the taped windows on the terraced houses he passed were the warehouses, dark shapes showing now as tier upon tier of brilliantly flaming windows.

Blazing stores of flour, sugar, timber and alcohol were sending thick smoke billowing hundreds of feet into the sky.

At the end of the street, he could see the docks where his father worked. The planes were getting closer, and when a crippled aircraft passed overhead; it was low enough for him to make out the recognisable shape of a Dornier bomber and see the markings on the wings, while the bells of the fire engines and ambulances clanged louder.

As he came closer to the conflagration, he could hear the firemen shouting and cursing. Barely audible above the great crackle and hiss of the fire, a man unrolling a hose shouted, "What's that bloody kid doing here?" He turned around, clutching his bottle tightly to his chest, and ducked up another street, then began to run again.

Just beyond the dock area, he found himself by the engineering shops where a paint shed had been hit. Unattended, it was burning fiercely. The heat was beyond anything he could imagine. Backing away, he was being fascinated by the sudden eruptions of enormous tongues of flames from doorways and windows when a rough hand grabbed him and almost wrenched his arm from its socket as he was dragged suddenly away from the building.

He turned to see an enormous wall crumbling into the ground behind him.

"Bit close for comfort, that one! What's a nipper like you doing out in this? Where's your parents?"

Mr Taylor was in the ARP and was always having barneys with his old man about the lights they showed. Now, Mr Taylor was crouching with him behind a wall and covering him with his helmet as exploding metal rattled onto the surrounding ground.

"Are you the Nicholson boy? Don't worry, we'll have you out of this in two shakes."

But now there came the ratcheting sound of machine guns, and across devastated yards he could see firemen running for their lives.

"Hold on, be brave, it'll all be over soon," Mr Taylor said, holding him tightly.

When the planes thinned and disappeared into the clouds and the only explosions were of things catching fire in the warehouses, Mr Taylor had taken his hand and led him across the yards towards the dock gates, where his ARP post was still standing. Inside the doorway, he could see the glowing arcs of cigarettes being smoked and hear the conversation of tired men. One of them was sipping from a tin mug as he came to the door and asked who Titch had got there?

"It's Nicholson's lad. Jim, ain't it?"

Julius nodded. He liked the name.

"Seeing him home?"

"It's on my way."

"Well, keep him away from the playground at St Winifred's. They must have thirty there already."

"Will do. Any more tea in your pot?"

"If you've got a smoke, there is."

Mr Taylor was rummaging in the deep pockets of his trench coat when Julius made his escape. Had you asked him, he wouldn't have been able to tell you why he did that, only that he didn't like being told what to do and that this seemed much like being run in by the coppers. He was through the dock gates before the ARP man had found his cigarettes.

He heard someone shouting after him, but people had better things to do than pursue a lost boy. He wasn't lost now, though. Dawn was breaking and beyond the dock gates he could see the roads which would take him back to the shelter, where he could finally get rid of the bottle under his coat.

All the same, St Winifred's wasn't really out of his way, though he encountered more unexpected obstacles on his route, an overturned milk-float, a gas-main on fire, some people in their night clothes loudly arguing. From over the playground wall at St Winifred's, he could hear voices.

A little further down the road, the wall became a scattered pile of rubble. He peered around broken brickwork at people gathered by a row of dark things covered by army blankets and tarpaulins. Someone was lifting the blankets and making notes in a little book with a pencil. He watched as a party of St. John's Ambulance men carried a stretcher into the yard and set it down by the other dark things.

Another ambulance man followed with a large canvas bag, which he set down with the things in the rows. He shook his head and lit a cigarette. Julius was nine years old, but he knew what was under the blankets, and he was grimly fascinated.

When the people had gone into the school, he approached the thing nearest to him. He crouched, looked and listened, and when he was sure no one was watching, he lifted the corner of one of the blankets and peered beneath.

A ghastly sickness overcame him.

Others might not have recognised her, but he did. Her jaw had gone but the dead eyes and the yellow hair belonged to Edith Collins, who worked at the corner off-licence where the old fuck so often sent him to get a bottle of porter and ten Woodbines. He stood up, dropping the bottle, which cracked and slowly emptied, and he vomited.

He'd peeked beneath the blanket because it'd be something to tell Chisel and Sol and the others. But that was all out of the window now. He wasn't going to tell anyone about this; he wasn't going to speak of it. He didn't know it then, but he wasn't going to speak to anyone for some time to come.

13

On the King's Road, the doors of PINZ were wedged open by a stack of Yellow Pages. Despite the bright oblique sunshine, it wasn't that warm outside, but the girl who seemed to run the place had declared that an open door was an invitation for people to step in. And at that moment, she really needed people to step in. Trade had bombed.

Outside, people swung shopping bags emblazoned with the logos of every boutique from here to the World's End, except for the one with PINZ scratched on it. For a short while, Chas Evans looked like he would fight back.

He reappraised and adjusted the stock, introduced special deals, vox-popped customers and gave huge wads of advertising flyers to the kids who hung about the place to hand out at gigs and pin up wherever they found a space.

He had spectacularly avoided the real issue, Juliet thought. Though no one at PINZ wanted to acknowledge it, everyone knew that punk itself had lost the spitting fire of its birth. People were moving on. But while everyone else seemed content to go on selling the safety-pinned fancy dress of last year, she was making efforts to update the place, ordering up a sideline of dark jackets and skinny ties and updating the tape deck's playlist. The playlist itself was another of her new and apparently contentious introductions.

Now, as she finished arranging a display of boots in a pyramid of purple-painted orange boxes, a note of dissension sounded from the tiny kitchen.

"Our *raison d'être* was always punk and nothing but punk," it chirped. "This New Wave stuff is nice enough, I grant you. But it's putting new spots on the fucking leopard."

At this, she had stalked over to the open doors and taken in deep lungs full of traffic-leaded air. Lighting a cigarette, she told herself it wasn't her fault. There were other forces at work, but that didn't stop her feeling like a total imposter who had supplanted a much abler girl.

Chas had told her not to sweat. That was life; these things happened. But he could simply close the shop and move on to the next big thing. Everyone thought he had one foot in whatever that was already. She was stuck here and must sink or swim.

"I actually bumped into her at Camden Lock," the voice from the kitchen was saying. "She's really sweet, nothing like the way she acts on stage. I mean, you couldn't be like that in real life, could you?"

Someone laughed. That would be the new girl. She and Ammo apparently got on very well, and what made this more galling was the fact that Ginnie Cunningham had been one of her own hires. In which case she should be more loyal, the ungrateful little bitch.

Treading her fag-end into the floor, Juliet took a last lingering look at the colourful *passeggiata* on the King's Road before turning on her heels and calling Ammo out from the kitchen.

"What's up, boss?"

She hated that.

“Nothing. But I thought you were going to deal with the delivery and get the new stuff out on a rail for tomorrow?”

“Yes, sure.”

“That’s not what it sounded like you were doing.”

“I was having my tea break. That’s still okay, isn’t it? Under the new regime?”

“I’m just saying we need everything right for tomorrow. Saturdays will make or break us, you know that. If you can’t be bothered, I’ll just have to...”

And then she followed the direction of the Scots girl’s gaze and saw that the items she had ordered, the jackets and shirts, had been taken from the packaging and arrayed not on a rail where she expected them to be, but all over the wall by the window. Tacked onto old wooden boards, they were already drawing interest from a couple of possible customers.

Why the fuck hadn’t she seen that? Above the garments, a painted sign, presumably of Ammo’s design, invited people to ‘Surf A New Wave.’ Ammo shrugged and went off to serve a customer.

When she got home, Maureen said, “Is that you, Julie? Pour me a drink, will you? Not a strong one, I’ve got to go out.”

“Your mother again?”

Juliet dropped her bag and her black PVC coat in the hall. She was tending to the drinks-tray with its bottles and novelty cactus ice bucket, but she still caught the look Maureen shot her. They both knew the score. It had been going on for years. Juliet had answered Maureen’s chirpy mother on the phone only last week; there was nothing wrong with her.

One night, in the days when Juliet used to steal down

the stairs to waste another evening at the Arndale, she'd glimpsed the broad back of a man in blue trousers and a white shirt standing in the kitchen, much too close to Maureen, who met her eyes over his shoulder. There was no way she would have told Gerry, but Maureen didn't know that.

In return for her discretion, Maureen put up a little shield around Juliet, telling Gerry not to worry about the bizarre things the girl wore or the places she went. It was all part of growing up. She didn't tell him about the time she'd had to go down the Arndale herself and sort out things with the shop manager after Juliet had taken a mascara from Boots.

If she and Maureen knew roughly where they stood in relation to each other, it was a different thing with Gerry. He had been a mystery to her from the start. "No, don't call me Daddy," he'd told her on what was probably her fourth birthday. "Call me Uncle Gerry. Or just Gerry." She had already learned that Maureen wasn't very responsive to 'Mum,' either.

If Gerry had been distant with her, he was different with Colin. They played football on the Common, and once or twice they had gone to Stamford Bridge. Gerry wasn't a Chelsea fan, so she guessed that had been Colin's idea.

Gerry bought Colin one of those airplanes with petrol engines that whirled around your head at the end of a wire. It was a kit; he and Colin were supposed to build it together, but Colin, who would have been ten or eleven at the time, told Gerry to build the stupid thing himself.

Going upstairs to shower and change, she remembered bits of a conversation she overheard when she was about that age or a little younger. Gerry and Maureen had rolled home pissed.

She had been sitting in the darkened living room

because she had heard noises outside and wanted to pretend there was no one in; for some reason, there had been no babysitter that night. The adults were in the kitchen. There were noises of glasses on the table, a cork being pulled. Maureen was talking.

"It's not just me, Gerry. I'm not sure you have feelings for anyone. Any feelings you do have, you waste on Colin. He's my boy and I love him, but you know what he's like."

"That's unfair. Maybe I just don't show them in the way some people do."

"And look how you behave to *her*. I'd be the first to admit I'm not the best of substitute parents, but at least I talk to her. I engage with her. We have a laugh sometimes. But you... is it because she's, you know..."

"Coloured? No, of course it isn't. It's not that at all."

"Then what is it? You barely say a word to her unless you want something from the shops or need a cup of tea."

Gerry's sigh was long and loud, she recalled. There was a moment before he said anything more. Then he said, "The fact of the matter is, Mo, that I can't see her without seeing him."

"Him?"

"You know who I'm talking about. In school, we were like the Lone Ranger and Tonto. In each other's pockets." He gave a little snort. "All those years, thick and thin, it was him and me against the world. I'm telling you, Maureen, we were brothers, or the next best thing."

"But that was all such a long..."

"And then, one day, he turns on me, just like that. He *suspects* me. *Me*, Maureen. I still can't get over that. It hurt then, and it still hurts now."

"Come here."

"And then what does he do? He foists his unwanted brat

on me, so I'll always have a memento of the way things were."

"Brat? That's harsh, Gerry."

"Yeah, yeah, I don't mean it. I swear I don't. Don't get me wrong, she's a nice girl. I can see that. And if things had been different... It's like I *want* to talk to her, be nice to her, take her to the park and that, but I just can't. It's beyond me, Mo."

"I know, I know. Come to bed. We can talk about it in the morning."

"I tell you this, Maureen. One day, there will be a reckoning for all this."

"I know, Gerry. Come to bed."

So, her father had been a friend of Gerry's. But why had he abandoned her with him? Of course, it wasn't a question Gerry would answer.

14

Later that evening, waiting for a District Line train at East Putney tube station, she told herself again that hers was not an existence that made any sense, and she wanted out of it. By the time the train had sunk underground near Earls Court and the curved window opposite was wildly distorting her short white skirt and army boots, badged khaki bomber jacket and green plastic beads, she had decided that this time it was for real.

She needed to start a new life on her own terms. A flat share, a bedsitter, or a room in a house would be a start. Anything had to be better than this. There was so much she didn't know about Gerry, and then there was his son.

She didn't think she could take any more of Colin. Every time they met on their stairs or in the kitchen, he seemed a little bit nastier. He had taken the news of her promotion very coldly.

"Say that again?"

"I've been promoted. I'm the shop manager."

"What do you know about managing shops?" Colin had spat.

"It's really good news," Maureen had said. "Isn't it, Gerry?"

Gerry had grunted, patted himself down and gone to find his car keys or his fags.

"Has someone got a fucking screw loose? You're only eighteen," Colin had complained. Later, when they were alone, he accused her of fucking or sucking her boss and then he went off on one about the way she dressed, like one of those tarts that did it for luncheon vouchers at that brothel in Streatham. "I don't fucking believe it," was all he said now. "The world's gone fucking mental."

He'd gone up to his room then and kicked the door shut behind him. Since he'd got a job as a hospital porter at St James' in Balham, his shift patterns meant she could go several days without seeing him, and when she did, he was sometimes too burned out to bother with her.

That night, as she got herself ready to go out, with a chair against the door, she wondered what the fuck was wrong with him. They had grown up together, for fuck's sake. It was in these last few years that things got bad and recently, much worse. She had already broached her plans with Maureen. "Anyway, I'm thinking of getting my own place," Juliet had said.

"But why? You've got your meals, your room and everything you could want here. I don't know what Gerry would think of that."

Juliet knew what Gerry would think. He wouldn't like it at all. Why, now there was the mystery.

There was the usual rabble queuing outside the Nashville Rooms, faces she had seen before at this and other venues, but no one she knew to speak to. She went straight to the bar and waved her pound note until eventually she got served with a Guinness and cider.

Up on the stage, the band was setting up, plugging in leads, testing mics, fiddling with knobs on amplifiers. The acts tonight were popular with the music press, so the place was rammed. She said 'hi' to a couple of people she vaguely knew from a gig at the Music Machine and then scanned the crowd for friendly faces.

Down at the front, the band and their female singer were launching into their first number. Moving seemed pointless, so she stayed by the bar, and when one of the guys behind hovered in her vicinity, she ordered the same again.

"Have one of these," shouted a voice in her ear. A skinny guy with spiky white hair, he was wearing an old jacket with silver threads running through the pinstripes, white trousers and green sneakers. He pressed something into her palm. A couple of small pills.

"What is it?"

"Just something that'll give you a lift. Looks like you need one," he said and winked.

The booze had dulled her senses, those that were still functioning after another shitty day at work. She swallowed the pills with a long pull of her snakebite.

She was dancing, pogoing, higher than anyone around her. She saw a photographer in the wings swivel his camera taking some crowd shots. Plastic glasses were starting to fly, there was the usual hail of spit too; the band was going down great.

The music was deafening, drowning. As fast as people climbed onto the stage, the roadies were chucking them off. She became aware of someone dancing with her, the boy who had given her the pills.

“It’s good, yeah?” he shouted in her ear. “Let’s have fun, now, yeah?”

“Yeah,” she shouted back.

She was lost in a maelstrom, the lunatic noise, the whirling colours, the jostling, jumping crowd and the manic hobgoblins hurling themselves about on stage. There was no sense to be made of it. Between the songs, she saw that her view had changed somehow. She was nowhere near the bar but in an alcove on the far side of the room and must have danced herself over.

As the band exploded into another frenzied blitz, she felt the cold, hard wall behind her back and the boy closer than he had been before, pressing himself against her, trying to kiss her, and then she felt his hand beneath her skirt. She tried to push him away, but the press of the crowd was too great. She screamed “No!” but she could hear nothing but the chopping guitars, and all the time he was busying himself down there, his hot, excited breath on her cheek.

She screamed again.

Then he was no longer there. A sudden, violent movement cut a hole in the crowd. She saw the boy smash his head against the wall. She couldn’t make sense of what was happening. First, he was there, in front of her, immovable, then he was smashing himself into the brick wall.

When he did it again, she saw he was being held by a big arm, and that arm was hurling him about like he was a bunch of rags.

Then a total blank. Later, she recalled seeing the same boy on the pavement outside, propped under a streetlamp with some girls, one of whom was holding a black handkerchief to his head. His trousers looked weird, dark with odd white patches. Maybe it was an effect of the flashing blue light, which was adding some nightmare colours to the onlookers' faces as the ambulance mounted the kerb nearby.

Then she blanked again and awoke in her own bed, with the morning sunlight streaming through the thin curtains and Colin leering into her face, saying. "Well, what the fuck happened to you, Princess?"

15

For a second, Julius Nicholson thought that the shattering of glass and the splintering of wood were part of his dream, the one where he was falling but had never, until now, hit the ground.

He sat up in bed, hearing heavy footsteps coming quickly up the open staircase.

Never mind the shouting, he knew who they were, and he knew what they wanted. The bedroom door crashed against a wall as four men crowded in, two uniforms, a DCI he knew of old and a DC not much older than Jimmy would have been.

The DCI, who was much the same age as Julius, took off his wet car coat and settled himself on the corner of the bed.

"You," he said to one of the uniforms, "Go and help the others in the kitchen." He turned to the younger detective. "And you, Vince. Can I trust you to take PC 49 and do the attic? You know what we're looking for."

When they were alone, Julius lit a cigarette and said, "What's all this about? If it's the broken wing mirror on the Jag, it's booked in already."

"Warrant. We're turning you over, Julius."

"I didn't think you'd come for breakfast, Inspector Harding. What are you looking for? Because whatever it is, I haven't got it."

"You know why we're here. That poor sod who had his guts shot out, Charlie Cooper. He was one of yours, wasn't he? Same M.O. as that blag in Stepney. Your dabs were all over the Gaskell's job."

"Don't give me that. If they were, you'd have pulled me in. Why don't you give Tom Adams a tug? He's been busy round here."

"I might as well tell you, Julius, you're our prime on this."

"I'm what? You've clocked me and Charlie, God rest his soul, having a pint and all of a sudden I'm back pulling armed robberies? You won't hang this on me, Andy."

"No? Why?"

"Because I've kept my hands clean. I pay my taxes."

"Maybe that's something the Revenue could have a look at."

There was a crash and a clatter downstairs and someone said, *Whoops*.

"You're overdue for a tug yourself, Julius. Why don't you save yourself some housework and..."

He stood up, went out onto the landing and called up, "You found it yet? It's got to be there somewhere."

Julius said, "What about our understanding, Inspector?"

Above their heads, they heard footsteps moving around, boxes being moved, and something falling over.

Harding said, "Times are changing, Julius, the Met's full of new brooms; you must have heard. Bottom line is, I must treat you the same as I treat everyone else. For the moment, anyway."

"Is that really it? Or have you been talking to someone

who's got it in for me? Keith Chadwick. Tom Adams. I hope they're not getting you to do their dirty work."

DCI Harding pulled out drawers in the chest, scattering unopened shirts, underwear and socks on the floor and then began to rifle through the bedside tables. When Harding didn't reply, Julius added, "Well, are you?"

"It's nothing personal, Julius. I'm just doing what I have to do."

"We did each other a lot of good back in the day, remember?"

"That was then, Julius."

Julius took a last pull on his cigarette and squashed the end in a pub ashtray as he looked the other man in the eye.

"Well, I hope living on your pay packet works out for you. Come and see me when you find it doesn't."

Steps rang out on the attic ladder. Harding met the younger detective on the landing.

"Well?"

From whispers, Julius made out, *What do you mean, it's not there?*

The younger man said out loud, "It's not there. He's clean."

"What about the paperwork?"

"Nothing."

"Are you sure? Because if I go up there and..."

"We'd have found a Penny Black if he'd hidden one."

A voice at the bottom of the stairs called up, "No luck, gov."

Straining to hear everything, Julius caught the sibilance of Harding whispering, "Someone is taking the piss."

Mood suddenly lifted, Julius called out, "Everything hunky-dory, Inspector?"

Harding's face was in his own, now. "We're going to

dismantle this place piece by piece until we find the glue that sticks your arse to this job."

But just then, someone ran up the stairs and delivered a message in low tones.

Harding listened and said, "I do not fucking believe it. I'm being done over. Alright, dust yourself off, Vincent, we're leaving."

Julius had taken up the newspaper he had been reading the night before. As Harding pulled on his coat, he said, "You'll be sending a joiner to fix the door? And a French polisher for the table?"

The front door slammed as the first of the cars started. Julius dropped the newspaper and lay back in bed, breathing hard.

Fuck me, he thought, over and over. *Nice one*, Carrot.

16

"Gerry said I was taken home by some Scotch girl."

This was on Monday morning, in the kitchen at PINZ.

"With a little help from a friend."

"Thanks, Ammo."

"No bother."

"I didn't think you were going that night."

"I changed my mind. I was backstage with Pauline 'til she went on. She's really nice, by the way."

"I really owe you. Did you see what happened?"

"No. First thing I knew about it was when the band stopped playing and Pauline was telling everyone to cool it, like Mick Jagger at Altamont. I thought it was just a tussle at the back there. Then there were people clearing a path and two big guys walking out. Heavies, you know? I went over to have a shufty, of course, and there's daft Donald lying in a swimming pool of his own blood. And you, of course. You didn't look too well either."

"No, I wasn't. Who's this daft Donald?"

"He's a fucking idiot. Doesn't know when to stop. Drugs, drink, whatever. Total space-waster. But he didn't deserve that."

"You think?" Juliet said, and for a moment, she was back there again, shoved against the wall with Donald's stubby fingers exploring, and she being totally unable to do anything about it. She'd give him what he got twice over, she was thinking. And then she'd do it again.

Ammo said, "Listen, J, I've been a wee bit of a bitch recently. Sorry for that."

"Fuck that, Ammo. I don't know what I would have done without you that night."

Ammo grinned.

"Sobered up and got a taxi home?"

"I don't think so."

Juliet didn't know how anxious she'd been about her estrangement from Ammo until they made up that morning. Following that, things had gone well; Ammo was more than helpful, and Juliet herself enjoyed a rare afternoon without any fuck-ups. They ended the day with drinks at the wine bar across the road to celebrate Ginnie's birthday.

Once again, Juliet had the feeling that if she had any real family, it was to be found here, among these people. By the time she stepped off the bus just before her stop on Wandsworth Common, she was in a rare, good mood and looking forward to her day off, when Ammo had promised to help her look for her own place.

Her mood didn't change when she began to daydream about her parents and to conjecture what they would have made of her starting a new life on her own. She imagined finally finding her father, who perhaps had done well for himself by now and might be as happy to buy her a sofa bed or a dining table as he would wrap her in his arms and tell her, *I've been looking for you all these years*.

Pie-in-the-sky, as Maureen would say, who actually knows what the future holds?

She walked by the Common where autumn leaves were turning to mulch, and crossing the busy road, she was quite unfazed to see Colin and three shaven-headed boys, in their boots and braces, clustered around the front door.

They watched her as she approached, daring her to come any closer, she thought. She slowed neither her pace nor stopped. Instead, she met their gaze and saw it flicker as she turned into the gravel patch outside the house and stood there for a moment, taking her time to find her keys, which were buried somewhere in the depths of her bag.

The other boys looked at Colin, but he said nothing; he was staring at the ground. The perverted imp in her head told her to speak to him.

"Hello, brother," she said as she let herself into the house. "It's a cold night. Don't stay out too long."

She let herself in. The door clicked shut behind her.

She could hear the *What the fucks?* from the hallway.

17

Julius had Carrot drive him to the pub in his Jag and drop him off at the harshly lit front entrance, where Benji's imposing figure was casting a shadow over a slice of the car park. Julius got out, leaving Carrot to deal with the car.

He took a gander at the motors already parked and wished he'd had the broken wing mirror on the Jag fixed. Carrot was parking the thing between Chip Thompson's gleaming BMW and Eddie Thoroughgood's Bentley, the one he'd had since becoming top dog up in Tottenham.

Arnie Thompson, he thought, you might as well tell Special Branch about your friends in New Jersey, you and your fucking Cadillac.

He was looking for a particular car and he found it parked discreetly by the exit, the Silver Shadow II belonging to Tom Adams. He was surprised Adams had come. It couldn't be to pay his respects. He'd be on his guard.

He ducked his head to avoid a huge sprig of mistletoe suspended on the porch. When Benji opened the doors for him, he saw paper chains and tinsel above a roomful of animated heads. For fuck's sake, Christmas decorations already? It was only December the second. It rubbed uneasily with the purpose of the night.

Well, Charlie was going to get a noisy send-off; that much was sure. From the speakers of the neon-blue Wurlitzer, Noddy Holder was exhorting everyone to look to the future.

He stepped into the crowded bar, one of three in the Chandlers Arms, a barn of a pub by any yardstick. The place was packed. He stopped and surveyed the room. He saw the big men by the bar, suited and booted and smoking cigars.

Looking beyond them, he took in the lairy, hairy, jack-the-lads, then the dangerous, quiet ones, and those who had come seeking alliances and opportunities. He noted the conspirators, talking in corners.

Fucking hell, he thought. He hadn't expected old Charlie to pull such a crowd, a shedload more than had gone to see him planted at Plumstead cemetery last week, by all accounts. But some of these boys would be here to size him up rather than say cheerio to Charlie.

Even he had heard the chat. People thought he wasn't the Julius Nicholson of old, that he was losing his grip.

Stepping down into the room, he felt all eyes on him, even if some people pretended not to be looking his way.

He had a certain walk that he liked to use in situations like these, ponderous, like each carpet-tile concealed a land-mine. When he did this, he turned his disability into a strength, his ornate, silver-topped walking stick into a symbol of power.

It was, in fact, anything but. Rather, it was a tangible reminder that someone had stood behind him as he waited for a tube at Oxford Circus one morning and pushed him in front of a slowing train. He was lucky to have come out of that so well.

He never found out who pushed him, a psychotic stranger or some nasty bastard out for his blood.

He waved away a pretty girl and her tray of fizz, nodded to one or two guests who tried to catch his eye but said nothing to anyone until he found Gillian, sitting in a corner, talking to Patrick's wife, Carol.

Steph, the assistant manager at one of his bookie's shops, was laying a consoling hand on her wrist and nodding every time Gillian said something.

"Gillian," he said.

The others looked up and shut up.

There was something in his throat. He had to cough before he spoke.

"I'm so very sorry for your loss. I just wanted to say..."

For a moment, he didn't know what he wanted to say. Carol said, "Well?"

He cleared his throat again.

"Charlie was a giant, a legend. Everyone's saying that. But I want you to know..."

He had to cough again. What was this—nerves?

"Know what?" Carol prompted.

"Charlie was more than that to me. He was my friend of mine. I trusted Charlie."

He waited for his well-rehearsed words to hit home and have the desired effect. But Gillian looked like she hadn't heard them. Which was misleading, because she said, "Did he tell you I've another on the way before you let him go on that job?"

Steph put her hand on her wrist again. "Gillian," she said.

"Did he tell you we was all set to move to Harlow? All set."

"Harlow? No, I don't think he did. Gillian, let's talk about this later. Charlie wouldn't have wanted you all upset."

"He was going to get his HGV licence. He kept telling me he'd do no more blags. It was a mug's game. I believed him. Then this."

"Gillian."

Julius gave himself a moment before he leaned closer and whispered, "It's no great comfort, I know, but we will take care of you and your baby. I promise we will."

He waited for her to respond, but she only stared at him blankly. He bent forward, touched her shoulder and moved on.

He worked the room, giving little backslaps to those he knew well, nodding to others and making jokes with those who would appreciate it, all the time keenly conscious of those eyes sizing him up, and looking to fill his shoes and squeeze the Island dry.

Tom Adams was a front-runner; he was sure of that, although Adams would probably have to put a spoke in Keith Chadwick's wheels first. There were others, too, lots of others. Suddenly, it seemed that everyone wanted a piece of the Island, and he had still to find out why. Thinking about this, he made another slow circuit of the room.

Between gaps in the clusters of drinkers, he caught glimpses of grainy photos of Charlie that had been enlarged, framed and hung on the walls. Charlie and his little boy (Marcus, was it?) in their Millwall strips, frozen in a park somewhere. Charlie and some people in the pub, one or two faces diplomatically airbrushed. Charlie with long hair in his Bermudas somewhere on the Costas, and Charlie with fellow revolutionaries in front of TV cameras that time they declared UDI for the Isle of Dogs.

He wondered vaguely what Charlie might have become had he been allowed to live. Not a fucking lorry driver, not if he had something to do with it. He'd had bigger plans for him.

The thing about Charlie was not what a nice guy he had been, but how useful he would have been to the firm. No, it was more than that; it was a matter of how useful he would have been to him, personally.

Since Chisel had been sidelined and Jimmy was tragically no longer a prospect, he had seen Charlie as the front-runner to be his number two, a resource of support at a time when he most needed it. Advancing Charlie would have been the next best thing to having someone with his blood coursing through their veins.

Oh, God, to have someone who had his back.

I need help, he said, habitually these days, to no one but himself. The angina seemed to be getting worse, but it was the loneliness that tore a new hole in him every day. God knew what he would do now.

He made a signal to Carrot; time to go. *Look to the future?* I'm sorry, Noddy, he thought, as he stepped out into a freezing December night, but I can't fucking see where that is.

18

On the cracked steps of Juliet's latest disappointment, Ammo said, "Well, what did you expect, on what you can afford?"

"Something a bit better than that. I mean, something with windows would be a start."

"It had a window."

"I've seen toilets with bigger ones."

"Clapham's going up in the world. You have to expect to pay for that. What about Wandsworth?"

"No way. I need to put some distance between me and my old life. This will be me, starting again and on my own terms."

"You'll be lucky to do that, hen. You always take a bit of the old life with you, I've found. You've ruled out that flat share in Streatham?"

"Didn't you see the way they looked at me? They might as well have hung a 'No blacks, no Irish' sign in the window."

"What a bunch of cunts."

Crossing the road, they scanned the postcards Sellop-taped in a newsagent's window. Among the usual ads for lost cats, bicycles, odd-job men and escorts, were a few for bedsits and flats. Ammo stood outside the nearby phone box and lit a cigarette while Juliet dialled a number and then thumbed a 10p into the slot.

"You waiting on this phone?" a voice said. Ammo turned and saw two boys, a few years younger than she was. She told them, "She'll be out in a minute."

"You with her?" the boy asked. He began to rap on the window. Juliet turned away to finish her call. When she tried to dial the second number, the boy ignored Ammo and pulled open the door.

"How long you going to be, sister?" he said.

Juliet turned and started to protest.

The other boy jeered.

"She ain't your sister. Look at her. She's with a white girl."

The best place to find a flat was in the evening paper. Without fail, Gerry came home with one, bought from the toothless old soldier who stood outside Gerry's local in all weathers, rasping *Ee'nin' Stanna'd! Ee'nin' Stanna'd!*

He leafed through the sports pages while he ate his dinner, and then Maureen might glance at the TV guide or the fashion section.

Until recently, Juliet had never bothered with the papers. Now, she eagerly scanned the ads for accommodation.

This evening, returning from flat-hunting, she saw that Gerry had already been home but was getting into his car again, wearing a smart new suit, with his hair newly trimmed. Something was going on, that much was obvious.

Dropping her bags and slipping off her coat, Juliet looked for the paper, which could usually be found in the kitchen or on the little teak table by Maureen's TV chair. Upstairs, the taps were running, and she could hear Maureen wailing *You don't have to say you love me...* as she prepared for her bath.

There was no response when she shouted up to ask for the paper. Then, remembering that Gerry sometimes spirited it down to the basement office, she opened the door under the stairs and descended the flight of steps.

The basement was originally a cold store with a secondary room and chute to receive deliveries of coal. This smaller room had been converted into a washroom with a compact handbasin and loo. Both rooms had high, narrow, horizontal windows, which gave poor illumination and a view of the weeds in the gravel outside the house.

The office occupied a footprint just a little smaller than that of the house above. An ideal place for Gerry to work at the big partners' desk or receive visitors, had it not been for the restrictive height of the ceiling. Men taller than Gerry had to bow their heads until they were seated in one of two club armchairs, or on the worn-leather Chesterfield sofa stationed opposite a sideboard laden with half-empty bottles of scotch and gin.

Juliet saw the place only when she showed down a client; Gerry liked to keep his little domain very private.

Now, when she entered it, she felt a chill. She had come in search of the newspaper, but it was impossible to be in this room without recalling Larry Hughes' corpulent physique and leering eyes parked in the chair nearest the door.

For a moment, she saw him lying on the floor where her feet stood now, a patch of colour on his baby-blue shirt where the bullet had torn into him.

She looked about, at the furniture, at the busily-patterned rug.

The room was in its usual state of disarray. It would test anyone, finding something out of its usual, wrong place.

The standard lamp was broken, its bulb shattered, the shade lying on the floor. But when that had happened or how, she had no way of knowing. The carpet was spotted with stains, but again, unruly evenings were frequently held down here, and stuff got spilt. She told herself yet again that she was being ridiculous.

She had come in search of the newspaper, but now that she was here, another thought struck her, one quite unconnected with whatever had happened, or had not happened, to Larry Hughes.

Gerry's desk would be an obvious place to begin looking for her birth certificate, the one document that would reveal who her real father was.

She was scanning the paperwork strewn there, invoices, receipts and open letters, when something scrawled on a yellow notepad caught her eye. Moving an overflowing ashtray, she switched on the desk light and saw her name and the date of her birth underlined twice in red ink.

Her birthday wasn't for months, so it couldn't be a reminder to buy another of the interesting gifts that neither he nor Maureen had ever acknowledged giving her.

Curiosity piqued, she tried the drawers, which were unlocked. Maureen would be in the bathroom for the best part of an hour, and Gerry looked like he was off to an important business meeting. She had the place to herself.

You didn't throw away a birth certificate; she told herself. That had to be here, somewhere.

Gerry's desk was as dishevelled as his appearance had been, up until this evening anyway. Among the mess he seemed to have swept into the top drawers she found phone pads covered with numbers and decorated with doodles, sheets of Green Shield stamps, half-eaten tubes of strong mints, sets of keys, sunglasses, lighter flints and a set of Polaroid snapshots of people at a party somewhere, one of whom looked like an actress she had seen on TV.

In a middle drawer, she found his passport with entry stamps for Palma Mallorca, Tenerife and Gibraltar. There was paperwork relating to the sale of some hair salons, correspondence from a firm of solicitors and a stack of double-entry bookkeeping ledgers.

In the bottom drawer, she found some curious old newspaper cuttings, one about a police raid on a Knightsbridge drinking club, another describing the arrest of a once-famous film producer and a third reporting the armed robbery of a Martins bank in Islington.

Apart from a single handwritten letter, which she found too intimate to read, the signature was all but indecipherable but might have read 'Gil'. Nothing that told her anything about Gerry or how the Hobsons came to be raising someone else's child, a child who happened to be black.

Perhaps the important stuff, such as her birth certificate, was kept in the two locked filing cabinets or in the small safe that rested on the floor behind one of the armchairs.

She could do no more without keys or Gerry's compliance. She found the newspaper under a cushion and went upstairs, wondering why her birthdate was of any significance to a man who barely registered her existence.

PART II

19

While Julius Nicholson was opening doors and switching on lights in his empty house, Juliet Hobson was looking for a niche in which she might try to sleep in the harsh concrete geometry of the South Bank.

She was wearing jeans and trainers and had put on a couple of T-shirts under a thick pullover, more for the sake of taking extra stuff with her than as protection against the bitterly cold night air.

She hadn't anticipated sleeping rough tonight, but she was no longer in a position to be certain of anything.

Leaving the house as silently as possible, she had walked up to the Common, where she took a night bus to Battersea. She found the Peabody easily enough and lugged her bags up several flights of concrete stairs to the floor where Ammo said she lived.

"You get a decent view of the river from the fourth floor," she remembered Ammo said that quite distinctly and looked across the road in the direction of the Thames. She couldn't see it.

People were still around, most of them coming back from wherever they had spent the evening, some noisier than others. An old man reeking of marijuana asked her if she was looking for something.

She shook her head and moved on. She had no idea which flat was Ammo's squat. She walked down the poorly lit outside landings and knocked on every door on the fourth floor, becoming increasingly anxious. There was no sign of Ammo.

Those people who answered their doors and listened to her said, no, they had not seen a girl of that description on their floor.

When a police car pulled into the yard below, flashing blue lights, she slipped quickly down the stairs and made her exit at the rear of the block. Shouldering her bags, she began to walk, distressed, confused, and with no idea of where she was going.

She followed the river without a particular destination in mind. The army-surplus rucksack and the bright turquoise holdall contained everything she thought she'd need for squat living.

In one bag were her underwear and socks, her toothbrush, deodorant, tampons, and nightwear. In the other was her building society savings book, a loaf of bread, some bananas, a knife, fork and spoon and a roll of toilet paper.

She'd also packed Marvin, a knitted bear she'd had since she was small. Someone might look at the contents of these bags and draw the conclusion that she had been planning this for weeks.

After wearily circumnavigating the National Theatre, a set of stops delivered her back to the waterside. She leaned on the concrete wall and looked out across the river, where London was still lit up.

People were walking along the Embankment, returning to their homes and beds from theatres and cinemas, restaurants and pubs. She ached to be one of them. This was so fucked up.

Tomorrow she would pull on her woolly hat, turn up her collar and draw out all her savings while that was still possible. That should be enough to buy her a bed for a while and some time to think. Tomorrow had never seemed more distant.

She tried to order her thoughts. The main thing was not to attract attention and to find somewhere to spend the night.

Under the theatre was a shadowy, cavernous area where she and Ammo had once watched some boys skateboarding. Inside, she found some old, flattened cardboard boxes which might make a bed of sorts.

Weak light filtered in from a lamp on the embankment. She looked about and listened. It appeared she was alone.

She collected pieces of cardboard and made a pillow for herself with her bags. She drew tight the cords on her coat.

She took a last look around before sandwiching herself between the cardboard sheets. She brought up her knees and, curling up like a caged hamster, she let the tears come at last.

She willed herself to stay awake and alert, but after all that had happened earlier that evening, her mind was drained, and she succumbed to sleep. Then, when she woke just before dawn, half-frozen and with the awful memory of the night before still playing in her head like a looped horror film, her head was on the ground, and her bags had gone. She tried to scream, but nothing came out.

Only a day before her life turned itself inside-out, everything had been going so well at work, anyway.

Things had been better since she and Ammo had made up. Even the shop's takings were up, marginally at least. They were working well together, Ammo nudging her gently towards becoming something like a competent manager.

They got their pay packets just before lunch, and Juliet insisted on taking Ammo out for something to eat. There was an Italian cafe a short walk up the road. Each ordered pasta and a glass of beer.

"We have a place like this just down the road from us in Glasgow," Ammo told her. "Well, a Glaswegian version, anyway. My dad used to love it there."

"Your dad did?"

"Aye, my dad."

"Is your dad still, you know..."

"Is he still alive? Yes, of course he is."

"Only you don't talk about your parents. So, I wondered."

"Both alive and well. And both annoying as hell."

"What do they do? If you don't mind me asking?"

Ammo took a moment to search in her bag for something she didn't find. Then she looked up and said, brightly, "Dad lectures in art history. My mam teaches in a junior school. And bang, there goes my street cred."

She laughed, but Juliet could see her waiting for a reaction. She added, "You might like to keep that between us, though."

"Don't be ashamed of your parents," Juliet told her, a hint of bitterness sounding. "At least you know who they are."

They had taken the bus home together, Ammo waving vaguely at the monolithic block where she lived and said Juliet really should come over some time, it might be fun, if she didn't mind the squalor.

She watched Ammo cross the road in front of the bus and the red light and then run across another road in the direction of the flats. The bus turned the corner and made slow progress in the Friday evening traffic as it climbed the hill towards Clapham Junction. She didn't see her friend re-crossing the road.

Gerry had been snoring loudly on the sofa when she let herself into the house.

"Christ, what time is it?" he said.

"Ten to seven."

"I'll be late. Why didn't she wake me? Is she here?"

"I don't know?"

He went to the stairs and called. Then he said, "I remember now. She's out with the girls. Hen night. A *male stripper*, if you will."

"Oh, have you had anything? Only I was going to warm up the shepherd's pie from last night."

"Eating out. Business. If I'm not already too bloody late."

He pulled on his blue blazer, straightened the collar of his pink striped shirt, and shook the hair out of his face. He took a glance in the mirror before snatching up his keys and his fags and said, "Right, then, I'm off."

She heard the front door slam behind him and tyres spinning on the gravel as he made his getaway, destination unknown, as per usual. Juliet hung up her coat, kicked off her shoes and opened the fridge.

The glass bowl with the pie wasn't there anymore. Looking around, she saw it sitting on the side, empty and unwashed. Colin, again. She wondered why he was home so early. Normally, he wouldn't be expected for another hour at least.

Annoying if he was going to be here tonight. She'd hoped to have a quiet night in, watching rubbish on TV and doing her nails. The set in the living room was still on; when she switched it off, she could hear Sham 69 clamouring from Colin's record player. There was some shouting, too; he'd got his mates round.

Returning to the kitchen, she put the kettle on. Well, there were no tomatoes, so just cheese on toast with a splash of Worcestershire sauce would have to do.

When the cheese had begun to bubble, she took the tray with her dinner and a mug of tea into the living room and settled herself on the couch, hoping there was something halfway decent on the box.

And then it happened. Again. The lights went off; the TV screen went blank. The music from upstairs abruptly stopped, and the swearing began.

There was some shuffling on the floorboards above, then heavy boots stomped down the stairs. There was more shouting in the hall, and then the front door opened and slammed shut.

Another power cut, for fuck's sake. Why didn't the government sort it out once and for all? Well, fuck it. There was a candle in her room provided for just such an eventuality. There was her big radio-cassette player, which ran on batteries, and a continental quilt to keep her warm. Early night, then.

She took her tray and went carefully upstairs. Opening the door of her room, she struck a match, found the candle under her bed and lit it.

The place looked nicer in the softer light. Going to the bathroom, she brushed her teeth and changed into her sleepwear. She could hear Colin stumbling about in the dark.

There was a crash and the sound of glass shattering,

most likely the low table that was usually stacked with football programmes, beer tins and ashtrays.

She closed her bedroom door and sat for a while removing her make-up before getting into bed. Reaching over her bedside table, Juliet turned on the big radio-cassette player. John Peel wouldn't be on for ages, but she could put up with Kid Jensen in the meantime.

The radio crackled as John Travolta and Olivia Newton-John chirped, *You're the One That I Want*. She turned down the volume when she heard his voice from the landing.

"So, you're in there, are you?"

"I'm having an early night."

The door opened, and there he was, using the door-frame to prop himself upright. He was wearing his bleached jeans, no socks, and nothing on his top despite the cold.

Someone had lipsticked a huge red swastika across his hairless chest. He was swaying now.

"Not going out then, with all your fine friends?"

She said, "You're back early," which he was supposed to take as an innocuous observation. After all, he must have got back hours before his usual time. She could almost taste the hostility in his voice.

"What if I am? I'll be early every day now. I'll always be here."

"Are you drunk?" Well, what was she supposed to say?

"I lost my fucking job, didn't I? So, I'm very fucking drunk. And I'm going to get a lot more drunk."

"You lost your job? That sucks. What happened?"

As if she cared, but...

"What's it fucking matter what happened? What's it to you with your fancy job in Chelsea? Fucking manageress. You? It's a fucking joke. You think you're fucking *it* don't you? You fucking lot, dossing in our houses, taking our jobs."

"Calm down, Colin. Look, you need to sleep this off.

You'll feel better about it in the morning. Hey, you were only saying yesterday your job was shit."

"What the fuck do you know about it?" he said, staggering towards her. "You can shut your trap. You and your fucking Chelsea shop. So, you're the boss now? I'll show you who's the boss."

He crashed into her bedside table, dislodging the radio cassette player and extinguishing the candle, but his flailing arms chanced to find her in the dark and take a firm hold.

"What are you doing? Colin?"

"I'm going to explain a few things to you."

He pushed her back down upon her bed, hard, his considerable weight pinioning her while he struggled to undo his belt. Juliet strained, writhed, and called on every muscle she had as she tried to pull away from him.

His hand was across her mouth as he whispered, "Don't make this hard on yourself, princess."

She panicked, screamed, but nothing escaped the fingers closing upon her mouth and her face.

There was no sound, only his grunts as he fought to free himself and the rasps of hot, excited breath she felt upon her cheeks.

Later, she would have time to consider how she might have done things had not the lights, the downstairs TV, and the music from Colin's room all come back on at once.

That was enough to throw Colin off his stride and for Juliet to tear herself from his grip. She fell off the bed and got up, expecting to have to defend herself, but he was just lying there, looking at her.

Behind the tattooed hand lying across his open flies showed a dark, wet patch of underwear. The dopey smile said it all.

"You cunt!"

He was grinning at her, rubbing himself.

"Get out. Get the fuck out of my room. Now!"

"Come here, sis."

"You tried to rape me. Get out."

"Don't know what you're fucking talking about."

"You should be locked up. Your parents…"

"You won't tell them. Who do you think they'd believe?"

"Me, you shit. They'd believe me."

She wasn't sure, though.

He swung his feet over the side of the bed and sat up. The dopey demeanour disappeared.

"You don't want to talk to me like that."

She could feel the menace. He was going to stand up, and when he did, he was going to strike her or do worse. He was too close for her to turn and run; he'd be on her in a minute. So, fizzing with adrenaline, she picked up the only heavy thing there was to hand, raised it as high as she could and smashed it down on his head.

The big radio-cassette player glanced off his temple before it crashed to the floor.

Colin was still sitting on her bed, bleeding and swaying. His last words before she picked up the broken machine and struck him once more, as hard as her draining strength would allow, were, "…the fuck?"

He fell forward, crumpling onto her bedroom carpet, where he lay still and landed on his face, the swastika against the floor.

Motionless her heart hammering and her breath coming in short bursts, Juliet squatted by the side of the boy, preserving a prudent distance in case he was shamming.

"Colin. Colin? Don't be stupid."

She sat down on her bed and watched him for movement.

There was none.

He lay where he was, perfectly still, a small pool of

blood on the carpet by his shaven head. She didn't know how long she had sat there watching him.

Then she touched his wrist. There was no pulse.

She bubbled with panic.

She hadn't meant to kill him, for God's sake. It was an accident. No, it wasn't an accident, exactly. So, what was it? She knew what had happened, but how could she put all that into words, and who would believe her? She might have light skin and green eyes, but she had never felt less white than at this moment.

What the fuck would Maureen and Gerry say? She had just killed their only son. This wasn't something on TV, though it seemed just as unreal.

There he was, lying in front of her with not a breath in his body. She had done that.

Oh, God. She had killed him. She had killed Colin.

A moment of lucid thought. Juliet entered Gerry and Maureen's room at the front of the house and peered outside.

No cars on the gravel, only a man walking a dog, who happened to glance up at her as he passed under a streetlamp. She would have to get out and get out before anyone knew she was gone.

Quickly grabbing everything she thought she might need in the unknown future, she switched off her light and closed her bedroom door behind her. Then she turned off Colin's music and shut his door, too.

20

A blast of icy wind funnelled along the river roused Juliet from a troubled sleep. Her eyes had no sooner blinked open than she saw Colin collapsing before her.

Waves of anxiety and chill, nauseating fear crowded in as she tried desperately to collect her thoughts.

She got up and looked about as if the slowly receding darkness had concealed her bags, but both were gone, and with them her savings book and her last dregs of hope. She scanned the embankment for someone clutching her bright-blue holdall.

She glanced at her watch: six fifty-two. At Maureen and Gerry's, no one rose before nine on Saturdays. It might be another hour before anyone got up to chivvy her into cooking their breakfast. They would find Colin the moment they opened the door of her room.

What the holy fuck had she done? She'd picked up that heavy machine and slammed it down on his shaven skull with dreadful force, as if this one awful act would balance the books for everything that was wrong with her life.

She pulled her legs up to her chest and peered at the

dirty grey river over the scuffed and threadbare knees of her black jeans.

On the Embankment, people with weekend jobs were already streaming towards the Underground stations, cocooned in warm coats and scarves. She would do anything to rewind the last few hours, to have back her crappy life, but Colin had killed all that just as surely as she had killed him.

She needed help, she needed food. She needed to see Ammo. She would know what to do. Where had Ammo been last night? Had she got the wrong floor?

No good going back there now. If the police went to PINZ, which they probably would at some time today, they would hear how close the pair had been and might watch the Battersea flats.

She needed the toilet. There was probably one in the foyer of the theatre or one of the other places around here, but nothing would be open now, so she squatted in a corner and accidentally soaked what might again be her bedding if she had to spend another night sleeping rough.

Pulling up her jeans, she zipped up her coat, it was too cold to hang about.

Her head down, hands thrust into the pockets of her coat, she started to walk along the riverfront. She had been down this section of the Embankment many times, but never before had it seemed so alien.

She had not gone far when she became aware of homeless people bundled into corners, sleeping in niches, curled up under clutters of cardboard, while others were on the move, loaded down with bulky plastic carriers and sleeping bags.

Walking on with no destination in mind, walking to keep warm. She was hungry, thirsty, and extremely frightened.

By eleven o'clock that Saturday morning, with the crowds beginning to be drawn into the gravitational pull of the West End, she was working on the assumption that all was discovered and that the police would be looking for a girl fitting her description. Her coat, one of Maureen's catalogue purchases, was a distinctive mustard colour.

As she negotiated the crowds heading towards Piccadilly and Oxford Street, she caught sight of McDonald's arches and pulled open the heavy glass doors, immersing herself in a blast of warm air, taunted by a cruel aroma of frying food.

There was a sign for the ladies, and once inside, she put her head under a tap and drank until she could drink no more.

Washing her face, she tried to bring some order to her hair with just her fingers, before taking off her coat and turning it inside out, so its dark-brown lining showed.

A woman with two little boys came in and hurried them into a cubicle.

The coat didn't look too bad. Without close inspection, it would pass, she thought, only now she couldn't fasten it up or warm her hands in the pockets. Not for a moment did she consider that rather than looking for a mustard coat, the police might be looking for a half-caste with green eyes.

She used the toilet, taking her time, in no hurry to be out again among the Christmas shoppers. For this little while, she was safe until she thought about what she had done, then she thought about her immediate and long-term future, and again, she cried.

That afternoon, she walked. She didn't know where she walked, only that all roads led her back into the West End.

She wandered up a street leading away from Soho and found herself on Oxford Street, amid tumultuous Christmas crowds. The early evening light had all but died, and above the jostling heads and the thousands of festive lights, blue and red lasers streaked into the sky.

She had hardly the strength to extricate herself from the carrying multitude, and yet somehow she found herself in a quieter street, back in Soho, somewhere. An alleyway took her out near the Windmill Theatre.

Here, there was noise and neon windows advertising girls, striptease, peep shows. Touts for clubs hustled on corners, but no one approached her. Exhausted, walking with no destination in mind, she was hungrier than she knew it was possible to be.

At last, she found a deep doorway of a closed shop and slid down onto the cold ground. Sitting there as traffic passed, shop-workers went home and two girls in thigh-boots had a laugh and a fag on the corner.

She saw people passing who couldn't see her.

The thought crossed her mind that she could walk into a police station and turn herself in. She would get a meal and a bed then. Ten or twenty years of them.

She let her eyelids droop, and a collage of images flashed up. Colin on the floor with blood seeping from his head, policemen asking questions, people in white body-suits moving methodically about her room, Gerry and Maureen's ashen faces.

She might have sat there longer, gone to sleep even, but a bright torchlight had shone in her face and a police constable said, *Come on, you can't sleep here, on your way, now.*

With nowhere else to settle, she found a space on the steps of the statue of Eros at Piccadilly Circus and huddled among tourists talking in different languages.

A plan took shape.

It wasn't so much a plan as an upgrading of the vague idea that Ammo could provide help into a conviction that the Scots girl could somehow save her and set things right. At 8.30 on Monday morning on The Kings Road she would intercept Ammo on her way to PINZ and the discovery that Juliet wasn't there.

'What's going on, Julio?' That's what Ammo would said to her.

She did not know what she would say to her. That something awful, something terrible had happened, and she needed a place to crash, just while she sorted her head out. That she couldn't tell her what it was, not just yet. That she needed a little money for food, because she hadn't eaten since they had their pasta lunch together and would pay her back as soon as.

As soon as what, she thought? There was never going to be a time when she would live a normal life.

As a fugitive, she would never work a normal job and get paid at the end of the week and have her own place, as she had dreamed.

Have her own place? She laughed aloud. Having a floor was a fantastic dream just now. She raised her head.

"What have I done?"

21

Sitting beneath last year's Pirelli calendar in the office, which had previously been Kath's dining room, Julius Nicholson scowled as the desk phone began to chirp.

He didn't like people calling him at home; he rather thought he had made that plain to everyone, so he tensed just a little as he picked up the receiver.

"Hello? Oh, fuck, it's you."

Leslie Shipham told him in a whisper that he was organising a 'Christmas do' for the firm, and how much could he put him down for with regards to the finger buffet?

Finger buffet? A Christmas sodding party? His head rang with 'fuck-me's. What did they think this was? The Isle of Dogs branch of C&A? They'd be having whip-rounds for birthdays next. What did they call those American puppets everyone was going big on, Miss Piggy and the frog? Muppets, that was it.

They were like a bunch of fucking Muppets. And they'd be just as funny if their rank stupidity hadn't gotten a good man killed.

"Emergencies only on this line. You know that."

"This is an emergency. It's Christmas in two weeks.

Everything's booked up; I had to pull a fast one to get The Swan. If I didn't book it, some other fucker would have."

"All right. Put me down for a bullseye, and I don't want to hear any more about it. And Leslie? Let's have another chat about that last little job. You know the one. Soon as you're free."

It was one thing after another, he thought. He had had enough already this morning, what with trying to work out the profit margin if he went into motor garages.

Only, he'd heard of a tasty venture going for an absolute song if he could come up with the readies as soon as. Its owner, Danny Mottram, had done a flit to the Costas. It was actually a chain of four garages, which should have been doing much better than it was. In the right hands, these places would make a mint, he was sure of it.

The opportunity was too good to miss, but because of his massive outlay on a chain of *Chez Michel* hairdressing salons, there was now a cash-flow crisis. True, there was money tied up in investments, but he couldn't release that without making substantial losses.

There were other parties interested; Danny told him he'd have to be quick. Any seller would say that, but the grapevine had confirmed it.

He ran his eye down the column of figures one more time. He had to have these garages, no question, but quite how he was going to manage that, he just couldn't fathom.

He didn't like what he saw coming, but everything told him it was unavoidable. If there was one person who could go over the books and show him how he could raise the money without fucking up everything else, that person was Chisel.

Talk about a last resort. He hadn't asked Gerry Hobson for anything except his regular bookkeeping services since they had parted company all those years ago.

The receiver was barely back in its cradle when the phone rang again. Les forgot to cost in the vol-au-vents? He smiled as he picked it up. He was going to enjoy telling Leslie Shipham where he could stick his sodding canapés.

"Yes?"

The smile disappeared. He stopped thinking about garages.

It took him a moment to digest what Carrot was telling him.

He didn't believe it, not at first. Was he having a laugh?

Desmond? No fucking way. Desmond had always been solid, no matter what some of the others thought of him. It made no sense.

Are you *sure*? He demanded. You had better be fucking well sure about this. If he'd had to guess who was sitting on the rail ready to jump ship, he would have backed any of the rest of them before Desmond. But there it was, and he'd now have to talk about damage limitations, find out what Desmond knew and decide how useful that information would be to his new employer, Tom Adams.

He knew what Leslie's reaction would be. He'd never liked Desmond, for no better reason than that his skin was darker than his own sallow covering.

"What did he expect," he'd be crowing, "They can't be trusted, that lot. He was always too quiet, wasn't he? They're the ones you have to watch."

Well, why didn't you, Leslie, he thought.

It was funny how little time he had for people who judged a man by the shade of his skin. Was Desmond's moonlight connected with simmering hostility from people like Les?

Ten-to-one, Les would say it had been banter, that Desmond liked it. It had taken him long enough to put aside the prejudices from his own youth and judge a man on his abilities alone.

He'd taken on Desmond because he was a good strong-arm man. He knew when to use force, and he knew when to stop, unlike some of them. A firm like his own needed someone like Desmond. It was a bitter pill, because he'd liked him, thought he was a loyal soldier up to now.

And going to Tom Adams, of all the people he might have betrayed him for. Adams himself had been getting cheeky of late, like he didn't know whose manor this was. He would retaliate, of course he would. Just how and to what degree was something he'd be giving some serious thought.

It was funny, too, how things turned out. Donkey's years ago, he'd gone to football with lads who liked to let off steam with a scrap. Saturdays over at Upton Park had been the best, there were always some clowns wearing the wrong scarves who had got themselves lost down a side street.

People who thought football hooliganism started in the late Sixties hadn't been down his way ten years earlier at a Hammers-Millwall game.

He'd always liked a scrap. Some of his teddy-boy mates had fallen in with some wankers who called themselves the White Defence League. The WDL didn't like the way the streets looked now, all those black faces and funny shops.

Now the scraps weren't just on Saturdays. Anyone whose face didn't fit was fair game. Blacks, Asians, anyone like that.

He'd gone along with them at first, just for the punch-ups. With him, it wasn't personal. They dragged him to a few of their meetings, always some bloke in a whistle and shiny shoes spouting off. Christ, those things were boring. But his mates seemed to swallow it all and went out looking for more trouble.

The thing was that a lot of them were sound geezers.

Some of what they were on about made sense, of course it did. At bottom, you were a white bloke. You didn't hang around with blacks and poofs because that's not who you were; it was as simple as that.

You may have given up cracking their heads, but you kept them at arm's length. Look, you were who you were.

So, when Angelica turned up at the Candy Kane wearing something that sparkled and green eyes lit up the club, he affected not to notice her.

But of course, he had.

When she passed his upholstered booth and their eyes met, it was like getting an electric shock. At first, he was angry.

Angry with her for looking, angry with himself for allowing the confusion which now raged within him.

There had been no connection; she was working, and he was just a customer.

She was black, and he was white, for God's sake.

His associates had seen her too, but when they made salacious comments, he just smiled and kept her in his sights and watched those dark, slender legs as she bobbed about the room selling cigarettes and cigars from her tray.

22

Juliet's whole world had crumbled away in the space of a weekend, so it seemed unfair somehow that Sloane Square remained unchanged.

The same buses were letting people off at Peter Jones, and morning commuters were bustling as usual from the underground station, seemingly oblivious to the chilling wind animating bare branches in the Square.

Snapshots of the last two days and nights overlay the shuttling momentum of rush-hour King's Road: the sympathetic face at the night-shelter door telling her to come earlier the next evening; lights on the river shimmering through her tears; the homeless young man who made a place for her under a railway arch; stale doughnuts glistening in a bakery bin and the hard bed with the red blanket where she had slept like the dead.

It was a moment before she could bring the Chelsea morning into focus.

If Ammo hadn't been delayed, she should be arriving any time in the next quarter-hour. PINZ, across the street and a couple of doors up, looked just as it had when she and

Ammo had been the last ones out on Friday night, laughing and joking and making plans.

She saw a police car stuck in traffic, slowly moving towards her, and slipped into the deep doorway at her back.

She'd made her plan. She'd tell Ammo to meet her at lunchtime in the Bricklayers Arms, a tiny pub tucked away in a backstreet behind Kings Road.

Ammo could be relied on to buy her a drink and would automatically ask if she wanted something to eat, and then she'd tell Ammo how she could help.

She wouldn't be asking for much; all she'd need was a blanket and any food that Ammo could spare until she got herself on her feet. Because that was what she would do. With Ammo's help, she would find one of those jobs that asks no questions. Scrubbing pans in a kitchen, handing out flyers like the kids did for PINZ, anything, to survive.

Crossing the road, she found another shop doorway and waited.

Buses came and went, but no Ammo.

A few doors down, she glimpsed a familiar knot of people standing outside the doors of PINZ. There was Ginnie, pogoing to keep warm and behind her, Christian, looking ill again. She must have missed Ammo's bus arriving because there she was now, only yards away, lighting a cigarette.

She stayed in the doorway, called her once and then a little more loudly. Just after one o'clock, she was exactly where she had planned to be, sitting in a corner booth of the Bricklayers Arms.

"So, what's happened that you can't come into the shop today? And is it catching?"

Ammo bought the drinks. "Are you hungry?" she said. The chalkboard by the bar screamed pepper steak, lasagne, Scotch broth, and mussels. Juliet swallowed and said she might manage a ham and cheese toastie, a diplomatic choice, given the enormity of the favour she was about to ask.

She could imagine how the tabloids would sensationalise Colin's death, herself the monster of the piece and still at large.

If Ammo was found to have assisted her, she'd be dragged into it, too. She'd lose her job, at the very least.

Any publicity is good publicity, Chas always said, but that was for the small stuff, not this. It has only been weeks since Sid Vicious apparently had killed his girlfriend in New York, and the papers had wrung that story dry.

The food arrived. Ammo had ordered herself a salad with chips on the side. Typical Ammo.

"So?" she said. "What's been happening, Julio? If you don't mind me saying, you look like shit. Your mascara's everywhere. Here."

She rummaged in her bag and brought out a little bottle and a packet of cotton-wool wipes.

"Nip to the toilets and sort yourself out."

Juliet took her time eating her sandwich, relishing the melting cheese, the salty ham and crispy toast like she was tasting everything for the first time. She watched Ammo nibbling on her salad.

She shouldn't do this to her; she knew that, but she was drowning, so she had no choice but to ask her for safe haven. This wasn't something she could just blurt out. If she did, Ammo would insist on knowing everything over lunch. No, she would have to work around the subject before going in for the kill.

"I had a rough weekend."

Ammo laughed and picked up a long, greasy chip. "Been there, Julio!"

"It started on Friday night. Things got totally fucked up at home."

"Do I get to hear the grisly details?"

You really wouldn't want to hear them, Juliet thought.

"How about you? What did you do Friday evening?"

"That gig at the Marquee. We were going to meet up there, remember?"

She did, though it seemed ages ago.

"And did you go?"

"No, did you?"

"Like I said, home life got a bit... So why didn't you go?"

"Oh. We had a little crisis at the squat. This guy overdosed. Not majorly, as it turned out, but we had to stay with him in case he got worse. So, like you, a fucked-up Friday."

Juliet bit her lip.

She hesitated before asking, "So were you at the squat all Friday evening? On the fourth

-floor flophouse, as you call it?"

"Sad, but true. Why are you asking?"

She hadn't meant to broach this matter at all. But she had to know.

"It's just that when things got really bad at home, I came looking for you."

Ammo put down the chip and wiped her fingers on the paper napkin.

"Where, exactly?"

"At the squat. In Battersea."

"You were there?"

"Yes, about nine. Maybe ten, I don't know."

"Go on."

"And I couldn't find you. I tried every door on the fourth floor. The were two flats I couldn't get a response from: one looked empty, and the lights were all off in the other. Had I got your address wrong?"

"Juliet, I don't understand why you're asking me all this. What I do at night is my business, okay? I'm not on your time. Or Chas'."

"It was just weird..."

"No, I'll tell you what's weird. It's you turning up in a doorway this morning and skiving off work. It's you wearing Friday's makeup and filthy clothes. That's weird. Fuck me, what have you been doing? You smell like a feral cat, by the way. And the weirdest thing of all? You get me to buy you lunch and repay me by acting like the fucking Gestapo."

She wriggled out of the booth and snatched up her bag. "I don't know what's wrong with you, Juliet. Who are you to give me the third fucking degree? I suggest you fuck off back to Wandsworth and sort yourself out. I won't tell Chas I've seen you. You two can sort all that out yourselves."

Juliet watched as her friend stormed down the barroom and into the bright day outside. The pub door wasn't the only one closing just now, she thought. One door closes, another one opens, so they say. Well, not this time. She put on her coat and was about to go when she saw the chips that Ammo had left in the bowl.

23

He flicked on the wipers and turned off the car radio. He was angry. Dangerously angry.

"So, who's in the frame for the bookie's job? Which of those impertinent fuckers thought it was okay to knock off one of my shops? I want names."

He was driving too fast; his gear changes were too sudden. Last week, everything had blown up when two likely lads with a sawn-off and a driver had jumped the queue at his Cubitt Town betting shop and caused Carol there to shit her pants as she slid the money over the counter.

Everyone knew whose business that was; she should have been safer than a nun in a knocking shop. He'd had to visit the place in person before it properly sank in that he'd been hit. He'd lost Carol too, apparently. It was more serious than lost takings. This was a message, a loud one.

"Somebody thinks they can take me on. Me. Here, on the Isle of Dogs. Who's the cunt, Carrot?"

Carrot spat out whatever he had been sucking on and dropped it into the ashtray.

"Well, we know Tom Adams wants in here. And you *have* stepped on his toes, as I understand it?"

He sometimes thought Carrot knew more than he should. Only last year, Julius bought a plot of land down by Canary Wharf for no better reason than he had heard Adams wanted it. This was his manor; Adams had no right.

God knew what he would do with half an acre of wasteland now.

"So, Adams, that Welsh bastard, Chadwick. Van Dijk. They've all been cocking their legs and pissing against my tree. And it has to stop."

He pulled over and parked on a dockside overlooking the Thames. Rivulets of rain were trickling down the windscreen, and the far bank of the river was shrouded in fog. Lost to view, a seagull was squawking.

"Oh, there's one more bit of news, though perhaps now's not the time..."

"Spill it."

"I leaned on DC Rogers, and he looked a bit harder at Leslie's printworks job."

"And?"

"Well, we could have a problem."

"How so?"

"A leaky ship, much as you thought. They knew something was going down where it did, and they had a fair idea of when, too."

"All right. So, who is our Judas?"

"He said he wasn't privileged to that level of information. But when I asked him if it might be someone with the initials L.S., he changed the subject. Very abruptly, I thought."

"Useless. So, if they knew, why didn't they scupper the escape route?"

"Lady luck intervened; it seems. The pursuit cars got

snagged in that traffic pile-up on the highway. Couldn't get through."

"This is bad. On top of Cubitt Town."

Carrot said, "It's hardly ideal, is it? Who are you going to trust now, I wonder?"

Julius glanced at Carrot's profile, a face on which some work might have been done by someone who wasn't a qualified plastic surgeon, he sometimes thought.

"So, what is this? Some slime spilling his guts? Or a pissed-up prat with a loose kisser? Either way, we get to the bottom of this, now. If I find one of our lot in the pay of Adams or any of those other cunts, I'll bury them in Millwall Dock."

Carrot was doing a decent impression of a nodding dog. "Perhaps that's what you need to do. Make an example."

"There's been too much of this lately. Desmond poached from under my nose. The bookie's last week. Is Tom Adams behind this? You remember that bent PI? Nally? I think we used him on the Martins Bank job, years back. Is he still about?"

"Probably six feet under now, the way he hit the bottle."

"Track him down. I want him to nose about on the quiet, find out who we're up against and who's feeding them information."

Carrot cleared his throat.

"No problem at all, if he's still alive and operating. But there again, why bring in someone we don't know? An outsider like Nally would be asking for trouble; that's my opinion. I think you should be looking closer to home."

"What do you mean?"

"I can do this for you, Julius."

"You?"

"Have I ever let you down? No, you just leave everything in my hands. You can trust me, you know that."

"All right, but this is important, Chris. I want results. Look at who needs cash. Who hates my guts? And which bastard wants my job?"

The car door closed quietly behind Carrot, and he pulled away. He recalled someone he had trusted completely until the time came when he stopped doing that.

Even after all these years, he felt the loss of him like an amputee feels a missing limb.

Earlier that day, he had seen Chisel on his own ground. He hadn't wanted to go. These days, Chisel came to see him, not the other way round. The man came on his set days, did his books, then drove home. There wasn't much chit-chat while he was there, either.

And now here he was, cap in hand, because he needed Chisel to show him how to manipulate his assets in such a way that he could see off the others in the running for those garages. All right, what he was asking wasn't part of their agreement, as Chisel had pointed out on the blower.

But that didn't explain why Chisel had greeted him like he had opened the door to someone he didn't know, or why he had been so strangely guarded.

"Juliet's at work, I suppose," he had said when they had run out of things to say. Chisel was putting papers in order on the dining room table. "She's all right, though?"

The place had changed since he had known it. The abstract prints and warm, moody colours had disappeared in favour of beige carpets and matching walls. Maureen's doing, he thought. He had picked up a framed photograph from off the teak sideboard. They were standing on a seafront somewhere, Chisel, his boy Colin and nearby, Juliet.

"When was this taken?"

"Maureen took it," Chisel said, "last year, maybe June."

"On her eighteenth birthday? June sixteen?"

"Not sure. Could have been. I've got it written down somewhere."

Could have been, he muttered as he swung into the car park of the Royal Oak. *Could have been*. He got out, slammed the door and eased through the bar crowd and ordered a pint and a Scotch chaser. He felt disappointed and, in some ways, disillusioned.

Maybe he had been right about Chisel all along. Didn't he even know the date of her birthday? What else didn't he know? It begged the question, who had he left her with, all these years?

He ordered another pint and carried it into the empty snug, his preferred refuge when he wanted to be alone. He slipped off his navy suit jacket and settled himself, letting go of his shoulders as he picked up his glass.

He had barely taken a sip when something moved in the periphery of his vision. An inquisitive baby's face appeared around the etched glass of the panelled door. Carrot, for fuck's sake.

He wasn't welcoming. "What do you want?"

Carrot said, "I've been hearing things."

He waited.

"I believe you wanted someone to check in on that girl?"

"Yes, have you found her?"

Carrot appeared not to have heard him.

"You might recall, I advised against using those Bermondsey boys?"

"They're cousins of Leslie's. He vouched for them."

"Leslie did? Oh, that's the case, is it? I see."

"Why? Has something gone tits up? Spit it out, Carrot."

“A while back, it seems, they sorted some kid who was trying it on with her. Ambulance job.”

“Oh, for Christ’s sake. I don’t need this. How was she—the girl?”

“Traumatised, I should think.”

“Right. Tell Les I want to see him. Not today, though. Go on, off you fuck.”

The door closed. He lifted his pint and drained half the glass. So, he couldn’t tell you her birthday, and he didn’t give a toss where she went or what she was doing.

Fucking Chisel.

The pain in his chest was back.

24

Juliet was aware of the stink before she rounded the corner and saw the enormous, illuminated sign on the Odeon, Leicester Square.

Christopher Reeve, Marlon Brando, Gene Hackman in SUPERMAN.

She looked about the square, keeping a wary eye out for police. The Odeon was disgorging a late-afternoon audience while at another cinema, a lesser crowd waited patiently in the cold to see *Close Encounters of the Third Kind.*

Between Juliet and this sign was the sort of huge mysterious shape that had played a key part in that film. She'd gone to see it on her own at Clapham Junction when it first came out.

It took her a moment before she recognised the dark, roughly pyramidal shape for what it really was, a mountain of bin bags, all filled with rubbish which was festering like the bodies said to be queued outside the mortuaries.

She hadn't seen the news for ages and had forgotten about everyone going on strike, the car workers, the gravediggers and the bin men. She must have walked past a dozen similar piles this weekend, but her eyes had been primed only for food and places of shelter.

She turned and cautiously scanned the crowd, moving this way and that around the square.

A half-hour earlier, walking down Tottenham Court Road, she thought she saw a man watching her and felt his eyes tracking her as she crossed the road.

She located the man's reflection in the window of an electronics shop. His clothing was dark and featureless, his features obscured by long hair and an olive-green woollen hat.

The only thing remarkable about him was that he stood motionless in the pedestrian traffic like a rock in a stream, and every so often, he glanced in her direction.

She was able to shake off the suspicion that she was being followed only when she turned into the narrow confines of Hanway Street and didn't see him come after her.

After that, she had walked without direction and was passing the *Superman* cinema when an exiting family of five stopped and waited for her to pass. The father, clutching a talkative boy of eight or nine, the mother holding tightly the hands of her two small girls.

She thought, how would her own father react if he heard she was sleeping rough on the streets of London? She smiled bitterly. In all likelihood, he wouldn't give a monkey's; he had, after all, lost no time in dumping her.

And yet there remained the other side of the coin, the one where he'd been unable to keep her because of circumstances entirely beyond his control. He might be anyone and capable, like Superman, or anything.

Why shouldn't he be an amazing lawyer, someone who could find her a way out of this hopelessness? At that moment, he seemed to be her last fragile hope.

But of course, finding her father was not even remotely possible if she couldn't discover who he was and where she might find him. The only person who could tell her that was Gerry, and that bridge was burnt to a crisp.

She raised the collar of her coat and was making another revolution of the square when a flock of startled pigeons rose suddenly from the ground. A police car pulled up just in front of her, blue light flashing.

She froze, heard the crackle of a radio exchange and presumed that it was about her.

She waited for a man in uniform to get out, turn her around and put her in handcuffs. Her heart stopped.

Then, when the car moved on again, she made her way down Irving Street, threading through the current of tourists flowing up Charing Cross Road before crossing over into Trafalgar Square, where muffled sightseers milled about, waiting for the lights on the colossal Christmas tree to be switched on.

She was cold, hungry and angry with herself for not pursuing Ammo when she stormed out of the pub.

She should have said something. Anything. Even if Ammo didn't live in the squat as she said she did, she must live somewhere, and that would do.

She ached for sleep and release from the awful thoughts which chased around her brain like demented furies. Mostly, those thoughts were of the scene with Colin.

Again and again, she saw her lime-green nails against the silver of the heavy ghetto-blaster, saw his leering, disbelieving expression morph into one of utter incomprehension as she smashed it down on his shaven head. He was going to attack me; she told herself, what else could I do?

It was then that she saw the olive-green hat again, the one she thought had followed her on Tottenham Court Road. Unsure if its wearer had seen her or not, she took a turn around the Square until she was walking in his direction.

If someone was pursuing her, she wanted to see his face. She wouldn't know if this were a policeman in plain clothes, but she might recognise an associate of Gerry's sent out to find her and bring her back to answer for Colin's death.

She resolved to find out that much, but as she approached the man, he turned his face away and lost himself among a huddle of tourists. She walked on.

Exiting the square, she crossed the road in front of buses waiting at the lights, unsure where her pursuer had gone.

Then, recognising the great building that towered over the Square as somewhere she had visited on a school trip, she climbed its steps and passing through glass doors and was embraced by the warmth within.

Doing her best to look inconspicuous, Juliet found a seat beneath an enormous painting of a blindfolded girl being led to the executioner's block. She looked at it for a minute or two before deciding that whoever had painted it knew something about hopeless situations.

25

The Candy Kane was tucked away in a Frith Street basement. Almost a week after he had seen her there, Julius made another visit, this time on his own.

In his head, he was already calling her 'Candy', after the club.

At first, he had tried not to think about her. What was wrong with him? She wasn't his type. He could imagine what the boys in Millwall would say about this. He could imagine what he'd have said about it too, just a few years back. Then, of course, there was Kath. Even recalling his niggling suspicion of last year didn't help him. That was when he'd thought that Kath might be playing away from home.

No, whichever way you looked at it, this was forbidden fruit.

Those bright eyes had looked right inside him, and whatever they found hadn't put her off, because they'd exchanged another look when he was leaving the club. But that was all they had been, looks. Not much on which to base the purchase of an expensive pair of brown wingtips and a new haircut by some ponce in Chelsea, but it was like he had no say in the matter. It had already been decided, somehow.

He had to see her, even if it was only to find out that he had been mistaken. So, late one afternoon, he'd done a bit of business in Stepney and then flagged down a cab on The Highway, the old Ratcliffe. Worth a couple of quid to keep his hair in place and his suit clean.

Tipping the taxi driver, he slammed the door. It was dangerous ground, but still he walked upon it, all the way to the steps that led down into another world.

She said there had been meaningful looks, that he had been imagining all that.

She looked at anyone she thought might buy a pack of Rothmans or a slim panatella from her tray.

This was when they were lying in bed together in a house he'd acquired as settlement of an unpaid debt.

She hadn't been there on that second night when he went to the club, it was her night off. The tall redhead who worked at the bar told him she would definitely be in on the following night. She told him that she was different from the other girls, and he thought, yeah, why not say the bleeding obvious? Then she winked and said that Angie liked chocolate.

Now, all these years later, he could not remember the line he used when he first spoke to her. It was cornier than a family-size pack of Kellogg's, he knew that much. She'd been taking a break in a booth at the back, resting her tray on the table above the pair of patent stilettos she had just kicked off. She wasn't smoking.

His opening gambit wasn't as funny as he thought it was. It didn't have the desired effect. She just looked at him, and if possible, appeared a little more tired than she had looked before. She ignored the box of *Terry's All Gold* that had appeared on the table.

He changed his tack. "Could I talk to you? Just talk?"

She couldn't stop him, she said.

And he talked.

How he got from talking about the beat group who had just shuffled off the tiny corner-stage to the sort of world he'd be bringing a child into, only months from now, was anybody's guess.

Well, she had said, at least there's Senator Kennedy. He'll make a good president. That surprised him.

Now that she had him on the back foot, she talked about herself and her childhood in Antigua and how she had come here to go to university (she was clever, too), but that had fallen through.

She had begun to explain how this had happened and how it had obliged her to take any job she could find but at that moment another girl had come along and whispered in her ear. She picked up her tray of cigarettes.

The next time he saw her; she appeared to have forgotten all about their last conversation. He tried to catch her at quiet moments, but the club was always busy. To her, he, was only another customer. He didn't want to try too hard, yet he couldn't bear to see other men around her, the ones who sucked in her cleavage as she offered her tray, the ones who cracked jokes only they thought were funny.

So, he waited until the club began its closing rituals, customers drifting out, waiters stacking chairs, lights going up, couples in corners disturbed and reminded of the time.

"It's all right, love," he said when the cloakroom girl came over with his coat. "I'm waiting for Angie."

The girl told him that Angie had gone home early that night. He nodded and left, but something made him pause before he reached the end of the road. He turned in time to see Angie doing up her coat at the top of the steps while scanning the street for a taxi. Seeing an amber light down the road, he began walking quickly back.

"I've been looking for you," he said, a little too breathlessly.

The black cab drew up, the engine throbbing. He opened the door, she got in.

"I don't know what you want with me," she said, "Customers are out of bounds, okay?"

"I just want to talk with you. Just a few words?"

"I'm tired. Not a good day. Sorry," she said. "Please, close the door."

But still he went back, if not night after night, then whenever his other activities allowed. She nodded and sometimes smiled when she passed his booth. He bought more cigarettes than he could smoke.

He asked, wasn't there somewhere they could have a chat? But she was always busy, and like she said, he was a customer. When she wasn't there, he found out what the other girls thought of her. She was all right in her way, the redhead at the bar said. Megan, on the reception desk, said she found Ange a bit stand-offish, but then she was different, wasn't she?

Sometimes he was obliged to come in with the crowd he'd been with on the night he first saw her. He didn't want to be seen with them now, not there, but some things you couldn't avoid.

So, he pretended not to see her because this lot would know something was up the moment their eyes connected.

He didn't speak with her until the following week when he dropped by, ostensibly to listen to the jazz combo that played there on Tuesday nights. While the musicians were tuning their instruments or perhaps had started to play, he heard raised voices in a nearby booth.

Looking up, he saw two young men harassing Angelica. By this time, he had found out her real name.

"Your *job,* darling," the one with a Billy Fury haircut was spitting, "is to entertain us. So, sit down."

He told her later that when he had bent down and whispered in the man's ear, all he had done was ask him to mind his manners. Whatever it was, it had an immediate effect, and the two men left the club soon afterwards.

The upshot of this little tête-à-tête was that he visited her again, and this time she agreed to meet him by the bandstand in Regent's Park. There, they walked about the flower beds, and when it started to rain, they had a cup of tea in the cafe, where they could hear the elephants in the zoo.

"Why the bandstand?" she asked him.

"I don't know." Not *I don't fucking know,* or *I'm fucked if I know*. It didn't seem right somehow, and not only because she was going to do a degree in economics at a proper university.

"A pub's a man's place. I thought if I said a restaurant, you'd think I was going too fast. Isn't there a film where some people meet at the bandstand?"

"If there is, I don't know it. I watch a lot of films."

"Oh, have you been to see *Psycho*? Everyone's talking about it."

"No." She laughed when he didn't. "I don't think I've met anyone like you."

She smiled gently.

He shrugged and said he could well believe that.

Some time later, naked in the brass bed at the West London house he had acquired as settlement of a debt, she turned to him and said, "You're quite mysterious, aren't you?"

"Am I?"

"Well, you haven't told me what you do for a living."

He thought for a moment. There were various ways he dealt with such questions, but none of them seemed to do the job.

"A bit of this, a bit of that, you know."

"Right."

"You might call it wheeling and dealing."

"I see. And what do you wheel and deal?"

"Oh, you know. It changes."

"So, you don't like talking about your job."

"Who does? Do you like talking about yours?"

"Do you make much money, wheeling and dealing?"

"It has its ups and downs, you know."

"Looks like you're on one of the ups, right now."

"Does it?"

"Your suit. The shoes. I don't think your mum cut your hair, either."

"Business is turning over just now, yes. I'm buying and selling a lot ..."

"A lot of what?"

"Stuff. Just stuff. Look, is it all right with you if we talk about something else?"

"It's all right, Julius."

She laughed again. He tumbled. She was winding him up. He liked it too.

"I know what you do. Or I've a pretty good idea."

"How?"

"The company you keep. Some of those men are quite well known. And it's not for giving to charities."

He sighed and fell back against the pillows.

"Nicked. Is that me fucked twice over, then?"

She laughed and put on her pants. "So, take me out, Al Capone. Somewhere nice."

And that was as close as he came to describing to her the

complicated and sometimes hazardous ways in which he got by. She didn't seem to want to know more. It was enough, or so he thought, that he spent so many afternoons and the occasional night with her.

His heavily pregnant wife didn't suspect a thing; he was sure. He was away so much anyway, for this reason or that. Now he invented a property development he was working on over on the west side, just in case anyone saw him heading in that direction.

He could tell her that with a straight face, as they had already had the old chain toilet ripped out and replaced.

He needed a change, and Angelica was all of that. She liked him too. They clicked.

He left his Ford Zephyr in the garage and took her out in his new two-seater, a Sunbeam Alpine. She liked being taken to see the sights, all the things she'd heard about but hadn't seen. You'd have been first with your head on the block; she'd told him at the Tower of London. She liked music. When they weren't frequenting her Soho coffee bars, they went to a club in Ealing.

Lying together, the pipe dreams came thick and fast. He'd get rich, and they'd have a house in Blackheath and one on the coast, Leigh-on-Sea, maybe. They'd take their holidays in Majorca one year and in the Caribbean the next. She'd have her degree and a good job. He'd go legit as he'd always planned.

She cuddled up to him and put out little feelers about whether he might leave Kath. She never got a straight answer to that one. And then he got nicked for handling stolen goods, literally a shed full.

He thought he'd get three years, instead, he got nine months and was out in six. It was worth paying for the services of 'Lenny' Wilkins QC. Kath came to see him, bringing baby Jimmy when she couldn't get her mother over to sit.

She said, "I didn't know I was letting myself in for all this."

Some of the visiting mothers had smiled at the baby, one or two of the old lags too, or they gave him a thumbs-up. Jimmy was cute when he was little.

Then Angelica said she was going to visit him. He asked her not to. It would complicate matters, he'd already been seen with Kath, for one thing. She had to come, she said, there was something she needed to tell him, face to face.

They watched her as she walked down the room, heels clicking, and sat down at his table. She'd made a special effort and she looked amazing. He'd given her some money and she was wearing a burnt-umber two-piece and the heels, make-up too, of course. There were one or two smiles, maybe a nod of respect.

They talked, and he thought she looked apprehensive. Across the hardwood table, she told him she was pregnant.

She sat there, awaiting his reaction. He was speechless. They'd been good with the condoms until that last time when he'd forgotten to get more. She'd left it till late in the visit to tell him, perhaps intentionally. And then, before he could corral the wild and conflicting thoughts chasing around his brain, the warders were shepherding the inmates back to their landings.

God strewth, he thought, as he lay on his bunk that night.

When he got out of stir, he went back home, praying that word had not reached Kath about his other visitor.

Being inside had given him the chance to take stock of

how things stood. He saw their likely course if he left Kath and took up with Angelica, and she had the kid. He'd lose friends on the Island; anyone who cared for Kath would cut him, and that was just for starters. He'd lose the Island, really; there was no way he'd be able to persuade Angelica to come and live there, even if he wanted her to.

There was only one sensible choice to make, and that was to stay put. Angelica would have to get rid of it. She'd see the sense of that. Bung her a few bob and an address where she could have the job done, and that would be that.

He said he'd come over; they needed to talk.

The plan was to install Angelica in the Wandsworth house. He wasn't thinking of selling it. The place would be his pension fund once the world discovered the charms of living south of the river.

The place was looking better already. He'd had decorators come in, but she chose the colours. They'd bought carpets and a few pieces of furniture; put a few bits and pieces on the shelves, and some pictures she chose on the walls. He rather liked what she had done with the place. It looked modern, but not at all like his drum.

He followed her into the front room.

"Am I about to hear something I don't want to hear?"

What was she, psychic? He slammed on the brakes.

"No, no, what are you talking about?"

She looked so lovely today. The bump was noticeable now, which thrilled him. Why hadn't he felt like this when his wife was up the stick?

"Can I...you know?"

"Can you touch it? Come here."

She lifted her dress to reveal the perfect curve of her belly and took his hand.

"Just there."

"I can't feel anything. Nice and warm, though."

"Wait."

"I can feel it! It kicked me!"

She let her dress down.

"Where have you been?"

He sat on the sofa while she poured him a Scotch.

"Busy."

"So, there's not a problem, then?"

"No, of course not. Why would there be?"

"It's just me being silly. I have too much time to think on my own here."

He nodded towards the bump.

"You'll have plenty to do soon."

"I'm going to need some help."

"Don't worry. Whatever you need, you'll have it."

"I don't deserve someone like you."

As he drove across Southwark Bridge, he thought, "That went really well."

26

On Christmas Day, Juliet joined the crowd filtering into St Martins to hear the carols, hoping to pass for another festive spirit. There would be warmth from the crush of human bodies if not from the church's heating system.

She'd had almost no sleep the night before, and her eyelids were becoming leaden when the wild-haired woman who had gone into the church before her shook her leg and said, "Soon as they're done here, head for the stairs. Last year, there were hot toddies."

Shelagh was a big, middle-aged, grey-haired woman in a weathered fur coat who carried several plastic shopping bags stuffed with clothing and whatever else.

As the service was ending, Juliet followed her out, down some steps and then into the vaulted crypt, where people like herself were queuing at a food counter. She could have eaten the smell itself. There were no hot toddies, but there was minestrone soup and warm mince pies.

Joining Shelagh at a deal table already claimed by a man with a bandaged head and a fidgeting boy who looked younger than herself, Juliet said, "You knew I was homeless, then?"

"It's not something you can easily hide, dear."

"Oh God, it's not the smell?"

"I stopped smelling other people years ago. No, dear. It's in your eyes and the way you walk. You mustn't walk into a place like you don't know if you'll be welcome. You need to walk in like it's your house."

"Does that work for you?"

She shrugged, smiled toothlessly.

"No, not if I'm honest. It's all this crap that comes with me. Otherwise..."

"Do you need it all?"

"Most days, no. But then there's a night where I'm outside with nothing to stop me from becoming a human icicle. That's when I'm glad of my newspapers. Always carry some newspapers, dear. You can stuff them up your jumper, you can sleep on them, use them for toilet paper, start a fire with them. You can read them too, if you have a mind to."

"Where do you sleep?"

"That would be telling. I have my places. Now, do you want that last mince pie?"

An hour or more after she had eaten her Christmas lunch, she was sitting on the Embankment, appreciating unseasonably bright weather and watching a man whose dreadlocks spilt from a big, woollen hat playing with his daughter.

There was a large pink dolly and colourful wrapping paper on the bench behind them, but now they were feeding pigeons from a sliced loaf of bread. The little girl screamed when a seagull swooped.

If things had turned out differently, might she have enjoyed something similar with her father? It seemed unlikely in the light of what Maureen had said. Her mother had been a hostess and black. He had been a white customer. What other explanation was there than he had used her for a night and then disappeared?

She gave out a bitter sound that caused the dreadlocked man to stop what he was doing and walk his little girl away. She let the tears run down her cheeks: her father had been a heartless bastard, and bringing recent events to mind, she wondered if she was as bad. She sat there for she didn't know how long, thinking about that.

She was picking up the tartan duffel bag she'd found in a bin and would stuff with her blanket and a few other necessities, when she saw her old bag, the bright turquoise one she'd lost on her first night on the streets.

The hooded figure who carried it, a street-sleeper she reckoned, was a little way down the Embankment, heading in the direction of the Houses of Parliament. Walking quickly, she closed in on the figure. A male. She was sure she recognised the little leather-edged address tag still hanging from the bright-blue bag.

When he passed under the wide span of a bridge, she was upon him before she knew what she was doing, the ferocity of her assault hurling his slight form to the hard ground.

Young eyes wild with alarm, he didn't struggle as she sat astride him. Raising her arm, she bruised his thin, unshaven face with the flat of her hand.

She slapped him again and grabbed at a bunch of material, violently shaking the thing beneath her while her voice resounded loudly under the concrete overpass. "You never came back," she screamed, "You never tried to find me."

At the close of New Year's Day 1979, Juliet slept fitfully on the floorboards of an abandoned house still used by junkies.

She had made a little more than six pounds the day before by smiling at Christmas travellers beneath the grand arch of Waterloo Station. Four pounds of this she had invested immediately in the purple-quilted sleeping bag she'd seen on sale in Millets' window. Unrolling it against the wall, away from the nest of crushed beer and cider cans, needles, old tobacco tins and strips of blood-stained cloth. The embers in the fireplace were as cold as the room itself. No one could have been in the place for a day or two at least, so she might be safe there for the night.

Even so, she settled herself where she had a good view of the door, with her back to a window. Remaining still for a moment, she listened to anything that might alert her to danger in the house or outside it, before attending to something she had to do before she slept.

The streetlamp directly outside the building allowed her to see what she emptied now from the bright-blue bag: some socks, a pair of pants, a grubby, grey tee shirt, a bottle of water, an opened packet of digestive biscuits, an old-looking lock-knife, a dog-eared A-Z; there was not a single item of her own.

The kid had probably found the bag empty somewhere. What the fuck.

Her rage had come out of nowhere. She felt like she had when she hit Colin not once but twice (*twice!*) with that heavy machine. She was alarmed to discover a side to herself that she neither knew, nor, it seemed, had much control over. True, there had been times at school when she had lost it, but nothing like this.

Lying on the hard floor, she watched car headlights as they fanned across the ceiling, heard the growl of the night-buses, listened to the nonsensical conversations of people rolling home from the clubs and whenever she drifted off, she was returned to consciousness by a sense of danger just beyond the window.

The third time this happened, she ventured a look and saw someone standing by the low wall, smoking a joint and muttering to himself. An hour later, some urgent whispering turned out to be a boy and a girl engaging in drunken intimacy.

The next time she was woken it was by the jumbled shards of a dream in which a kinder version of Gerry was whispering a secret in her ear.

Tired, filthy and painfully hungry, she made her way back to Waterloo Station and used the facilities.

She felt better after she'd washed thoroughly, brushed her teeth and brought some order to her hair. This was good, as today she had a definite purpose. She knew exactly where she wanted to go and as soon as her cup was more than half-filled with silver change, she bought a small white loaf and a pack of cream cheese at a convenience store and headed West.

Later that morning, having passed through Lambeth, Vauxhall and Clapham, she was on Nightingale Lane, approaching Wandsworth Common.

The Common itself was empty of all but a scattering of dog walkers and a few mums pushing strollers. The local paper probably had been full of what she had done. If she was going to be recognised anywhere, it was surely here.

Nevertheless, she had to go on.

She thought that by seeing the house and maybe glimpsing its remaining occupants, she might glean some idea at least of the hornet's nest she had kicked.

Some little part of her, against all she believed was true, hoped that she might detect some movement in Colin's bedroom. It would be dangerous to go any closer and yet she was more exposed standing out on the Common than she would be on the pavements near the house.

She went closer.

While she was still some distance off, she saw there was something different about the place. The curtains had been removed. Crossing the road, she edged a little closer.

From where she stood, she could peer into the living room. Maureen was often to be seen there, touching up her lipstick before going out, or making herself another gin and tonic.

Gerry's Ford Capri was missing from the gravel patch outside.

Closer now and she could see bare floorboards and stacks of tea-chests. She was aware of having stood there long enough to attract attention and so she moved on. Against her better judgement, she allowed herself to gravitate towards Wandsworth town centre and the places she had known so well only weeks ago.

At the bottom of the hill, where the Arndale Centre towered over everything, she turned onto Garratt Lane and from there into St George's Park, where she found a secluded bench. She stayed in the park until mid-afternoon, at which time she was rested and had spent some of her coins on a restorative tin of Coke and a chocolate bar.

She would see the house one more time before she consigned it to memory. That awful thing had happened within those walls and yet the rest of her existence, for what it had been worth, had happened there too.

So confident was she that nothing would have changed since she was there just a few hours ago that she rounded the corner too quickly and was startled to find herself almost in the middle of a hive of activity.

A big, brown removals van was parked in front of the

house, its loading gate open, and boxes were already stacked inside. Men in overalls were carrying more from the house.

She watched, mesmerised, as the stacks in the van grew and the men went through the front door and emerged lumping sofas, chairs, table lamps and the dismantled wall unit.

Everything she remembered was in their hands or in those boxes. All her own stuff, too, if they hadn't thrown it out or burned it in the garden.

One of the men called, "Oi, love, you can lend a hand if you've nothing better to do."

Another said, "Like watching blokes get a sweat on, do you?"

She barely noticed.

Gerry and Maureen were going. She didn't know where and imagined the Hobsons themselves didn't care where they went, so long as it was away from the place where the monster they had harboured all these years had turned on them and murdered their son.

She heard, "Cheer up, darling, it may never happen."

She walked up the road, away from the house.

Then she heard her name called and turned again.

It was Gerry pushing a wheelchair. Gerry was clearly as startled to see her as she was to see him and the person in the chair.

So strange was the scene that seconds passed before she recognised its occupant as Colin, or some strangely wizened version of him.

Colin was alive, but he looked terrible. He wore a blue woolly hat presumably to cover the wounds she had given him, and looked pale, thin and confused. He stared at her and said nothing. There was no fight in him at all.

Her first thought was to run.

Gerry saw that and said, "Stay. I want to talk to you."

"I'm sorry. I really am. So sorry. I didn't mean to. He..."

Gerry looked up at the clouds and took a lungful of air.

"I think I know what he did. Or tried to do? It wasn't hard to guess."

She looked at the boy in the chair, so frail-looking now, so little left of the Colin she had known, for good or bad, all her life.

"I didn't mean to do that, I swear. I'm so sorry. I just wanted him to stop. Oh, God, I thought I had killed him."

He looked at her for a moment, like he was really seeing her at last, she thought.

"Well, for what it's worth, you didn't do this. Not much of it anyway. You gave him a nasty knock, which maybe he deserved. But you didn't do this. Someone else will pay for this."

"Who? What happened?"

He turned, gave some instructions to one of the overalled men and appeared not to have heard her.

He said, "Where are you living now?"

"Nowhere."

"I'm sorry about that. But you can't live with us anymore. Not after this."

"I know. I said I'm sorry, and I meant it. I did."

"It's not because of that."

"Then why?"

"Look. I must be getting on. We're moving today, as you can see. Busy, busy."

"Where are you going?"

"Essex. I can't explain. We just can't stay on here."

She looked at Colin, who didn't seem to be there. He gave no sign of having recognised her, or even of having seen her.

Gerry ran his fingers through hair, that still needed cutting, and said, "Juliet, I'm sorry it's turned out this way.

Sometimes, that's what happens. Things have become complicated, and you can't be with us anymore. You shouldn't be here now."

"I don't understand."

"I'm sure you don't. It's time you were with your own people. Lines have been drawn. You'll have to make your own way in life."

She saw her opportunity and took it.

"My own people? I don't know who they are. You would never tell me."

He hesitated, perhaps deciding his next move.

"Oh, fuck the lot of it."

"What?"

"It doesn't matter anymore. I can give you a name, Julius Nicholson. Remember that and ask for him on the Isle of Dogs. Everyone knows him there. You deserve..."

"I deserve what?"

"Doesn't matter. Listen, what you do after you meet him will be your decision. It'll be a big one, too."

27

A crowd had gathered on the street corner.

Nicholson wasn't ready for a meeting with newly homeless tenants, so he stayed in his car parked across the road and looked at what remained of his slice of Notting Hill from there.

The firemen were finishing up, taking off respirators, coiling hoses. One of them was talking to Carrot, who was nodding away like the toy dog again.

After some more nodding, Carrot gave a little hitch to his flared slacks, skirted an enormous puddle and slid into the passenger seat.

Julius said, "What's the damage?"

"There's about half the house still useable, but you'll have to stick a new staircase in and get the place rewired. That was long overdue anyway. You'll need to get the gas supply checked, too. Then you can start renovating the toasted bits."

"How many tenants will we lose?"

"Six rooms are kaput for the foreseeable."

"Six, then."

"More like twenty-six. There was a lot of subletting going on. Two of your tenants are now in hospital."

"Fucking hell. I'll need you to sort out the insurance claim."

"Insurance? They won't pay out on this. We weren't insured against arson."

"Arson? Is that what it was? Are you sure?"

Carrot nodded at the firemen, who were looking his way. "They are."

"They know that for a fact?"

"There'll be an investigation, of course."

"Christ. This is getting serious."

"Could have been worse. Could have been the whole block, but only your properties went up."

"Just mine?"

"Looks like it."

"Then I'm being targeted. Who is it, Carrot?"

Carrot was leafing through the pages of a tiny notebook he carried.

"Well, we know who poached Desmond. My guess is the same gent had you turned over by the Sweeney, too."

"I can see Adams doing over my bookies, too. And this?"

"Not necessarily. But he's the odds-on favourite."

Maybe, Julius thought.

He tightened his grip on the wheel. It seemed the only thing he could get a tight grip on. He said, "And the wages job?"

"I thought you were looking into that?"

"Too many questions, Carrot. I want answers."

"I am looking into it. These things are awkward; they take time."

"I've got a fucking headache. Got any aspirin?"

"Not on me."

"Then get out and find me some, will you?"

Carrot got out of the car, and as soon as he had walked around a corner, Julius drove off.

He eased the Jaguar onto the Westway, where an infant's face on an advertising hoarding lit up memories of Angelica and the times he visited her while the baby grew inside her.

To step into her house, the one he made available for her, the one Chisel lived in now, was to escape from his world into another, a world of exotic scents, Charlie Parker records and conversations he would never have dreamed of having on the Isle of Dogs.

It was to get away from the life he lived back East, though something about that side of him fascinated her. And it was to slough off his cares and collapse onto cushions in a ruffled heap of good tailoring and accept the reefer of sweet-smelling hashish she offered him and think to himself, this is possible, I could change everything for this. I could be someone else.

He took her out to restaurants in Fulham and South Kensington.

They still went to the club in Ealing and to another one they liked on Eel Pie Island. But he didn't like her to dance now that she was showing so prominently; they had a lot of evenings in, when she would cook, and once or twice she even tried to show him how to cook, too.

When the signal was good, they watched *Emergency Ward 10* and *Danger Man* on TV. They went for walks by the river in Putney when he might look eastwards down the waterway and think what a long way he had travelled.

He put his hands on her belly and said, "I love your bump."

She said, "It's your bump. What are we going to do?"

"Well, I don't know, not yet."

"You won't leave your wife for me, will you?"

"I don't know. Sometimes I think I..."

"Don't ever lie to me."

"No, really, I sometimes think to hell with everything. If we are meant to be together, then..."

"But we are not meant to be with each other, are we?"

"What do you mean?'

"You know, Julius. Have you not seen the looks we get in the places you take me to eat?"

"Fuck them, fuck them all."

"A white man. A black woman, and one who happens to be pregnant."

"I'd kill any man who said anything."

"Do you think what we are doing is wrong?"

"No, what are you talking about? Of course I don't."

"And yet when we went to your precious Isle, we never got out of the car."

"That's different. Everyone there knows Kath."

"It's no different, and you know it. So, I ask you again, what are we going to do?"

He looked at his shoes, scuffing the concrete on the hard outside the riverside rowing clubs, the way they had done on the parquet flooring outside the headmaster's office at school.

Then he looked up, looked at her in her white dress with matching boots and hat, so beautiful against the backdrop of the river. She looked like a model in a magazine.

"You'll have the baby and I'll provide for it. For him. Or her. I'll see you right and I'll come as often as I do now. Nothing will change."

"Of course it will change, Julius. Everything will change, sweetheart."

She kissed him on the nose and looked in her bag for a tissue.

28

"Why didn't you come last week?"

"I told you I might be busy. It's not always easy."

To some extent, that was true. Things were beginning to take off for the Nicholsons, as he already liked to call his business, even though Jimmy was still a toddler. It was easy to become distracted from increasingly complicated affairs of the heart when you were considering such weighty matters as whether it was time to put away the pickaxe handles and carry a shooter on a bank job.

She asked him, "How easy do you think it is for someone like me on my own? I don't know anyone here."

Someone had told him that the *Daily Herald* had £150,000 delivered by Securicor to its wages department every Thursday.

"Well, it's not like you'd be wanting to go out that much, is it? In your condition?"

"I was thinking of inviting Sonya over. From the Candy Kane."

"That's an idea."

It was, too. Charlie had already finagled himself a girlfriend in the *Herald*'s wages department, and Chris Grayson had found a solid place to intercept the van.

"But it'd only be for an evening. The rest of the week, I go slowly mad if you're not here. All I can think about is the baby. Julius, I keep thinking there's something wrong."

"What do you mean?"

"I don't know. Sometimes I don't feel quite right, that's all. It's probably because I have nothing else to think about."

"Look, I'll come over more as soon as I've got things sorted out."

It was worth taking risks for that kind of cash. Shotguns, then.

"I sometimes wonder if this is going to work. Are you listening to me?"

"Of course, I am. And the baby's still due on the 24th?"

"Thereabouts, yes. You'll be there, won't you? To take me to the hospital?"

He put his arms around her much-changed shape and felt her fingers press into his shoulders.

"Of course I will. Now don't go worrying yourself on that score. They'll have put your phone in by then, so you won't have to use the call box."

"I should hope not. And I'll see you next week as usual?"

"Yeah, of course you will. I've told Kath I'll be out every Tuesday until the end of the month."

"On the construction job."

"On the job, yes."

They both laughed because they were still having sex.

He wondered how strong they should make this team. He was thinking that six men should do it nicely.

On the Isle of Dogs, he took a phone call.

"Joey, my old mucker, how's it hanging?"

He'd thought it was social.

We've got a consignment. Imminent. We need to talk.

"Call me on my other line in ten minutes."

He got his coat and picked up his car keys.

"That's better. Can you hear me?"

Loud and clear.

"So, there's another lot coming in, then?"

On the Esmerelda, out of Bilbao. Docks tomorrow morning at about ten.

"You know what to do, Joe. Once the gear's loaded onto the lorry, the driver can shunt it over to the car park behind the football ground and your boys can empty it there."

The driver's sound, is he?

"As a pound. Give him a slap, make it look real, but don't go overboard, alright? Any problems your end?"

Not if you can meet us tomorrow morning, nine thirty, behind the engine sheds.

"What you want me there for?"

Your connection from the shipping line wants to meet with you. He won't trust anyone else. Wants reassurance, I think.

"Or more money. Look, Joey, tomorrow is dicey for me. Can't you go?"

It's got to be you, he says. The boss man. It won't take long, but we don't want him getting cold feet at the last moment.

"Christ, I wasn't expecting this. What time did you say?"

Nine-thirty.

"Let me see. Yeah, okay, if we sort that out double-quick, I can still make it."

Make what?

"Another appointment. Nothing you need to worry about."

———

It was only another prenatal checkup. It wasn't like she was having the baby that day.

Even so, he didn't want to make her late. He would be cutting it fine.

The following morning, he ignored the bells of his alarm clock and rose later than he meant to, cursing himself as he flew downstairs, still buttoning his shirt, and went to his meeting on the docks.

As he closed the door behind him, he heard the phone ringing in the hall, but whoever it was would have to wait. The man he was to meet was late anyway and then complained at length about the arrangements.

When he had sorted everything, he got in his car and drove west, loudly damning every red light and traffic jam he encountered.

He let himself into the house at Wandsworth, expecting an earful for being so late. They would call the hospital, apologise and reschedule the check-up.

He'd tell her not to get so worked up over nothing.

"Angie?"

He called her name again. He went through to the kitchen, peered through the window into the small garden.

"Ange!"

Louder this time.

He went up the stairs, three at a time.

He said, "I'm sorry, I got held up."

Something made him stop on the landing.

He didn't know why; he just stopped.

Then he opened her bedroom door and was shot through with dread.

On the tangled sheets of the unmade bed were long, dark streaks of blood.

He looked about for a clue, anything that might tell him something about what had happened.

He was out in the street before he knew it, hammering on the door of a neighbour. The coloured lady was in a terrible state, the neighbour reported. They'd sat her down and one of them had gone out to call an ambulance. No, they didn't know if the lady was all right; he should go to the hospital.

Which fucking hospital?

They didn't know that either.

There was still no phone in Angelica's hallway, so he sprinted up the road to the phone box she used.

Sweating, purple-faced, he reached into his pockets and pulled out half-crowns, shillings, ha'pennies, but none of the big pennies he would need to make his calls.

He looked for somewhere to change a ten-bob note, but this was the Common and there were no shops he could see.

Throwing himself into his car, he drove blindly until he pulled up sharp outside the newsagent's shop, where he came out clutching a copy of *Reveille* and a fistful of coins.

When he hammered on the window of the red kiosk at the end of the parade, the old lady using the phone looked alarmed but carried on talking.

"Sorry, love, but this is an emergency."

He cut off her call and bundled her out of the booth.

Now, which fucking hospital?

He dialled 999.

St James, Balham. Okay, then.

He opened the door of the booth and was accosted by a man in a butcher's apron. The old woman he'd dragged out of the box was standing behind him.

The man said, "Here, mate, you can't do that to a pensioner."

He hadn't hit anyone for a while, but now the man's florid face caught the full force of his uppercut and the edges of his gold rings.

He said, "Which way is Balham, you cunt?"

There were more lines going into her than Clapham Junction, he told someone, long after it had happened and when he could talk about it.

She was conscious, but barely.

They must have filled her with drugs, because her eyes looked dopey. There was none of the sparkle and the assertiveness he had come to know and to respond to.

He said, "Hey, baby, I'm here."

He couldn't bring himself to say, "It's going to be alright" because that wasn't the way things looked.

The staff had intercepted him on the way in, taken him into a side room, and told him in medical detail what had happened.

He didn't understand a word of it and wasn't really listening. He wanted to see her.

The good news, they said, was the baby had been saved. It was a girl. She had been taken to another ward, but given time, it looked like she would be okay.

Yes, but the mother? They told him it was too early to say and that the next day or two would be key.

He sat by her bedside while she drifted in and out of consciousness.

Doctors and nurses came and went. When she surfaced, she rarely talked, so he did that.

Mostly, he said he was sorry. It had been business, he said, important matters of business, although never had such matters seemed less important than now.

He was sorry, he said again. He felt her fingers squeeze his own and was grateful. The machine at her side bleeped.

The nurse at the desk went over her details. "Angelica Cazenove? But you are Mr Nicholson?"

"We're not married," he told her. "Not yet."

The nurse wrote on a form and then asked if he would like to see the baby.

He wasn't sure he did, but now he was being led into another room and past several cots filled with tiny bundles until they stopped at the one on the end.

Her eyes were open, though she appeared to be looking at some invisible thing six inches from a pretty little nose. Was she smiling, or was that just wind?

Would he like to hold her?

And then there she was, in his arms.

She looked the very image of her mother.

Don't squeeze her, the nurse said, laughing.

He stared down into tiny bright eyes and thought the shade of her skin was perfect. How could a little thing like that be so pretty?

When they asked him what she would be called, he said Juliet, because they had talked about that.

He slept that night in his car and was beside her bed as soon as they would allow.

When he had taken the lift to the ward, he found his way barred and was ushered into a side room where he was told to wait.

After the nurse had left, he opened the door of the anteroom and peered through the small round window of the door to her ward. There were curtains around her bed, doctors more active than he had seen them, nurses hurrying this way and that.

He grabbed the arm of one who bustled through the doors.

"What is it?" he said. "What's going on?"

"You're hurting my arm," she said. "You'll have to talk to

the doctor, but they think it's sepsis. The antibiotics don't seem to be working, but we're doing everything we can. Please, Mr Nicholson. Wait there until we have news."

He panicked. "She'll be alright, though?"

"We're doing everything we can, Mr Nicholson."

She woke and looked at him with eyes that were unclear.

Angelica's voice was barely audible.

"How is she?"

"The baby? She's going to be fine. She's bonny."

That was how he had heard babies described.

"She's well?"

"Yes, she's very well. And she's beautiful, like you."

They told her they would bring the baby to her, but by the time they had, she had relapsed again and was out cold.

Later that day, she opened her eyes and looked into his.

It was an effort for her to said softly, "Look after her, won't you?"

"What do you mean? You'll be looking after her."

"No time, Julius. Promise me. You'll look after her."

"Of course I will. Save your strength now and get well."

She closed her eyes. He went to answer a call of nature, and when he got back, the curtains were still around her bed and inside the doctors in their white coats were there; they told him that Angelica had passed.

"Passed? Passed what?"

Their faces said it all.

29

Once again, Juliet sought refuge in the National Gallery.

It was warm, the soft seats were preferable to hard paving, and she liked to think that anyone looking her way saw a scruffy art student rather than a friendless pariah who slept on the streets.

Sitting on her favourite bench, she had fallen under the spell of one of the exhibits. *The Execution of Lady Jane Grey* depicted the teenage Lady Jane blindfolded and reaching out uncertainly to find the block on which her head would immediately be cut off.

There was something about the hopelessness of the doomed girl's situation that seemed to put her prospects into some sort of perspective.

This afternoon, eating a tuna sandwich she'd bought for pennies before a lunch counter closed for the day, she crossed Westminster Bridge and walked up Whitehall towards the Gallery.

Sitting before the familiar, awful scene, she tried to make sense of what Gerry had told her.

I can give you a name. It's Julius Nicholson. Remember that and ask for him on the Isle of Dogs. Everyone knows him there.

Who was Julius Nicholson, and where on earth was the Isle of Dogs?

She dwelled on that until a warder approached and told her that the gallery was about to close.

Something happened that night which caused her to put all thoughts of Julius Nicholson aside for the next three days.

She had joined some people gathered around a fire beneath a railway arch. There were about a dozen rough sleepers, all talking and sharing bottles. Some faces were already familiar to her. Shelagh was sitting closest to the fire, guardedly sorting the contents of her plastic bags.

Also present were Brian, who claimed to have owned a van-rental company, and Shelly, a scrawny teenage addict who had lost her baby.

She warmed herself, chatted with Shelagh and sometime later went off to relieve herself behind a wall.

It was when she emerged with her bright blue bag over her shoulder that she saw the boy again. There was no sign of bruising on his thin face, but she recognised him immediately. He recognised her, too, or maybe it was the bag, and he backed away.

"Don't go. I want to apologise."

He looked behind him, checking his escape route, she realised.

"I mean it. I'm sorry. Don't go. I want to explain."

He said, "I don't want any trouble."

"There won't be any. It was a mistake. I have your things."

She knelt and emptied his possessions from her bag.

He approached them warily.

"It's alright. I don't bite."

"I think you might," he said.

"What's your name?"

"What's yours?"

"I'm Juliet."

"I'm Arthur. Hello, Juliet."

"Hello, Arthur. I'm sorry about what happened. I made a mistake."

"Your mistakes hurt."

"I know. I'd like to make it up to you."

"How?"

"I have enough money to get us both a McDonald's."

"And a shake?"

"Think so."

"All right."

She led him over the bridge and onto the bright and busy Strand, where they found a booth at the back of the noisy restaurant.

The Christmas lights had been taken down, but shop windows were blazing, the pavements still pulsing with people returning from work or the January sales.

She bought the food and carried the tray over to the table where he sat, expectantly.

He looked different out of the shadows, skinny but quite good-looking, with fair, spiky hair and an unblemished complexion.

Under the old black coat, he now unbuttoned a cotton shirt with a mattress-ticking print which he wore under a blue waistcoat and jeans which had holes in the knees. A gold-coloured hoop hung from his right earlobe.

She wasn't sure if the look was intentional, but it suited him; he looked like an underfed cabin boy on a pirate ship.

Juliet watched as he opened his hamburger box. Seeing her looking, he returned a hungry smile.

"All square now? I'm forgiven?"

"If you've got some ketchup."

"Where are you from?" she asked, watching him eat.

"Cornwall. Up by Tintagel. So, obviously, I was called Arthur."

"What's Tintagel?"

"Doesn't matter. Where are you from?"

"Wandsworth."

"Can't you just go home?"

"No."

"Something bad?"

"Yes."

"Do you want all those fries?"

"Yes."

"That's a shame."

"You can have them if you're hungry."

"I've not eaten today."

"Do you often not eat?"

"Some days. I don't find it easy to ask for money."

"You can get over it if you try."

"Did something bad happen to you?"

"Mum died and then Dad married a real queen bitch. It got so bad that I couldn't stay in that house. I left." He licked the last of his ketchup off his little finger.

"To go on the streets?"

"Of course not. I was going to crash on sofas and floors just until I got myself fixed up. A lot of people I knew had moved up here. Well, that all worked out, obviously. I still haven't got myself fixed up."

"So where do you sleep now?"

"Everywhere and nowhere. Those sofas and floors, when I can get them. Usually just for a night, though I house-sit whenever I get the chance. Trouble is, I've been doing this for a long time now, and the people I used to stay with don't always want to see my face on the doorstep. So, there are a lot of nights I have to sleep out. You?"

"Some nights, in a shelter. Others, wherever I can."

"If there's any way I can avoid sleeping out, I do. It's too dangerous. Down by Waterloo, I saw this guy's tent being set on fire by drunks. He was screaming when he got out and they were standing there laughing. That kind of stuff happens."

"I've heard. But a lot of nights, I've no choice."

"You've got a choice tonight."

"What do you mean?"

"Tonight, I have a flat in Kennington to myself. You can come back if you want. There's some food and a few bottles of beer."

"Wow, Kensington?"

"No, Kennington. But it's good enough."

She wasn't sure what the invitation meant. If it only meant shelter, comfort and warmth, that was enough. If it meant something more, well, that could be good, too. She gathered her stuff and followed him up the steps and into the bright street.

It hadn't hurt like she thought it would, maybe because she had already half done it with Sayed from the burger bar in Wandsworth or was too distracted by the sensation of a warm, giving mattress and soft pillows.

In the morning, she extricated herself from clinging bed sheets, feeling good, for a change.

He had used a condom both times, so there were no worries on that score.

She showered—"for about an hour" he told her, after—and found coffee, milk and a kettle. There were eggs in the fridge.

Over breakfast, she told him what Gerry had said about a man called Nicholson who lived on the Isle of Dogs. What

Arthur told her about the Isle of Dogs wasn't inspiring. It was a tip, he told her. Disused docks, abandoned or demolished buildings, second-rate housing and the reek of decay. He'd gone down there looking for empty buildings to squat in, but he'd quickly decided he couldn't live in that place, even rent-free.

She said, "Still, I have to go."

Arthur was packing things away; he had to vacate the place that morning.

"Why?"

"I have to find this Julius Nicholson. There's some connection."

"What kind of connection?"

"I don't know. That's why I have to go."

"Well, you'd better take this."

He pulled a tatty book from his bag and put it on the table for her.

"Your *A-Z*?"

"You'll need it more than I will. I don't know, this all sounds funny to me."

"I can't argue with that."

Arthur was fastening straps on the bag he'd acquired to replace Juliet's blue one.

"So, you don't have any ideas about this bloke at all?"

"I sort of have one, but I don't want to say anything about it in case it's not right."

"You're counting some chickens, maybe?"

She buttered a third slice of toast.

"I don't know. I might be."

He picked up his bag, looked at her and said, "Well, this is it, then?"

She said, "Yep."

"See you around, then."

"Yep."

Walking away from the house, she thought the wind blew harder and the ground looked colder. She might have stayed with him longer, she supposed; he seemed to like her. But she would only hamper his sofa-surfing, and besides, liking her didn't necessarily mean he wanted to be with her.

In any case, she was getting used to being on her own and was becoming increasingly self-reliant. No, she thought, as she threaded her way through crowds heading towards the tube station, she would leave it at that.

Last night had been a matter of two people coming together for warmth and whatever else, nothing more; she'd see him around.

Pulling her coat around herself, she began walking towards Waterloo Station and the South Bank.

30

"Carrot, those papers you moved from the house."

Carrot appeared not to hear him, so Julius reached down and unplugged the Flymo. Carrot looked about, puzzled.

"What's that you said?"

"Those papers, the ones you moved."

"Yes, all safe."

"I want them back. Also, you moved my flit kit. It's in a hold-all. I want that back in my attic, pronto."

Carrot frowned.

"Of course. But it makes no sense keeping the paperwork there. What if we get a knock?"

"I'll take the risk. I want that bag back today and the papers as soon as."

"I'm not sure this is a good idea."

"Do I have to go down your lock-up myself?"

"You'd be wasting petrol. It's not there anymore."

"What do you mean, not there?"

"I had a funny feeling I was being watched, so I moved your stuff."

"Fucking hell, Carrot, where?"

"Camberwell."

"All right, just give me the key and I'll go down the lock-up there, then."

"It's not a lock-up."

"Well, what is it, then?"

"It's a caravan. I've stowed everything in my caravan."

"You've got a caravan? In Camberwell?"

"Elddis Crusader, four berth, a little beauty. It'll be quite safe there. And the beauty of it is, if ever we think it's not, we just hitch it up and go somewhere else."

"Where's it parked? I want to sort this today."

"Ah, that's just what you don't want to do, just now."

"What do you mean?"

"The thing is, I took Mum down to Camber Sands over the weekend. Ruddy disaster. Her old problem playing up, she said, the jellied eels, I thought. Toilet's in a dreadful state."

The headache was coming back.

He ducked back into the house to find the aspirin in time to hear the doorbell chiming and to see a familiar face through the frosted-glass panel in the front door.

"Leslie. Carrot's out back. Have a word with him, will you? He's got a lot of papers of mine I want returning and he's playing silly buggers. I haven't the strength to deal with him today."

Leslie said, "I'm telling you straight, Jewels, you want to watch him. I wouldn't trust him with my laundry. I didn't know he was here. It's him I've come to have a word with you about."

"You can say what you want while the mower's going."

"Well, it's like this. He thinks he's in charge of his own little Operation Countryman."

"Operation what? We're hardly the filth."

"He's conducting an investigation of his own, though, just the same. He says you authorised it."

"I thought it would keep him quiet for a while."

"Well, it hasn't. He's been talking to everyone about the wage's job. And when I say talking to everyone, I mean accusing everyone."

"Oh, fuck me."

"And obviously, they're not happy. The boys. Carrot's got the idea he's your main man now. There's nothing in that, is there?"

"No, there bloody well isn't."

"Well, he's making people nervous."

"I'll bet he is."

He's making me nervous, Julius thought.

"Leave it with me, Leslie. I'll talk to Carrot. Oh, and Leslie?"

"Yes, boss?"

"I want to see Reggie and Ronnie."

"Who?"

"That pair of clowns you dropped on me. They're giving me headaches."

"Right you are, boss."

He'd talk to Carrot and to the Malone brothers but not today, he thought as he took another couple of aspirin and washed them down with a finger of Scotch.

Beyond the window, Carrot was winding up the orange electrical lead, carefully, like it was his own. And now he was hanging the mower on a hook in the shed that he'd assembled in a corner of the garden.

"Do something about that, will you?" Julius had told him, waving his hand in the direction of the jungle that had sprung up after Kath had died.

He had to admit, Carrot had worked wonders.

There was a patio where it was nice to sit with a drink while the new fencing complete with a rear gate stopped prying eyes. He watched as Carrot bent to squirt weed killer along the borders and then stood up straight to survey the garden.

Not for the first time, Julius received the impression that he was looking it over like it was his own.

Did he hope it would be his, someday, somehow?

———

Turning off the shower, he towelled himself dry.

The bathroom mirror returned an overweight, middle-aged man with more wrinkles than last year's potatoes. Down below, his penis dangled uselessly. Switching on the portable in his bedroom, he lay on the bed, naked, brooding.

An early night with Kath had typically meant some energetic sex, some God-awful rubbish she'd find on the TV and then more sex. He remembered how he sometimes fell asleep with her legs still clamped about him.

What a sorry sack he had become, he thought, as sleep finally claimed him.

Julius paid the price for retiring early by waking at five.

Now it was Angelica he was thinking of. He could not possibly have seen it coming: Angelica dying and leaving him holding the baby. Because that was what happened.

He'd had to sort out a quiet funeral for Angelica; she was cremated and her ashes interred at Putney Vale and then he'd had to talk to the hospital about the baby. To his surprise, no one had questioned whether he was the father. No doubt, he was viewed as some sort of progressive.

"Do you have any relatives who can help you with the baby? She'll need a wet-nurse." The ward sister was adamant on this point. "They become vulnerable to all sorts of diseases if you don't get them a wet-nurse. Just for a while, until they can take formula."

He said he had, because he had already made his plan; he only needed the parties involved to agree to it. The main thing was to have this settled without delay and before Kath had gotten wind of any of it.

For the time being, the baby stayed at the hospital.

He saw Chisel later that day. It wasn't an easy conversation.

It went on for too long; you were supposed to get these things over quickly, before they knew what was happening to them, like they did in the prison topping shed. But this was complicated.

Once Chisel had digested the idea that he was no longer to be his old mate's right-hand man, that he was, in fact, suspected of insurrection (a charge he flatly denied), Jewels unveiled the carrot.

There was a house in Wandsworth.

He'd get someone in to clear out the place, and then Chisel and Maureen could move right in. Much bigger than they were used to and situated in what optimistic estate agents were calling an up-and-coming area.

He would get a monthly cheque, quite a large one, ostensibly for continuing to do Julius' accounts.

In return, he and Maureen would look after the baby. Maureen was already breastfeeding their new baby, Colin, they called him. So, one extra shouldn't be too much bother?

"What's Maureen going to say about this?"

"Thank you for my nice new house? When are you taking me for dinner now we can afford it? Something like that?"

He'd tried to inject a little humour and lighten the

mood, but they both knew and accepted this for what it was —a parting of the ways. The Hobsons went west.

Parting with her was harder than he could have imagined.

He stood in the bare hallway of Chisel's new house, distracted by memories of being there with Angelica, as Maureen took the carrycot from him and went into the front room, where another baby was crying.

Chisel nodded, shrugged.

It was time for his visitor to go.

Was that all there was to it?

He hadn't said goodbye.

In his mind's eye, he'd seen them sitting in the room where Maureen was now presumably feeding her own baby, discussing Juliet's future in sombre tones, because, there was now of course an atmosphere between himself and the Hobsons.

As he had remembered the scene, he had taken Juliet out of her cot and held her one more time, looking into those extraordinary green eyes, and reluctantly allowed her to be taken from his grasp.

Perhaps it was better this way. This way, he wasn't going to get emotional. Instead, he felt empty.

As he was leaving the house, he heard Angelica struggling to say, *Look after her, won't you?*

Sometimes, he drove over to Wandsworth and watched the house.

Or he parked up by the school and waited for her to come out of the gates, bag over her shoulder, talking to an

Asian girl with glasses. It would have been awkward for them both if he had stopped her and told her who he was.

When she left school, he heard she was working in a Chelsea cafe, and twice he had gone there for his lunch and watched her serve customers. She had grown into a smart-looking young woman, and he ached to recognise so much of her mother in her cheekbones, her eyes and slender neck. A pity she wasn't doing something a little better than running plates to tables.

Once, when she brought him his bill, he forgot himself and said, "You look so much like..." and she waited, questioned him with Angelica's green eyes.

He apologised, said she'd reminded him of someone he'd known long ago.

He let the moment go; there was Kath to consider, and besides, there was no way of knowing if Juliet would want to see him after all this time. The next time he went to the cafe, he discovered that his daughter was no longer working there.

He didn't know what to make of the changes in her appearance when she got that job in the shop on the Kings Road. The colour in her hair, that wild make-up, those clothes.

She was still doing menial work, but he thought he could do something about that, so one afternoon he took Carrot with him and risked meeting her, though in the end that didn't happen. The ponce who ran the place had all but shit himself in his rush to promote the new girl.

He wondered what she would have said to a father who had given her away and had had nothing to do with the first eighteen years of her life, except for sending her nice presents, anonymously, at Christmas and on her birthday.

As she grew older, he saw she was starting to have a life of her own and was going out in the evenings. He had no idea where she went, only that she left the house dressed like something from a horror film.

All sorts of possibilities occurred to him, none of them very nice.

There seemed no way to satisfy his morbid curiosity until he heard Leslie mention the Malone brothers, cousins of his who did a little door work and who also liked to participate in any activities likely to bring in significantly more than the average national wage.

The Malones were keen to make their services known to Julius Nicholson.

He wasn't sure he needed them except for this one little job; he told Leslie. There was a young woman he wanted to know about. Where she went, who she was with, and how safe she was. If these Malones could do that, he would see them right.

He would have interviewed them himself, but he didn't want to give them a toe in his door. So, he left it in Leslie's hands, and that had been a mistake. They had found her with some punter at a club and had mangled him. God knew how she had taken that.

Then he received two bulletins of news concerning Juliet. The first informed him she had left the Hobsons. No wonder Chisel had been so awkward when he went over there.

He wasn't unduly concerned, though; she'd be sharing a flat with a friend. That was what they did at that age. But now he heard a second and much more ominous piece of news.

From what he gathered, the Malones had connected

with some skinhead mates of Chisel's lad. When these boys had gone round to see Colin, they'd walked in on a blistering barney between Chisel and Maureen.

Chisel had not been welcoming, telling them, no, Colin couldn't come out to play, he'd been playing with Juliet, and she'd damn-near killed him. Then it seemed that Leslie Shipham had twigged that Colin had tried it on with the girl.

Already fairly sure that she was Julius's bastard child, he'd seen a chance to improve his standing with the boss. So, he'd had a word with the Malones, who had had more than just a word with Colin. And now Julius was having a word with him, Leslie Shipham.

"I cannot fucking believe it," said Julius.

Leslie sat on a grey plastic chair beneath a picture of a bare-breasted calendar girl. Looking like a pig in the slaughterhouse, Julius thought.

Behind him were buckets of paste, a ladder and some rolls of wallpaper, which Carrot had been using to redecorate the boss's new office, relocated now to the commodious back room of the flashy motor-garage Julius had acquired on Rainham Road.

"Do you have *any idea* of what you have done? Do you have a fucking *inkling*?"

Leslie started to said something, "He had tried to..."

"I don't want to hear it."

"He deserved..."

"He deserved fucking eviscerating. But not by you or your country cousins. And certainly not without my say-so. I'll ask you again. Do you know what you have done?"

Leslie's eyes were on the table.

When he entered the room, Julius was cleaning the revolver he was known to have, a souvenir of his National Service, it was said.

He hoped this was a piece of theatre, but with Julius, you never really knew. Now it lay there next to a bottle of Johnnie Walker, absorbing light from the green rise-and-fall fitting which dangled over the desk.

"What?"

"You've fucked up my world, that's what you've done."

"I don't get it."

"You've given Chisel's kid brain damage. He's in a fucking wheelchair. He's a fucking vegetable."

Julius poured himself a generous measure of Scotch.

"I didn't know it was that bad. I didn't think they would go that far. I'll sort the fuckers out, Jewels, no sweat."

"I've sorted them. You won't see Heckle and Jeckle in these parts again. Not upright, anyway. No, it's you what needs sorting, Leslie."

"Me? What have I done?"

"Do I have to spell it out for you? You've fucked up any chance there was of repairing bridges with our friend in Wandsworth, just when I needed him. You've blown that out of the water, you worthless cunt. He won't forgive this. Ever."

"But I thought you two were dead to each other anyway?"

"Given time, some things can change. And that might have been one of them."

"I'm truly sorry. I didn't know. And it was the fucking Malones did his boy, remember that."

"Your hires, Les."

He drained a large glass of whisky.

"What you doing with that?"

Julius had picked up the revolver. His forefinger rested

on the trigger as the heavy gun swung towards the man in the chair.

"Open your mouth."

"Now, come on, Jewels. It's me, Les."

"Open wide."

Les did what he was told.

"Say 'Ah.'"

"Ahh."

"From what I have heard, Leslie, old Chisel's been making himself busy over in SW18."

Leslie tried to spit out the barrel which tasted of gun oil and cordite. Julius gave the weapon a little push and broke a tooth. Leslie squirmed.

"As you were, soldier."

He shoved the barrel further in, so that Leslie gagged.

"Getting friendly with people who are no friends of mine."

He wasn't watching as Leslie's eyes bulged, and nor did he seem to hear the noises a man makes when he chokes. He cocked the hammer.

"There's been a Silver Shadow outside Chisel's gaff more than once. Tom Adams's. I smell a dangerous alliance in the making. So, what you may just have done, Leslie." He cocked the hammer, "is to have fucked our future as surely as I'm now going to fuck yours."

He pulled the trigger.

There was a metallic 'thunk'.

Leslie fell to the floor, blood oozing onto his chin.

Julius reached for the bottle.

"Go on, fuck off. Before I change my mind and fill the chamber."

Leslie dragged himself to his knees, ashen and sweating, then all but fell out of the room, leaving the stink of the farmyard behind him. Julius put down the gun.

“Carrot. Get in here, now.”

Carrot had been standing outside the door and would have heard everything, just as Julius had intended that he would.

“Those papers. I want every piece here on this desk this afternoon. Do you understand?”

“I’m on it,” said Carrot, scuttling towards the door.

The mist is lifting, Julius thought. “I know what to do.”

31

She saw Arthur in the same place she had seen him last time, beneath the railway arches, almost as if he had been waiting for her. He got up from the pile of tyres where he'd been sitting and ambled over to her.

"I've been having another think about what you said," Arthur said

"About what?"

"About going down the Dogs."

"What of it?"

"Well, maybe you shouldn't go by yourself. Not if you don't know the place."

"I can't know it until I've been there."

"So, I was thinking, maybe I could go with you."

She could have hugged him.

"That would be amazing."

He smiled.

"When were you thinking of going?"

"Tomorrow morning, unless you've got something else on?"

Arthur scratched at his blond scalp. "I'll check my diary."

They walked along the Embankment together. The morning's rain had stopped, and sunlight sparkled in puddles. The two policemen walking towards them didn't frighten Juliet, because she had not killed Colin.

She asked Arthur when he might get another house-sit, so they could sleep together again. Soon, Arthur said.

When Arthur stopped to browse a second-hand bookstall, Juliet's eye was caught by a tatty paperback. She picked it up. *The Isle of Dogs: Its Rise And Fall.* She flicked through to the first section of black and white plates.

Isle of Dogs, Yesterday, offered pictures of workers crowding dockyard gates, a street party celebrating the Queen's coronation, half-naked children playing in the river, an ocean-going ship dwarfing terraced houses and a lattice of docks filling up with steamers and tugboats. Then came *Isle of Dogs, Today:* buildings in varying states of demolition, high and medium-rise council estates, prefabricated houses, great swathes of disused land, bored teenagers backgrounded by boarded-up flats, corrugated-iron fencing daubed with racist graffiti and empty docks.

Her mood fell; it didn't look promising.

The next morning, she and Arthur boarded a bus heading East. They sat in silence as the furniture of bleak East London streets rolled past the windows, motor spares dealers, bookies, TV rental places, kebab shops, pawnbrokers, scrapyards, dilapidated Victorian pubs plastered with flyers.

She had no idea where they were.

When they saw a strip of grey water lined by cranes just like the ones in her book, Arthur rang the bell, and they got off.

The bus had dropped them on a street with few obvious

landmarks beyond some monolithic blocks of flats. They walked alongside a waterlogged park and then down a street where drifts of wind-blown litter banked against walls, and three cars parked together had been set on fire. Gerry had sent her to a ghost town, she thought.

She followed Arthur, asking herself how she was going to find Julius Nicholson in a place like this. Who would she ask? Who *was* there to ask? Then, as they were passing another row of identical flats and boarded-up shops, Arthur stopped and turned to her. "Listen, you hear that?"

"What is it?"

"I don't know. Down there. On the main road."

She followed as he quickened his step, hearing music and a man's voice barked over a PA system. Then, a wider street and a different world, where a dense crowd lining the street was cheering and heckling a motorised procession of gaudily-decorated floats.

Juliet stopped, mesmerised by rackety noise, the vivid colour and sudden activity. Somewhere down the procession, a steel band was playing. Juliet threaded her way through noisy spectators and arrived at the kerbside.

"Ahoy there!"

She looked up.

Shouting down from the deck of a galleon which had come to a stop in front of her, was a big man with a boxer's face and a pirate's hat. A red-and-blue stuffed macaw had been strapped to his shoulder. Before he could say anything else, the truck was moving off again.

More floats rolled slowly by with footballers in Millwall's strip, big men wielding hooks among hardboard cranes, a Pearly King and Queen sharing a pearly throne. Then Juliet realised she'd lost sight of Arthur.

She began to walk in the direction of the procession, negotiating mothers pushing strollers, children eating ice-creams, and men tipping back cans of beer, while calling out Arthur's name as she scanned a mosaic of heads for a spiky crop of blond hair. Again, she wondered how anyone would start to look for a man called Julius Nicholson.

"Oi, darling, how's about 50p for the widows and orphans?"

She had caught up with the pirate ship where the middle-aged buccaneer with the parrot was reaching out his plastic pail from the slow-moving lorry.

"I'm sorry, I've got no money."

He shook his head.

"It's like that, is it?"

"'Fraid so."

"Well, how about a smile, then?"

She smiled. She liked his face.

"That's better," the man said as the procession came to another halt. Perching on the edge of the flatbed, he reached under his plastic jerkin and extracted a packet of cigarettes.

"Want one?"

"Do you mind?"

"You look like you could use one. Hold it still."

As she blew out smoke, he said, "You from round here, then?"

She shook her head.

"Thought not. Been on the Island before?"

"No."

"Like it?"

"Looks alright."

She nodded towards the crowd and floats.

"You won't find a friendlier place in London. What brings you here, then?"

He seemed friendly himself, so she took a chance.

"I'm looking for someone. Someone who lives here."

"I've lived on the Island all my life. Everyone knows me. Go on then, what's the name?"

"Julius Nicholson."

The lorry began to move. The macaw wobbled as the man dropped his cigarette and remounted his flat-bed galleon. She repeated her question, thinking he may not have heard her correctly over the jubilant noise of the steel band.

"Julius Nicholson?" She had to call out loudly as he was looking away, over a sea of heads. "Do you know him?"

She was aware of people around her taking an interest in their conversation and heard *Nicholson!* repeated by a woman standing somewhere close. The man bent towards her. "I don't know him," he said in a low voice, "And that's the way I want to keep it."

He reached out his bucket to someone else in the crowd. Juliet was watching the float move off again and puzzling over the man's reaction when she felt a hand on her shoulder.

"Everything alright?" asked Arthur.

"I'm not sure."

Up ahead, the Jolly Roger pennant disappeared around a street corner.

"Where did you get to?" she demanded. "We need to make a start."

"We're looking for someone called Julius Nicholson. Can you help us, please?"

They had begun their enquiries at a large newsagent's first, reasoning that if Julius Nicholson had a paper delivered, he might be on their list. He wasn't. They tried another, smaller shop.

Juliet went into a launderette and asked the women emptying dryers.

They asked random individuals, a school caretaker, the owner of a cafe, the caretaker of a block of flats, a bored traffic warden, and some chatty girls in a solarium. People frowned, shook their heads, said they'd never heard of him or acted like Julius Nicholson was the queerest name they'd heard in a long time.

By early afternoon, Arthur was looking like he'd had enough.

He said, "I thought your Gerry said everyone would know him?"

"He did,"

"Gerry was over-optimistic, it seems. You sure he didn't say the Isle of Thanet?"

"We'll try the pubs."

"Money?"

"So don't buy anything. I need to do this."

Nearby pubs were heaving with revellers from the carnival. In the first pub, Juliet asked a skinny old man incongruously attired in an *Incredible Hulk* tee-shirt.

He listened, grinned toothlessly and called out, "Young lady here's looking for someone called *Julius Nicholson*. Anyone know a Julius Nicholson?" and the name had daisy-chained around the pub like it was a game.

People laughed, gave them looks.

"No such person living here," he told her, and turned his back on them.

They were watched as they extricated themselves from the crush and left the pub. There was little doubt that drinkers at the next two pubs had heard of Julius Nicholson; it was there in the doubtful looks, the exchanged whispers of bar staff, and in eyes that followed them, but no one would admit as much.

"They're like the Masons, this lot," Arthur said. "We may be better off cutting our losses and going."

"No. I have to find him."

"Have to? Why's finding this geezer so important to you?"

"I don't want to speak about it, not until I've seen him."

"He could be anyone, you know that. And I'm not getting good signals."

"I have to know who he is. I need to see him, if that's all I do."

"We're getting nowhere. Come on, let's go."

"Not yet. If there's nothing doing at the next one, we'll call it a day. Okay?"

"I get the feeling we're not welcome here. One more pub and that's it."

Walking up the road in the hope of stumbling across another pub, Arthur pointed out a blue Hillman Imp which had just driven slowly past them and said the driver had ducked down to get a look at them.

"They're just curious. We're strangers, I'm black."

"So was the steel band. I don't like this."

They walked away from the carnival district and chose a place called The Vulcan.

The Irish girl who served them with two halves of bitter gave no sign of knowing who they were talking about. Had they tried the phonebook?

Juliet sighed. There was only one other customer in the place, and he slipped out the door as soon as they sat down.

"So, are we done here?" asked Arthur. "It's getting late."

"Didn't you think we were getting close at times?"

"Too close, maybe. There's something wrong with all this. To be honest, Juliet, I don't understand what we're doing here."

"I should never have dragged you with me."

"Come on, let's go. You can come back another time."

"You'll come with me?"

"I don't know about that. Listen, I'm going to pop out and check the bus timetables. You stay warm. I'll be back soon."

Juliet sipped her drink and reviewed their options. She was thinking they might come back the next day and try another part of the Island when the pub doors burst open and Arthur stumbled through them, knocking over her drink as he crashed into his seat.

"Jesus! What happened to you? Are you hurt?"

"Came out of nowhere," he mumbled. She saw the open wound just above his temple and, stifling her panic, she reached into her bag and pulled out a length of toilet paper, staunching the wound as she called out, "Please, somebody help me."

The Irish girl, who wasn't as shocked as Juliet to see Arthur in this state—he was shaking now—rummaged behind the bar and bustled over with a first-aid kit. "Another one been in the wars," she said as she settled herself next to Arthur and turned his face to hers. "Come on, let's take a look at you."

"What happened?" Juliet asked him.

"Ah, don't you go worrying about him. It's not half as bad as it looks. Hold that there while I find the TCP."

"Does it hurt?"

"Stupid question."

"You were attacked?"

"Yes."

The girl said, "I'm sorry to hear that. It's generally a safe-ish district around here. We just need a big sticking plaster, now."

"I should never have brought you here," said Juliet.

Two young men in cheap suits and pork-pie hats entered the bar and looked about for staff.

"I'll be with you in a minute," the barmaid called to them.

"What's happened to him, then?"

The Irish girl smoothed the plaster into place.

"You fellows wait a moment there; I've only one pair of hands."

"It's all right, we're going," Arthur said.

"Are you sure you won't rest here for a little while?"

"No," Juliet said, "But thank you for your help."

"It's a pleasure. Now, if you'll take a word from the wise, you'll not go reporting that to the police. People don't take kindly to that kind of thing around here, and to be honest, it'll do you no good anyway."

32

"So, one more time. The Securicor van drives round to this rear entrance every Thursday?"

Patrick said, "Yeah, it's always Thursday. But they vary the timings to make it harder for anyone trying to knock 'em off."

Julius pored over the map drawn in thick felt marker on the reverse side of the wallpaper that hung over his desk.

Don Garbutt said, "So in fact, they could pitch up any time on a Thursday?"

Julius looked up from the map. "No. There will be a pattern to those deliveries. There will be a rota of times. That way, they can arrange the shifts for their guards. We just need to pin it down."

"Already sorted, boss," said Patrick. "Malc and me have spent the last five Thursdays parked up in Sainsbury's across the way. Clear view from there."

"And?"

"Next delivery should be sometime between 11 am and 11.20 this Thursday. If we're right."

"And are you?"

"I'd put my house on it."

"Nice work, Patrick. And you, Malcolm. Thank fuck someone's on the ball."

"Who's going on this outing?" asked Dom.

"The team will be you, Donald, Malc, Patrick, Carrot and Peter. Inner circle only. Peter, here is in the last-chance saloon on this one. Malcolm will have the shooter."

The boy coloured but said nothing.

"Carrot?"

"Why not? Let's see what he's made of. He'll be our lookout."

"Where's Leslie?"

"Leslie's on a new career path."

Patrick lifted his glass. "I'll drink to that."

"Okay. I'll sort the motor," said Malc. "Something like Leslie used to get us? Volvo? Vauxhall Viva?"

"No, something fast."

"Got you."

"Another thing. I want you to make yourselves familiar with every route in and out of that bingo club and all exit routes once the job's done. I want the whole thing over and done with, the cash stashed, and the vehicles gone before they know what's hit them. We are going to kick Tom Adams in the balls so fucking hard he'll still be singing like Aled Jones when next Christmas comes around."

They laughed together, like a team.

"On it," Malcolm said. "Fuck me, boss?"

"What?"

"Like the old days, innit?"

Later, in a relatively quiet corner of The Waterman's Arms, Malcolm said, "There was someone in here asking questions. About you."

"Who?"

"Don't know. Black girl and a scruffy little geezer. Young."

"Don't sound like friends of mine. I don't like people asking questions. Let me know if they turn up again. No, get some details."

Carrot returned from the bar with a tray of drinks and gave Julius his change. Julius handed the glasses round.

"That's yours, Malcolm. Brown and bitter, wasn't it? And here's your rum and Coke, Peter. Don, yours was the Special Brew? Patrick, your usual. That leaves Christopher with his lager and lime and me with the Scotch. Cheers."

"Cheers."

"Cheers."

"Fucking lager and lime, Carrot!"

"Peter. None of that. We're a team now. It's us nasty fuckers against the world. Not each other. How's Brenda, Malcolm? Still wearing you out?"

"She's unnatural."

"Lucky bastard."

"So, we're all up for this, then?"

"Yes."

"Yes."

"And we all know what we're doing?"

"Yes."

"Thing is, he needs teaching a lesson."

"Who does?"

"Tom Adams. Where have you been, Carrot?"

"I was thinking."

"Well, don't. It worries me."

"Jewels."

"Something on your mind, Donald?"

"Who's that, corner of the bar there? Geezer with the mutton chops and lairy shirt?"

"Fuck knows, I don't. Why?"

"I've seen him somewhere before. Can't place him."

"He's nobody."

"He's been looking over here. Listening, maybe. I don't like him."

"Where did you see him?"

"I tell you what, if he looks again, I'm having a word."

"No trouble tonight, Donald. We can't afford to draw attention just now."

"All right. Looks like he needs a slap, though. Just saying,"

"Who's ready for another one?"

"Wait, I've remembered where I clocked that bloke."

"Where?"

"At Charlie's send-off. He was making himself comfy at Tom Adams' table."

33

She sat in the cold with her head against a broken brick wall, thinking of how, only yesterday, she had clung to the possibility that Julius Nicholson was someone who might, for some reason and in some unguessable way, do her good.

Now she couldn't make him out.

People didn't want to talk about him or not with strangers, anyway.

She asked herself what sort of man might inspire that level of loyalty. It was hard to dismiss the possibility that this was someone people feared.

She told herself she was being paranoiac again when she tried to connect him with what had happened to Arthur. But if he was a dangerous man, then why had Gerry been so keen on sending her to see him? It was only now that Juliet completed Gerry's unfinished sentence. *You deserve...* he had started to say, that day in Wandsworth. She filled in the blanks out loud, feeling warm tears on her cheeks, *Each other. You deserve each other.*

They had returned from the Isle of Dogs too late for beds at the hostel, so they sheltered instead under the railway arches where they had first met.

The fire someone had lit earlier had burnt out, leaving an acrid smell for the men and women bundled against walls and buried under cardboard and cloth.

Every so often, an old man broke the silence and began screaming.

Juliet pulled tight the drawstrings on her sleeping bag and huddled against Arthur, who had gone straight to sleep in the recess of a brick buttress, despite the bitter cold.

She shivered uncontrollably, drawing up her knees and clenching her teeth. From a van parked over the road drifted the tantalising smell of frying onions.

She felt for the length of metal tubing she had put between them, because at night, you never knew what might happen.

Unable to sleep, she paid attention to the noises of the night, the traffic on the nearby road, the rumble of a tube train deep underground, and the incoherent shouting of drinkers at closing time. The shouting seemed to go on and on and get louder and nearer.

She sat up with a start and shook Arthur.

There were streetlights nearby, and peering around the buttress, she could see the young men who were doing the shouting.

Arthur sat up.

"What's up?"

"Trouble, maybe."

Quietly, she sloughed off her sleeping bag and watched. There were four of them, all wearing suits that must have looked smart a few hours before. Belligerent tones, loosened ties, and untucked shirts spoke of a night of hard drinking.

They lurched and stumbled.

One of them kicked at something she couldn't see.

He raised his voice, shouting at whatever was beneath him.

"You know what you are?"

The young men shifted positions, allowing Juliet to see an old man on his knees, his bald head and gaunt face white in the streetlight. It was the man who had woken up screaming.

"I said, you know what you are?" Louder now, "Are you deaf as well as stupid?"

The man on his knees gave a little shake of his head.

"I'll tell you what you are; you're a fucking parasite. You hear me? A fucking leech."

He kicked again at the man on the ground, who yelped and cowered.

Another man stepped forward and bent a little. "You hungry, mate?"

She heard the man say yes.

"You want a burger from that van over there?"

Again, an affirmative noise.

"With or without onions?

"Onions."

Now the man was kicked again, this time with more violence than the first had offered.

"Then why don't you get off your lazy arse and earn one?"

The men all laughed.

"You smell of piss, you useless cunt. When did you last wash? Have you even heard of soap? Get up, you fucking stain. Go on, get up."

The man stood up slowly, and even from where she crouched, Juliet could see he was shaking.

The one who had kicked last said, "Fucking hell, these people," and then, in a singsong, wheedling whine, *Have you got any spare change, have you got any spare change?*

"This lot want to fucking work, like normal people. You

want a handout? Well, here's a handout. See how you like that."

The man remained standing after he was struck in the face, so another man hit him and he went down, falling on his knees and then keeling over as he was kicked again. He groaned.

Juliet turned to Arthur, saw his wide eyes, and saw him trembling. "We have to do something."

Arthur shook his head.

"There's nothing we can do except get hurt. There are four of them. Just keep your head down."

"We can't let that man..."

"Leave it. You'll only make things worse."

It was like some switch had been thrown. She had no memory of shaking off Arthur's restraining hand, of having stood up with the length of metal piping in her grip, of having begun to walk.

Now, suddenly, she was there, behind the drunks still taunting the man on the floor, who had curled himself up with his hands about his bloody head.

She touched the shoulder of the one who had last kicked the man, and when he turned, she smashed his nose with the metal pipe.

She stared at the blood that pumped through the fingers he held to his face and spilt on his shirt, heard him screaming as he spun away.

Addled by booze, the three others were slow to react. Before they had made a move, Juliet struck again, lashing out with no plan, gripped by the same uncontrollable rage she had experienced when she had beaten Arthur and almost killed Colin.

She hadn't seen the third man until he had thrown her to the ground, shouted, "I've got the bitch, I've got her."

Crushing the breath from her body, he sat astride her,

pinioning her hands as he waited for the others. She tensed, awaiting the kicking and worse that was to come.

At the same moment, someone shouted, "Behind you!" and the man's grip fell away.

She rolled over and broke free, got to her feet and saw Arthur, grasping his old lock-knife. The men saw it too and waited to see what the skinny kid would do.

Juliet expected him to throw down his knife at any moment and run off, and for a moment it looked like Arthur was thinking that too, but instead he took a step forward and then another, swinging the blade as he muttered, "Who's first?"

The men hesitated only a moment, still unsure if he meant it, but then they backed off, shouting, *black this, black that* and *little queer* as they stumbled back up the street, still hurling insults and promising they would be back. Juliet watched them go and then sank to her knees, rubbing her head.

When Arthur could control his hands, he knelt and did what he could for the injured old man.

They had no sleep that night. They walked and sat on benches and walked again when police patrols moved them on.

As dawn began to sculpt office blocks and roof-scapes, a new mantra was sounding in her head: *I can't go on like this, I must make it stop.*

Sitting on a bench in a bus shelter, with Arthur now asleep on her shoulder, she made two resolutions.

Firstly, she would search again for Julius Nicholson. Not until she had seen the man face to face, and had learned from him that no help was to be had from that quarter would she give up.

If she'd encountered people on the Island who were uncooperative, she'd find others who were.

Then, there was still something else she would try, something which would only hurt her pride. Soon after she woke, she told Arthur that she was going back to the Isle of Dogs.

"What's the point? Whoever this bloke is, he doesn't want anyone looking for him."

"So, you won't come?"

"Why go looking for trouble? I've had my fill."

"I'd sooner not go on my own."

"Then don't go. I tell you, Juliet, something always happens when I'm with you. Something bad."

She yawned and managed a tired smile.

"Kennington wasn't bad."

He grinned. "No, Kennington was all right." He spat on his hands and tried to smooth sleep-ruffled hair. "But you're on your own this time."

"You're sure?"

"I've got to see a man about a sofa in Finchley. Just be careful, all right?"

"You're going, then?"

"Yeah." He buttoned up the old coat, began to walk away and then came back and kissed her on the cheek, said, "It's been all right, Juliet. Maybe I'll see you around, yeah?"

This time, luck was on her side.

A little more than an hour after she had begun to make enquiries in steamy cafes, still-empty pubs and on big housing estates where the wind whipped off the river, she was talking to the kindly tenant of a sub-post office, who swallowed her tearful story that she was due to start her new job today as Mr Nicholson's cleaner but had left his address on a slip of paper in her other coat.

The postmistress opened a book and found the details she needed.

In some ways, she hadn't been ready to succeed so quickly and was almost reluctant to take the next step.

According to Arthur's *A-Z*, Nicholson lived about a mile and a half from where she was now.

What would she do if she saw him? Would he know who she was?

Gerry had seemed to think so. Wiping grit from her eyes and cursing herself for the fool's errand she had gone on with so little forethought, she soon found herself down by the river near a development that must have looked startlingly modern some ten or fifteen years ago. This little outpost of modernity was unlike anything else she had seen on the Island, a failed speculation in riverside living, perhaps.

The detached house she identified as belonging to Nicholson was all white-painted weatherboard and glass and had a driveway leading up to the metal doors of a big double garage. The windows were huge and would afford the owner a cinematic view of the river.

She walked past slowly, not wanting to stop and attract unnecessary attention.

She'd said nothing to Arthur, but she knew why she was here. She might be a stone's throw from finding out everything. And if so, would she like what she discovered?

That was another matter.

Still watching the house when she heard a metallic clank and the faint hum of an electric motor. The door of the garage was slowly opening. An engine started up, and a sleek red car slid out. At the bottom of the drive, it turned in her direction.

She slipped into a doorway before the car passed her, slow enough and close enough for her to ascertain that the suited driver was the man she'd seen at PINZ, the man with the heavy-framed spectacles who had frightened away kids at the door and rattled Chas Evans.

The bag she had been clutching slipped from her fingers as she experienced the vertiginous feeling of standing on a cliff edge which was beginning to crumble away. Now everything was thrown into confusion.

She cursed, stamped her foot, and said, "No, no!" as if accepting what she had discovered was entirely optional.

If she was in any way connected to this man, she decided, she would disavow that connection.

As she walked back up the Island, past disused factories, junkyards and empty warehousing, she decided to act on her second resolution, which was to swallow her pride and see Ammo one more time. She'd apologise for doubting her and throw herself on her mercy, if that was what it took.

34

Julius Nicholson wasn't sleeping.

The tightness in his chest was back, and his mind was racing.

A job like this was always dependent on too many factors. There was always something which might go tits-up. He turned over. Don't be a prat. You've done all you can. Go to sleep.

Things would be different once they had pulled it off, once Julius Nicholson had pulled it off. It would be a big one. There was no doubting that. 'Colossal Cash Prizes' and a fat staff payroll all on one delivery? Which clown had thought that one up? He was just thankful to the bingo-caller who had sold him the information.

They'd be in the money after this, no doubt about it. Everyone would know who had done this one, even the heavy mob, but they'd be in and out before anyone knew it, everyone in gloves, plates changed and leave nothing for the Sweeney to take to the DPP.

Everyone would know who had done it, and everyone would know who the top dog was.

And once the money had been scrubbed clean, he'd live like a top dog for a while. Pick up a nice little bolthole in Marbella, why not? He'd be happy, wouldn't he? He reached out and switched on the lamp at his bedside, fumbled for his glasses and flipped open a pack of Player's Gold Leaf. He'd have everything he wanted, then.

Striking a match, he studied the flame, his features clouding in the yellow light.

That was utter bollocks. He'd have everything except for the only thing he really wanted, the thing he had craved ever since Jimmy had been killed in that car and Kath had got cancer, which was someone to share his success, tell him he had done all right, shoulder some of the weight and maybe carry on the business after he was gone.

He was building his empire for no one.

Oh God, he thought, if only Angelica had lived.

Lighting the cigarette, he inhaled deeply, coughed and blew away the ash, which rained upon his forest of chest hair.

Except.

Except that now, he was beginning to think differently because, just maybe, there *was* someone.

He had been cautious, doubtful at first; it was a crazy idea. But now he was hearing strange things that suggested this person was not so unlike him after all, that there might be something in this wild idea of his, an idea which would leave the world in no doubt that the Nicholsons were back in business.

After all, what did it matter what people thought now? Kath was long dead, poor cow. No, it was high time he introduced himself to his daughter.

The next evening, he had his supper at Terry's down by the river.

He had the place to himself. The cafe had been a different place only a few years ago, when the demolition men had set up camp on these streets and Terry Shaw had employed four or five local girls to cook up the pie and mash and slosh steaming hot tea into big mugs.

Terry's was always full of big men in orange overalls, and you might find yourself fighting for elbow room with builders from Bermondsey or rubbing shoulders with excavator operators and dumper truck drivers.

There was a big, blue jukebox by the counter filled with stuff that he liked and he enjoyed nothing better than lingering over a mug of tea and a bacon sandwich while Brenda Lee sang *Sweet Nothin's* or The Righteous Brothers lost that Lovin' Feeling one more time.

The jukebox had gone now, as had Tel's clientele. It wasn't even Terry running it anymore, but a family from Cardiff. The tea was still good, but the soul of the place had moved on.

He took his mug to a table by the window overlooking the river, now that the old dockside offices had been pulled down.

He'd been here with Chisel. When was that, now, must have been after that social up west, when they'd met Barbara whatsherface and some others off the films and they'd made a night of it, stumbling into Tel's sometime after seven in the morning, still in their evening wear.

Chisel had been pissed as a rat, and he hadn't been much better. They must have looked a sight. But Tel had just twitched his moustache, waved his greasy spatula and said it was nice to see some people still making an effort.

They had sung along to every record they stuck on the

jukebox loudly, never mind anyone else who had come in for a quiet cuppa before work. It had been one hell of a night.

It could have been the night when Chisel said he loved him.

No, not like that, of course, not like *that*. It was just one of those things you say when you're plastered... you know; I *love* you, mate, I *really* love you—that kind of thing. But even so, he never forgot that look in his old friend's eye.

In the months and years that followed, it gave him cause to wonder about him more than once. Well, it mattered how Chisel felt about him now. Leagued with Tom Adams and his boys, he could make things very difficult.

Chisel would have known there'd be a tariff on Colin trying to rape his daughter and would have been expecting some sort of comeback, but not what the fucking Malones had done.

Surely to God, Chisel would know this was none of his doing.

Maybe he should send him a message. He could have the Malones kneecapped, he thought, and then pulled himself up short. Perhaps that sort of thing wouldn't do now. Not if he was going to be working alongside his daughter?

He was mopping up the last of the thin liquor with a slice of white bread, wondering whether it might be possible to set in motion the wheels that would bring his daughter into the business, when Carrot bustled in, dragged up a chair and said, "Saw your car."

"Well?"

"I've got some news."

"And?"

"She's been seen."

"Who?" though he was sure he knew.

"Her."

For Carrot, this was far too sensitive a subject to say more about than that. He knew Julius had never liked to be direct on this subject. Carrot could understand that.

"Where?"

"Battersea."

"When?"

"This afternoon."

"Who saw her?"

"Alex Ryan, one of mine. Used to see her when he was in with Chisel. He reckoned he saw her up West, then he lost her again. I must tell you, Julius, she wasn't in the best of circumstances at the time. Not according to Ryan."

"What do you mean?"

"Sleeping rough. On the streets."

"Jesus Christ. Chisel never said..."

"So as soon as he clocked her this time, he was on the blower to me."

"All right. Battersea, you say. What's she doing there?"

"Bit of a change in those circumstances. Consorting with the upper crust, it looks like. Tasty place on Prince of Wales Drive."

"Who with?"

"Some girl, about her own age. She's with money, I'm telling you."

He smiled to himself. "That makes sense. Good work, Christopher."

So, he was feeling about as good as he could when he drove into the garage the next morning and saw the cars Patrick had brought in the night before. A white Cortina estate for the cash and clobber and a black Saab Turbo—they'd need something quick as well. He found Patrick crouching behind the Saab. He looked up and said, "That's the plates sorted."

"Nice one. What about the motors?"

"Cortina's good. Peter picked up the Saab, a bit distinctive for my liking. What do you reckon?"

"It's no great distance from here to the job. No distance at all from the first change of motors. It'll be sweet. Who else is here?"

"Peter's round the corner at the phone box, just in case."

"Patrick? Don?"

"Back room."

"Everything sorted?"

"All set. Just waiting on Carrot."

Julius smiled. The bad years were over. Watch out, Tom Adams, I'm coming to get you.

Then, rapid steps outside, and Peter ran in, wearing white overalls. People don't look at geezers in overalls, Leslie had said before the last one.

"Don't run, walk. Decorators don't run."

"It's Carrot. On the blower. Wants to talk to you. You'll have to be quick on your toes before someone else uses the phone."

"What's he want?"

"Wouldn't say."

He wiped condensation from a glass panel of the phone box as a police car sped by.

"Bit of an unexpected problem, I'm afraid."

"What is it, Carrot, tell me!"

"It's my old mum. She's not at all well. I think she's caught something, because now I've got it. I've been turning myself inside-out on the toilet, and didn't get a wink of sleep. Feels like I'm at death's door."

"Fucking hell, Carrot, you will be soon. You can't call in sick on a fucking armed robbery."

"No one is more upset about this than I am, Julius. But what am I to do? I'd be no use to you at all. I've practically had to crawl to the phone."

Julius crashed the receiver onto its cradle and began to formulate Plan B.

PART III

35

Juliet was sitting with her boots off and her feet up on a very expensive sofa.

She could tell that from the nice material and the way it felt solid beneath her. This wasn't something Maureen would have picked out if ever her Premium Bonds came up. It looked classy, like the rest of the furniture in this enormous fourth-floor flat of a mansion block in Battersea.

The place even smelled expensive. There were lights and cushions like she'd seen in shop windows on the King's Road.

There were paintings like those she'd seen in gallery windows.

Going home, she had sometimes wondered who had the money to shop in the elegant places she saw through bus windows, and now she had her answer.

People like the owners of this flat, people like Ammo's parents.

They had taken off their coats and walked down the hall and into this gorgeous apartment with a view over the bare trees of Battersea Park.

"I'm sorry, I really am. I should be ashamed." Ammo sighed.

"This is your *squat*, then."

"Don't. Don't rub it in, alright?"

"Because this place isn't cool, like a squat is?"

"I could hardly work at a place like PINZ and tell everyone I lived in a palace like this, right?"

Juliet couldn't help herself. "And your uncle didn't walk to London on the *Right to Work* march?"

Ammo said, "He did, actually. Not all our family made it out of the tenements."

"Why didn't you just tell me? The last time I saw you?"

"I was going to tell you. But at a time of my choosing. When I was ready. I wasn't ready; I didn't enjoy being interrogated about the squat."

"You wouldn't have liked it anyway."

"What?"

"Squatting. I couldn't see you living in those flats."

"I know, I tried it. I need to work on my bohemianism."

"Your what?"

"Doesn't matter. You want a coffee? And there's some cold pizza in the fridge, if you can still eat anything?"

"Yes, to both, thanks. Where are your parents? The lecturer and the junior schoolteacher, I think you said?"

Naughty, but it had to be said.

"Ah, did I say that? Well, mum does work in a junior school, but it's a private one. She's the head and she's on silly money."

"And your dad?"

"He *is* in art, and he does sometimes give lectures, but he's a senior partner of a Mayfair auction house. He earns more than he knows what to do with. Come on, Julio, I was hardly going to tell you that, was I? Anyway, they're both out at the moment. Some charity event, I think. They'll be back later."

"Won't they mind? Me?"

"No, I've told them about you already, and I phoned Dad just before I left work. All's good."

"I can stay here tonight, then?"

She was already wondering if the beds might match the sofa's blissful comfort.

"If you have a shower and borrow some of my clothes. Sorry, you probably don't notice it yourself, but..."

"I do. Coffee first and shower after. Do you have a washing machine, or does someone do your laundry for you?"

"Fuck off and find the kitchen yourself."

Earlier that day, she had walked into PINZ like she was turning up for a day at work.

Ammo had seen her first.

"Julio."

"Can we talk, somewhere? Stockroom?"

"Sure."

They could hear the excited whispering out in the shop, which began the minute they left the shop floor. Ammo sat on a table; Juliet took a stool.

They said, *I'm sorry I...* in unison and both laughed, the ice broken.

"So, Juliet. What the hell has been happening? There are folk here who thought you were dead."

Juliet smiled. "There were probably people here who wished I were."

"Not true. So, can you tell me anything? Or maybe tell me over lunch? I'll buy. Again."

She was the one smiling now.

"God, yes please. And I'll tell you everything for that. But first, I need to see Chas."

"Chas? You want your job back?"

"No, nothing like that. I must ask him something about those visitors we had. The guys in the suits. Is he in?"

"I think so. Let me go see."

Ammo chose the bar-and-grill across the road for lunch. It was filling quickly with the usual Chelsea types, leisured ladies, loud-talking men enjoying long, business lunches, shop-workers celebrating a birthday.

There was one small table with two chairs behind the door to the kitchen. And when the young men wearing loosened ties had slipped their jackets from the backs of the chairs, crushed their cigarettes into the glass ashtray and left, they took their bags and settled in.

Ammo said, "I get the feeling you'll need a drink if you're going to spill your guts?"

"God, yes. I can't remember the last time I had a drink, unless it was glugging someone else's tin of cider. Oh, wait, I had a beer with Arthur."

"Arthur?"

"Not important."

"So, are you going to tell me the whole sordid story? From the beginning? I'm hoping it's not sordid, by the way."

She laughed.

But Juliet's attention was elsewhere. Every time the door to the kitchen swung open, she was tantalised by the aromas of frying fish, meat on the grill, vegetables steaming, herbs, spices and the zip of roasting coffee beans.

She hadn't eaten since the night before when she'd spent begged coins on a portion of chips.

"Oh. My. Lord."

"Order whatever you want. I'm better off than you think."

"So, you got my job? On my pay? That's a result anyway."

"Something like that. Now, what takes your fancy, Julio?"

She ran her eyes down the blackboard. With so many luscious possibilities, it was like reading porn. When she had weighed up the imagined tastes and textures of every item on the board, and despite what Ammo had said, she was still looking at the prices too, she picked out the moussaka, with a side order of chips and salad.

Ammo said, "Starter?"

"No, this is good. And thank you. I'm not used to eating so much these days. I've dropped a waist size."

A slim girl in black smiled as she put a terracotta bowl of warm, freshly-baked bread rolls on the table. Juliet tore off a huge hunk and buttered it generously.

Ammo's brow furrowed. "My goodness, you *are* hungry."

"My table manners are pretty shit now, I know."

"They were never great, hen."

Ammo ordered two large glasses of house red.

They laughed. They ate. Juliet began to talk, just a little at first, about her old life in Wandsworth and then, as the first sips of wine began to embolden her, she opened up and talked about Colin and what he had tried to do to her. She found it harder to speak of what she had done to Colin.

She described how she had left the house with nowhere to go.

She didn't revisit what had happened next, when she had tried to find Ammo. She attempted to put into words the shock of finding herself on the streets of London, which were colder than she could believe. She told her about being hungrier than she had ever thought was possible.

She also told Ammo what Gerry had said to her and spoke about her experience on the Isle of Dogs and what had happened to Arthur. Then, about the man driving the Jaguar.

"And you're sure this was the same guy who gate-crashed Chas's office that time?"

"It was him, all right. Chas told me just now that it was Nicholson who got me your job. Why do you think he would do that? He doesn't know me."

"I imagine you'll find out, one of these days, watch yourself. I used to hear of people like him in Glasgow. You didn't have to live in those areas to know what was going on there. The evening papers were full of it. People were living in fear of some of the big men down there. You'd see faces wearing Glasgow smiles, cheeks slashed with razors."

"Criminals?"

"Criminals, gangsters, whatever. Bullies are what I call them. Your man's one of these lowlifes, depend on it. Listen, Julio, if you'll take my advice, you won't go near the Isle of Dogs again."

"But he knows who I am. He found me at PINZ. He'll find me again. "

"Do you know what he wants?"

"No."

"Do you have any ideas?"

"I have one. How about you?"

Ammo put down her fork, her meal unfinished as usual.

"I have one, too."

"Let's compare notes, then."

36

Two days before Julius Nicholson had outlined his new plan to rob Tom Adams' bingo club, Juliet Hobson was shaking a man's hand and wondering if his fingernails had been manicured.

"So, um, you're Amelia's friend, the one she's been telling us so much about?"

Ammo's father, younger than she had imagined and wearing designer jeans and a nice blue jacket rather than the pinstripe of her imagination, sat on the corner of the sofa and crossed his legs. His shoes were visibly expensive, like his watch.

"You've had her worried, you know."

"I'm sorry. I never meant to do that."

"The last time she saw you. Meli thought you might be sleeping outdoors, living rough? Was that right?"

She nodded.

Ammo's mum was perched on the arm of the chair in which her daughter had curled herself. Her mother was petite, elf-like, with a small nose and Ammo's grey-blue eyes, which met hers as she said, "That must have been pretty awful at times."

"It was..."

She didn't know how to describe it. Harsh, frightening, freezing, surprising, disheartening. Heartening. It had been all those things, at times.

Ammo said, "Don't believe her hard-luck stories, Pops; she's been spending her time developing an interest in your line."

"Now you do have me curious."

As Juliet seemed reluctant to speak, Ammo told her father about Juliet's visits to the National Gallery.

"And was there something there which took your eye? Some picture that sparked this interest?"

Juliet nodded.

"In my experience, there usually is," Ammo's dad said. "In my case, it was one called *Christ and the Adulteress*, probably painted by Titian. I stood before it on a school jaunt to Kelvingrove Art Gallery, absolutely spellbound, gobsmacked. Which was yours?"

"*The Execution of Lady Jane Grey*."

"Ye-es. Paul Delaroche. Rather melodramatic for my tastes, but I can see how the subject matter might have resonated with you. A girl, same sort of age, in the dark and fearing the worst."

"Was that why I liked it?"

"Well, she knew what was coming couldn't be any worse. You've only been wondering in the dark. But in London on a freezing night, that can't have been nice."

"It wasn't."

"We can save all that for later. Amelia's already told us more than she probably should on the phone today," Ammo's mother said. "You poor thing. Now, I've put you in the box-room at the end of the hall. There's not a great deal of space, but the bathroom's next door. Is that all right?"

"You're so kind. Thank you. I'll be gone in the morning."

"No, you won't, not until we've sorted you out. One way or the other?"

"Alice, the girl's old enough to sort herself out," warned Ammo's father. "We can't go interfering..."

"But she needs help, Vaughan."

"We can give her that," he said, "But let's also give her the chance to make her own decisions. What I want to say is—Juliet, isn't it? It's up to you to decide where you go from here. Your future is no one's decision but your own. Although, for what it is worth, we're more than happy to advise, if that's what you would like. In the meantime, will you stay here with us? I'd like to open your eyes to some more pictures, if you will let me."

"And Vaughan's cooking lunch on Sunday, aren't you, Vaughan? Highland beef, isn't it?"

Ammo's father gave her a warm smile, the sort that a father had never given her.

"We'll be very happy to have you. I won't say 'any friend of Amelia's', because she knows a lot of riff-raff." He pretended not to see Amelia stick out her tongue. "But you are very welcome. Believe us."

Oh, my God, Juliet thought, and fought back the tears.

Snug under a continental quilt in the small but cosy bedroom at the end of the passage, sated with food and just a little tipsy from the wine, Juliet nestled into soft pillows wearing Ammo's pyjamas and revelled in warmth, security and the knowledge that Ammo was her friend again.

She switched off the lamp by her bedside and listened as Ammo's family made their preparations for bed. She heard dishes being collected, glasses chinking, a voice, Ammo's father's, saying, "Leave all that 'til morning, come to bed."

She heard Ammo and her mother laughing and people using bathrooms, doors closing, and then was aware of a pleasant silence spreading through the flat.

In her little room, the clock on her table ticked loudly, the bright, luminous hands reading five minutes to midnight.

She was in limbo; her life was in balance. As she turned her pillow over, she wondered which way it would go.

37

If Securicor is sticking to the schedule Patrick and Malcolm have worked out, he has got there bang on time.

Julius crosses the busy road and takes his time reaching the top of the lawned slope above the back of the *Fat Fortune Bingo Club*. The grassy knoll, he thinks.

The bus stop here affords him a perfect view of the scene below, both the entry and exit route of any vehicle delivering to the cargo-bay or the office doors at the rear of the bingo hall. He looks at the timetable and checks his watch.

The raincoat and empty briefcase lend him the appearance of a harassed commuter anxious to board his bus and be off to work. He glanced up at the clouds, as if checking for rain. He looks up the road as if searching for the bus, then down the road as if interested in an unusual vehicle. All the time, of course, he is watching for the dark-blue shape of the Securicor van, or the distinctive livery of a police car.

He waits.

Time seems almost to have broken down. He wonders if they have got this all wrong. But it is no more than six minutes before he sees the van approaching. He puts down his case and stretches his arms wide, as if taking exercise.

Below him, he sees Malcolm and Peter in the Cortina read his signal and drive slowly into position just around the corner from the office doors.

Now he runs his hand slowly through his hair and in the Saab across the road, Patrick and Don release their seat belts and roll down their ski masks.

The Saab moves out, signals a right turn, crosses the stream of city-bound traffic and follows the van down the slip-road towards the front of the club.

Now he can only wait and be ready to bundle himself into the Saab once the thing is done.

Here we go, he thinks.

It is like watching some old action movie where everything plays out in slow motion, *The Wild Bunch,* he thinks.

The van halts by the office window, but the doors of the van remain closed.

The Saab accelerates wildly as Patrick slings it around the corner and cuts the van off at the front, just as Malcolm slews the Cortina across the road behind it.

Malcolm is already out of the car and hammering on the van's window with the shotgun butt. The gun's not loaded this time, but the guards won't know it.

Peter's behind him, but he doesn't seem to know what to do.

He turns and sees Patrick hefting a crowbar. Swinging it at a side window, he cracks the strengthened glass.

There are muffled cries from the men inside. They're all up for it, and they'll be in that van in a minute, one way or another.

No one is watching their backs, so only he sees what happens next: the police cars which steam in from both ends, trapping the trappers, and the eight-armed officers who leap from the loading bay, Heckler and Koch firearms at the ready.

Malcolm sees them; there is a split-second of indecision before he hurls his empty gun to the ground and follows it.

The rest of them are on their knees, hands behind their heads, while the cops reach for handcuffs.

Up the slope above them, Julius is about to flee when he clocks a copper in a helmet following Peter's gaze.

The copper sees Julius standing on the knoll and understands.

Julius turns as a double-decker passes him by. He runs after it, shouting for the conductor to stop the bus, runs despite having one leg which won't.

His heart pounding like a jackhammer, his breath coming short and fast. He can't risk a second to look behind to see where the copper is. His body isn't up for this; he fears its imminent failure.

Just when he thinks the game is up, the bus slows, and he lunges at the pole, pulls himself aboard, and almost falls into the arms of the conductor, who tells him that was a silly thing to do.

38

The following day was Saturday, and in Battersea, there was frozen orange juice, croissants and coffee for breakfast.

They had set a place for her, but that didn't stop her feeling like a magpie in someone else's nest. Ammo's mum was still in her pyjamas, her hair unbrushed. "Help yourself to coffee, Juliet. Or there's Earl Grey in the pot if you prefer."

She wasn't sure how you operated the cafetière; Maureen had never had one, so she poured herself a tea.

Ammo nudged her. "We've been talking about you."

"Amelia!" Ammo's mum calls.

"Well, we have, haven't we? We're always talking about someone. Anyway, the good news is you have somewhere to stay until you can get sorted out."

"That's amazing. I'm grateful, really I am."

"Don't be," grunted Ammo's dad, "you haven't tasted some of the cooking around here."

"Ammo, I haven't got a job. I can't pay..."

"No talk of money." Alice jumped in.

Ammo's dad was hidden behind that day's edition of *The Guardian*. She could hear him smiling as he said, "Not the done thing, talking of money."

"Anyway, you'll have money, a little, anyway. I saw Chas after you went back and unburdened yourself to him. He's talking about putting you back on the payroll."

"Seriously? Don't tell me he's seen my potential again."

"I think it's more like insurance against another visit from you-know-who."

"What's all this?" asked Alice, looking from one to the other.

"Doesn't matter, Mum. Looks like Julio will have a job. That's a start, isn't it?"

"I just wish for her sake it wasn't at that extraordinary place you've chosen to work at. Vaughan, we can give her another year, then she must think about university. What do you say?"

"I say there's been an armed robbery. Another one. A bingo hall in the East End this time. They've caught them, that's something."

"You wonder what the police are doing," said Alice.

"I did say they caught them. All except one, anyway."

"But really, Vaughan, it's getting too bad. People think they can take the law into their own hands..."

"You've been reading that red-top again, haven't you?"

She laughed. "I just feel sorry for the people they rob. Imagine having a loaded gun pointed at you. That sort of experience won't go away in a hurry."

"I can't remember when we last had a day out together. He must like you." Alice whispered to Juliet.

"Do you really think so?"

Ammo said, "I wish he didn't. I'm bored stiff."

Juliet hadn't been afforded the opportunity to be bored.

In the National Gallery, the Portrait Gallery, the Courtauld Gallery and a private one normally inaccessible to the public, she had listened to Vaughan enthusing about pictures and artists she had never heard of.

He showed her heaven and hell, angels and devils and everything between.

The sudden and profound change in her life left her unable to think past her gratitude to this family for taking her in.

The life she had been rescued from backgrounded their progress up Charing Cross Road. As Vaughan was walking at her side, talking about Caravaggio while Alice and Ammo were following behind, speaking about shop shortages, Juliet recognized the doorways she slept in.

The feeling of detachment persisted, as if she were floating high above them all, unable to believe she was part of this happy family group, in which no one was hungry, everyone had a bed to go to, and there was leisure to think of things beyond the basic needs of life.

As they passed Foyles' bookshop, she saw Shelagh dragging her assorted bags in the direction of St Martin's. Juliet stopped.

"Shelagh?"

The woman looked at her with eyes that were tired and confused.

"What do you want?"

"It's me. Juliet. We had Christmas lunch together."

"Did we?"

She looked her up and down.

Dressed in Ammo's clothes, bathed and well fed, she must appear very different from the street girl she was only yesterday, it seemed.

Juliet noticed that Ammo and her family had taken a step back.

"I think I remember you." Shelagh regarded the nicely-dressed people now standing in the doorway of a camera shop. "So, you've gone home, have you? I said you should."

"How are you?"

"As well as, you know. My hips are playing up again, but that's age and the weather, I suppose."

"Are you going to St Martin's?"

"I am, but there's some confusion about whether the soup kitchen will be there today. I will try my luck anyway."

"It's going to be a cold one tonight," Juliet said. "You need to be inside. Saint Jo's."

"I've got no money for hostels. Besides, I like the fresh air."

Vaughan stepped forward and looked at Juliet. She had no idea that he could look unsure of himself.

"Would you be good enough to accept this?" He held out a twenty-pound note.

Shelagh put down her bags and looked at it doubtfully.

Juliet was looking in Foyle's window. What a lot of books.

She heard, "Do you have two tens? Or four fives? Everyone will think I robbed it otherwise."

And then it was Vaughan's turn to see people he knew. As they walked down Piccadilly towards Mayfair, where he wanted to show Juliet his auction house, he was twice greeted by well-spoken and undoubtedly prosperous men.

Alice rolled her eyes when an expensively dressed woman greeted him with a kiss on the cheek. Then, outside the doors of the auction house itself, while Vaughan was expounding on the extraordinary amounts people would pay for what was, of course, only paint and wood and canvas, a silver car drew up beside them, causing an obstruction in the road.

The driver beckoned to Vaughan. He frowned as he bent to the open window, while drivers held up behind began using their horns.

The two men spoke in low tones, and then the car slid back into the traffic.

"Who was that?" Alice asked.

"Nobody. He doesn't matter," Vaughan replied shortly.

"Doesn't matter, but drives a new Rolls-Royce?" Alice said.

"Will you get off my back, for once?" Vaughan erupted.

Recovering himself, he said they could see the auction house another day. Just now, he needed to deal with something back at the flat.

She had expected them to settle down and watch TV in the evening, like at Gerry and Maureen's. Instead, they ate late.

Vaughan and Alice seemed to enjoy cooking the meal as much as they enjoyed eating it.

Half aware of knives chopping, glasses breaking and two people laughing in the kitchen, she sat on the couch, hugging a cushion and watching Ammo knitting a multi-coloured sweater, her senses teased by the sharp aromas of sizzling spices.

"I didn't know you knitted."

"Something else you didn't know about me."

She glanced at the high ceiling with its fancy edging, at the big ornate fireplace, the great bay windows with their heavy, deep-red curtains, the leafy plants on the mantelpiece, the intricately patterned rugs that covered large parts of the darkly stained floorboards.

"Knitting gives me time to think, sort my head out."

"What are you thinking of now?"

"I'm thinking of how we'll get you back on your feet again. Have you thought about what Chas said? The job?"

"He's serious? He actually wants to hire me again?"

"Yes, he does." She fiddled frantically with needles and yarn. "Damn, now look what you've made me do. And not just for protection. He liked a lot of the stuff you did. So?"

"So?"

"So, what do you think, Julio? Do I call Chas?"

She laughed. "I don't think I have a choice in this matter, do I?"

"Not really. It's a deal, then?"

"Deal."

"Good, because I've also been thinking that you and I might get a wee place of our own. South London, probably. What do you think?"

"A flat? With me? Why would you leave all this for a poky place in The Elephant and Castle or somewhere?"

"Because I'm nineteen years old and I'm still living off my parents. I need to get real, if you know what I mean."

"I've known *real,* and it's not always fun, believe me, Ammo."

"We'll be okay. Two wage-packets and no one to tell us what to do. It'll be great."

"But look at this place. And your parents are amazing. Why leave?"

"It's a gilded cage, Julio. Help me out, hey?"

There was a bottle of lager for everyone to accompany the aromatic chicken tikka masala that Alice had made. Vaughan contributed potatoes with spinach and a steaming dish of lentil dhal. There were all sorts of accompaniments, crispy papadums and spicy pickles. Let me at it, she thought.

"This is incredible," Juliet said after tasting everything.

"I agree. Quite inedible," Vaughan said, whose good humour had been restored.

"Stop it, Vaughan," Alice said.

"They love making curries," Ammo said.

Vaughan looked up. "It's about time you did some cooking around here, young lady."

"Here we go."

"No, I'm just saying that it's a lovely thing to do. A warm kitchen, a little music, a recipe. There's nothing like it for clearing the mind."

"All right, all right. I'll cook something next Sunday."

"Will it be your chilli con carne again?"

"What's wrong with my chilli con carne?"

"Nothing, nothing at all. And at least Juliet won't have had it before."

Vaughan uncorked a bottle of red wine and poured Juliet a huge glass.

"Vaughan! She's not used to drinking like..."

"Us?"

"Like you. Do you want a smaller glass, Juliet?"

Vaughan had his eyes on her. He had an impish smile for an older man.

"I think I'll be all right with this."

But of course, she wasn't. She was barely down to the lees before she had revealed more than she intended of her empty existence in Wandsworth and her struggle for survival on the streets of London.

She told them how she had injured Colin and why, and about the people like Shelagh she had met in shelters and soup kitchens, and under railway arches in the rain. And then she told them everything she knew about Julius Nicholson.

Vaughan said, "It sounds like you came here in the nick of time. And your stepfather says there is some connection between you and him?"

"He's not my stepfather."

"Can I ask *what* he is, then?"

"I don't really know."

"Let's put that to one side for now. So, hearing of this connection, you wanted to pursue it."

"Yes."

"Understandable, when you had nowhere to turn. But believe me, this man will bring you only grief. Yes, he may be an undeclared relative of yours. I think we all see that as a possibility. But if he's done nothing for you up to now, he's unlikely to do anything in the future, yes?"

"I suppose not."

"And the advantage you sought by pursuing some possible connection was what? Food, shelter, care, something along those lines?"

"Yes."

"Well, thankfully, that's all now taken care of. You can say goodbye to Mr Nicholson, whoever he might have been. Now let's talk about something more hopeful. And let me help you to some more saag aloo. It's very good, if I say so myself. Amelia tells me you're chewing over whether to take up your old position at her shop?"

"I've been thinking it over, yes. And I probably will take it up."

"All right. Now, you say this Nicholson character has seen you there. We don't know how likely he is to reappear, but if he does, I want you to call me. Any time of the day. I may know some people who can persuade him to leave you alone."

"Dad?"

"It's all right, Amelia. Just some old friends from Glasgow. They're very nice people. When they're not working."

He laughed. Ammo laughed too. Alice gave him a quiet look and got up with Juliet to clear away the plates.

39

Slowly, the memories of the weeks she'd lived on the streets started to fade.

She forgot some incidents entirely until something caused them to be recalled.

There was always something to distract her from thinking of those days, a tiresome customer at PINZ, an ear-splitting gig at the Rainbow or the bliss of living with Ammo's family.

It wasn't long before whole days passed in which she forgot entirely about the bitingly cold nights under cloudless skies and the fog of hopelessness that had so often shrouded her.

And then, at the end of an afternoon spent mostly in the back of the shop, sorting out the new stock and arguing with Ginnie about what should go in the window, she got a shock.

Ammo had burst into the stockroom wearing a face that told Ginnie she might be wanted elsewhere.

"What is it?"

"What indeed. Thank God you were in here."

"Why?"

"You had a visitor."

"Who?"

"Not the big fellow, Nicholson. The other one. Ginger hair, bad teeth."

"What did he want?"

"He wanted to know if you worked here. I said, no, you'd left weeks ago. No idea where you'd gone."

"Did he believe you?"

"Difficult to tell. He said that was a shame, because someone he knew wanted to talk to you. He left a phone number in case you came back here."

"Do you think he'll be back?"

"On balance, I'd say no. But I'll tell everyone to keep an eye out. Everyone's on your side. If he turns up again, we'll deal with it, somehow. Anyway, I wanted to talk to you about doing some flat hunting on Sunday."

The first flat they saw had been advertised in the *Evening Standard* as a two-room apartment in Tooting Bec.

Ammo pointed out the plaster ceiling rose in the main room, which was intersected by a flimsy stud wall to create the bedroom, where the rest of the rose made an unusual feature.

They would share the scruffy bathroom with the occupants of four other flats in the house; the bath itself was heated by a rusting, gas-powered geyser. They had arrived there at the same time as a Transit van, from which speaker cabinets and a drum-kit were now being humped into the ground-floor flat by long-haired men with tattoos and Motorhead tee-shirts.

"I think this is what you call oversold," said Ammo, peering through a filthy window at a litter-strewn street.

"Or a shitheap," Juliet said. "You could call it that, too."

Nor was the place they saw in Streatham that same day any better.

The next day, a Sunday, they went out to see a flat in Forest Hill with two bedrooms and a tiny bathroom, which they liked and could just about afford, but soon after they arrived, the couple in the downstairs rooms began breaking things, and the woman started screaming.

Monday evening, they went to Camberwell.

This one was on budget and sounded perfect, but they reached it just as the new tenants were being shown out.

Then they got lucky.

Word of mouth had given Ammo an 'in' on a place in Peckham. The owner would hold the flat until they had seen it.

The plan was to go from PINZ to Battersea, change into something that sober-living and responsible tenants might conceivably wear and take a mini-cab to Southeast London. It would be worth the expenditure.

Ammo was cashing up, so Juliet went home alone that afternoon to redo her makeup and wait for her.

As she walked down Prince of Wales Drive, she noticed a brown car, conspicuous for its dreadful colour. The man inside was energetically winding down the window. A hand appeared and a blue sweetie wrapper floated down into the road.

40

"Excuse me, miss."

She recognised the man getting out of the car immediately. Her heart sank.

"What do you want?"

The doors to the mansion block were only over the street. She could ignore him, cross the road and be safe in a minute.

But curiosity got the upper hand.

The man, who wore an ill-fitting brown jacket with beige, flared slacks and a pair of shoes with old-fashioned stacked heels, was holding open the passenger door for her.

"If you would be so good as to step into the car, it will be my pleasure to reveal my purpose," he smiled.

"You can tell me here."

"Well, yes, I suppose I could, but I'm put off doing so by the pedestrian traffic. I tell you what. Why don't you and I have a little stroll together in the park, and I'll explain why I have accosted you?"

She glanced up at the big bay window of Ammo's room and considered her options. She knew what she should do but she didn't do it. In days to come, she would often ask herself why.

Striding down the rain-shiny paths in the park, he said to her, "Where do I begin? Where do I begin?"

She kept a little distance between them as they walked.

"Not at the beginning this time," he decided, "That's for him to tell."

"What's this all about? Only, I have somewhere I need to be tonight."

"Tonight? Oh, no, that would never do. Not tonight."

"I have someone waiting for me."

"Well, if that's your beau, he will just have to wait. This is of much more importance than a Friday evening tryst, I can assure you of that."

"Please. I'm in a hurry."

"Why is everyone so impatient these days? Deary me, the times we live in. It's about your father."

"What?"

"Your father. He's not well, and he's been asking for you. Although, between you and me, I told him it would do him no good seeing people, not the way he is now. But he was insistent. As far as he was able to be, anyway."

"My father?"

He looked a little taken aback.

"You did know he was your father? I do hope I am not the deliverer of a bolt from the blue."

"Who is my father?"

"Julius Nicholson. I thought you would have worked that out by now."

There was all the difference in the world between working it out and having someone confirm it, she thought.

"How?" she said. "And even if he is my father, why would I want to see him?"

"Why? The bonds of blood, of course. Nothing more natural."

She stopped and turned.

"I'm going back."

She needed to sort all this out, she needed to talk to Ammo. Maybe to Alice and Vaughan, too.

"Don't go. He's very poorly. He needs to see you. It might be the last chance he gets. Last chance you'll get, too. Won't you jump in the car, and I'll take you to him? I'll run you back right afterwards, I promise."

An overpowering stench of TCP and camphor was what she noticed first. He led the way down a short hallway and into a sitting room, brownly illuminated by late-afternoon sunlight filtering through thin cotton curtains.

"She doesn't like anything bright. It's her eyes, you see," nodded Carrot.

The flat had last been decorated hundreds of years ago, as far as Juliet could see, the faded flamingo wallpaper was almost exotic. Edged around an old oak table, he sat down on one of two boxy, faux-leather armchairs.

"Sit yourself, sit yourself," he said.

She took the matching sofa opposite his chair, and in the crepuscular light, she distinguished the recognisable shape of a gas fire standing in front of a disused fireplace, over which hung a framed print of Buckingham Palace in the rain.

As her eyes adjusted, she could make out hundreds of brightly-coloured umbrellas opened before the tall iron railings.

On the tiled mantlepiece were arranged several more

framed photographs, a large one having pride of place in the middle.

"Ah, you've spotted it, have you?" The man got up and opened one set of curtains. "We'll need a little light on the subject."

He stepped over two dinner plates encrusted with a brown sauce and picked up the large photo frame, in which a vaguely familiar face was pictured with a formidable-looking lady with blue curls and a man with untamed red hair wearing an oversized sports jacket in a herringbone pattern.

"What do you think of that, then?"

"It's very..."

"You see who it is?"

"I've forgotten his name."

"You're pulling my leg, aren't you? Anyone can see that's Bruce Forsyth in the middle. And that's Marjorie on the left and me on the right. He's not at all like you'd think, you know."

"Is he not?" she said, out of politeness.

"Mum and me appeared on *The Generation Game* on the twenty-second of November 1975. You probably saw us. Millions did."

"Did you win?"

"No. There was talk of unfair judging, but I'll leave it at that."

There was a thoughtful silence before Juliet asked if she could see her father now. The man said something about sleeping dogs, she'd have to be patient a little while longer.

They sat in silence for three or four minutes and then a lavatory flushed loudly. A door opened and closed, and slippers shuffled down the hall. The man jumped up.

"Juliet, this is my mother, Marjorie. Marjorie, this is Juliet, the young lady I was telling you about."

Juliet stood as the old lady entered, who appeared not to see her as she lowered herself carefully into the other armchair.

"She'll have to take us as she finds us," Marjorie said. It was early evening, but Marjorie was still in her nightdress, which showed under a blueish housecoat. She looked shrunken, just a shade of the resilient-looking lady who must have given Bruce Forsyth pause for thought only a few years ago.

"It's my bowels again."

"She's a martyr to her bowels. Shall I switch on the television, Mum? *Porridge* will be on."

Christopher fiddled with the controls on the TV. "Such a funny programme. Do you watch it? It's all about life inside."

Marjorie watched critically as Ronnie Barker's old lag engaged in playful banter with the prison warder and then shook her head.

"Getting all chummy with screws," she said, "I can tell you this, Julie Andrews, it wasn't like that when I was in the cunt."

Juliet sat quietly and waited.

Marjorie had taken herself off to her bedroom. The man, Christopher, seemed to hear a noise, though Juliet heard only the rumble of heavy traffic on the street below.

"He's awake," he said, "I'll see if he's up for seeing you," and disappeared into the room across the hall.

Juliet had half a thought of getting up and going while he was in the other room; it would be worth hopping in a cab to be away from these people and this awful, cloying place. Now the moment had arrived. She wasn't even sure she wanted to meet him.

But then a face appeared in the doorway, a yellow hand beckoned. In the bedroom, the curtains were drawn shut, and as these were much thicker than the ones in the sitting room, she could see little at first but the outline of a single bed in which someone lay.

A gap in the traffic outside allowed her to hear breathing, slow and stertorous. Christopher approached the bed, lowered his head, and listened.

"He's going back to sleep, it seems. What a pity. Come closer, closer and meet your father."

He stood back and opened a curtain just enough to illuminate the bedhead.

She took a step forward and then, seeing no movement in the bed, she took one more step.

In a greying white vest and with his hair unbrushed and his thick glasses on the bedside table, he was unrecognisable as the man who had commanded the shop in Chelsea that day.

His hard, potato-like face was sallow, his big chin blue, and there was a little flow of spittle oozing from the corner of his pale lips.

Satisfied that he was unconscious, she regarded him as she might an animal she had never seen before.

Her mouth hung open a little, the way it had when she discovered a family of armadillos in a glass case at the zoo.

She tried to equate this man, this broken thing before her, with the images she had conjured as a kid, when she tried to imagine what her father might look like. She had imagined him in a thousand guises, but never had she imagined this.

She turned to the man, Christopher. "How did it happen?"

"As I understand it, Miss, he over-exerted himself, running to catch a bus."

"He collapsed on a bus?"

"Oh no, first thing I knew, he was playing knock-knock

on my doorstep looking dreadful. I said he couldn't stay at mine for reasons which I thought should be obvious to him. It wasn't until I got him here that he took so badly."

"He should be in hospital."

"He won't go to hospital, for reasons he had best explain himself."

"Why am I here?"

"You're one for the questions, aren't you? Well, he woke up yesterday and started rambling. It took me and Marjorie an age to understand that he was asking for his daughter. I told him at first that it wouldn't do. I could look after him, and as you can see, I am looking after him. But he became so agitated that we had to hold him down to stop him from falling out of bed. He remembered your name and used it, Juliet, Juliet. It was like listening to Shakespeare, *Macbeth*, or whatever it was. No one else would do. He had to see you."

"Why?"

"Must be blood, like I said. It's not like he needs anyone else, not with me around. I know his needs, his little ways. After rambling on a bit, he went back to sleep, and I thought that might be the end of it, but when he awoke, we were treated to the same performance all over again. It was doing him no good, I could see that. So here you are."

"Here I am."

The breathing became laboured.

"Can't you get a doctor to take a look at him?"

"I think not. There would be questions."

"About what?"

"He'd be the first to say he wanted to be left here in peace until he gets better. Maybe for longer, I don't know."

"This place is too small. You must be sleeping on the sofa as it is."

"Oh, no, Marjorie's bed is quite big enough for the two of us. He's no problem. Almost one of the family, now."

"Is he going to wake again?"

"It's hard to tell. He can sleep for hours. Then he wakes when we're least expecting it, and that's usually at an awkward time."

"You said you'd take me home."

"And so I will. But we need to prove you've been here. In case he doesn't wake until after you've gone."

He bustled off and opened a cupboard in the hall and came back wielding a Polaroid camera.

"Stand by the bed," he said, "and say 'cheese.'"

41

Two weeks after they had moved into the first floor of a neat Victorian terrace in Peckham with two small bedrooms and shared use of a rear garden, Juliet and Ammo were again in Battersea.

The lure of a proper Sunday lunch and the prospect of having their clothes washed for free became too much, which was when Ammo remembered that she had been neglecting her parents.

Vaughan was uncorking a bottle when they let themselves in.

He looked at Alice and said loudly, "The freeloaders are back." And got out two more long-stemmed glasses.

Ammo and Juliet sank into deep cushions and revelled in the warmth of a family united. Ammo said, "Cheers." They clinked glasses and sipped the chilled wine.

Juliet looked anew at the spacious sitting room with its expensive wallpaper, framed oil paintings and shelves crammed with hardback books and LP records.

The life Ammo had so readily abandoned was the model that now fuelled her craziest fantasies. It was ridiculous, and she knew it; in what kind of crazy world could she aspire to this?

She released a hollow laugh. Vaughan, stylishly dishevelled in jeans and an expensive, open-necked striped shirt, glanced up from his Sunday supplement. "And what's amusing you? Let's hope it's not me."

Juliet smiled. "Just something Ammo said. Amelia, I mean."

Vaughan put down his magazine. "So how is it, then? Out there, beyond the pale?"

"It's really good. We have our freedom," Ammo said, much too eagerly.

"Beware freedom. She's a slippery customer."

"What do you mean?"

"Well, haven't you only made yourselves free to be uncomfortable, free to be poor? When you might have stayed with us?"

"We couldn't stay here forever, Pops."

"We might have stood you for a little longer." He turned to Juliet. "And are you happy to be free?"

She hesitated. Ammo frowned.

"It's not like here," Juliet said.

"But nothing is rotten in the state of Peckham?"

"It's okay, Da. It's not Hillhead, but it's nae Govan either, you know."

Vaughan's face was sometimes hard to read, Juliet thought, as he turned to his daughter.

"I do wish you would speak as you've been raised to, Amelia. You didn't grow up in a Glasgow gutter."

Alice joined them, sitting down with her glass of wine, still untouched. She was wearing a beige-and-green kaftan with her long, chestnut hair tied back with amber beads.

"It's nice to see you both looking so well."

"Did you think we would fade away, Ma?"

"You know what I mean, Ammy. We worry, you know. And how about you, Juliet? I hope you've had no more visits from that man. Nicholson, was it?"

Ammo sighed. "You might as well tell them."

Bringing Julius Nicholson, the awful Christopher, and his mother into the conversation was the last thing she wanted to do. But already, Vaughan was sitting up.

"Tell us what?"

Juliet didn't know what to say; she didn't want to say anything.

"He sent someone in a car to take Julio to see him."

Alice sat up. "And you went?"

"Yes."

"Do you want to tell us what happened? Did you find out who he is?"

She took a moment.

"He's my father. Unfortunately. And he's not well."

"Okay. I think you had better tell us all," said Vaughan.

Vaughan listened, nodded, and said nothing for a moment. She couldn't imagine what he was making of this. Nothing good, she imagined.

Then he stood and went over to the windows, where he appeared to examine the view over the trees in the park.

"I wasn't sure whether to tell you this, Juliet."

In the corner of her eye, she saw Ammo mouthing, *what the fuck?*

She waited. Vaughan's attention was still held by something somewhere down in the park.

"It's merely this," he said, turning to them. "I have some contacts. I wouldn't call them friends, rather people I've had some dealings with at one time or another. The art world is very *chiaroscuro*. It has its dark fringes, you know."

"Forgers, that sort of thing?" Alice said.

"Well, whatever. The thing is that I sat down with a man

I know and I asked him if he had any knowledge of your Mr Nicholson."

"My father."

"Yes."

"And had he?"

She wasn't sure she wanted to hear the answer.

"Quite a lot, as it happened. Apparently, Nicholson is something of a big wheel on the Isle of Dogs. In the criminal fraternity."

"Oh," Juliet said.

While she hadn't known for sure, there had always been the chance that she had been mistaken about Julius Nicholson.

"Do you want to hear any more?" asked Vaughan.

"You've started now, Pop."

"From what I can gather, Nicholson's had his fingers in every pie you can think of, from petty larceny to fencing goods pinched off the docks. He's dabbled in the protection racket, too. It seems he funded his first businesses with money from the armed robbery of a newspaper wages department in the early 60s. Now he's wanted in connection with another armed robbery."

"He's wanted by the police?" Alice shuddered

"Christ, Julio, you're Mister Big's daughter."

"Shut up, Ammo. An armed robbery?"

"That's what I heard. The men they caught in the act of robbing that bingo hall are known associates of Nicholson. The police are waiting for one of them to talk."

"And will they?"

"Who can tell? The 'supergrass' is hot news; there's immunity on the table. Maybe cash too. I wouldn't like to be in Nicholson's shoes."

"Are they going to arrest him?"

"I don't think they have a case against him yet. But my

contact says they want to bring him in for questioning. Once they find him, of course."

"What are you going to do, Juliet?" Ammo asked.

"Do? I don't know."

"Vaughan, might she be implicated in some way? Assisting a felon or whatever it is?"

"No, she's done nothing to assist him, have you?"

"No."

"But doesn't she have a duty to inform the police of his whereabouts?"

"Juliet, don't worry," Vaughan said. "You're not in any trouble. So long as you stay away from him in the future. Is that possible? He is, of course, your father."

"He's not my father. Not in any way that means anything."

"Well, then. You've nothing to worry about."

"So why the long face, Julio? What are you thinking about?"

"I'm thinking," she said after a while, "About whether it's possible for people to change. I mean, will he always be like that? If he fully recovers, I mean. Or can people reinvent themselves? With help, I mean?"

"Vaughan?" Alice said.

He turned away from the window.

"For some people it is possible," he said, "But for Mr Nicholson? I'm sorry, I don't think so. Not from all I heard about him."

"I have another question."

"Fire away."

"Will I turn out like him? I mean, I am his daughter, with his blood."

Alice looked shocked. "What a thing to say!"

"But why not? I don't always trust myself to make good decisions. I've made a lot of bad ones."

"Juliet, don't forget, there was your mother, too," began Alice. "You may have inherited more from her than you did from him. And I don't suppose she was a criminal too?"

"I don't know who she was or what she was like. Only he can tell me that."

"As I understand it," Vaughan said, "It's not always blood that settles things like that. There are other considerations. Where you were brought up, for instance. Environmental factors. How you were schooled. That kind of thing."

"Nature versus nurture," Ammo said.

Juliet looked at them all, Vaughan standing there with his hands in the pockets of his designer jeans, Alice sitting with her arm around her daughter. She looked around the room, at the world that was theirs. She thought of her own world, of Gerry, his associates, and what she thought had happened to Larry Hughes.

"Well, that's it, then," she thought.

42

"You can't just go swanning off God knows where, like you used to."

"I need my time, Maureen. You get yours."

"What if he wants something?"

"He's in bed. He's catheterised. What's he going to want?"

"I just feel like I'm doing everything. Your head's somewhere else these days."

"It's work, Maureen. There are things I must do and places I need to be. Don't ask me more than that."

"I'm serious, Gerry. You missed the last hospital appointment. I had to get the neighbour to help me with his chair; it was embarrassing. I can't get him into that van on my own."

"Well, talk to them next time you're at the hospital. They can arrange a pick-up and drive him back."

"It's not enough, Gerry. I need you to go with me to every one of those appointments. I need you to take your full share of this. Or isn't he your son as much as mine, now that he's like he is?"

"That's unfair, girl. I'm doing what I can under the

circumstances, but the cold, hard fact is, he needs proper treatment. 24-hour care. For the time being, at least."

"Now I've heard it all. And where are we going to get the money for that?"

"Be patient, Mo, I've got something in the pipeline, something big. Give me a chance, love, just give me a chance."

All right, Colin had tried it on.

But Jewels had gone too far, like he always did.

Jewels had gone too far at school, and he had gone too far in his business dealings.

When there was a proper way of doing something, a route which might take some time but would fill their coffers without immediate consequence, Jewels would choose the shortcut through the quicksand and over the snake-pit.

He'd never listened to sense, and he'd have them all in trouble before too long.

Gerry remembered that time twenty years ago, now? When he had sounded out the boys, a fatal move on his part, as it turned out.

"If this goes on, we'll be taking our summer holidays on the Isle of Wight this year," he'd said, "and next year, and the year after that." But a pocketful of cash blunts the senses. *Don't give us that;* they came back. *Jewels has done alright by us, and he's done well by you, mate. You'd do well to remember that.* By and large, that was true; they had done well under his leadership. But that was more down to luck and police incompetence than through any brilliance on Julius' part. To Gerry, that was all too obvious. According to his way of thinking, the day was coming when the law would come down on them like a collapsing brick shithouse. They were getting too big for the expensive boots they all now wore. Which switched the lines under his train of thought. Boots and other such considerations were important to everyone in that decade, he recalled.

Julius in particular liked to spend a lot of the money on looking good, and he did look good in his mod-ish tailored suits, his skinny ties, dark sunglasses and razored sideburns.

He looked really good; he was slim as you like in those days. Fashion wasn't Gerry's own thing, but for a while, he had gone along with it. He needed to look sharp in the company they now found themselves keeping.

Those were strange days.

There he was, hanging out with faces from the newspapers in places he couldn't have imagined himself going in a hundred years; ritzy West End nightclubs, Knightsbridge casinos, a Twickenham film set. He'd even spent three exhausting nights at a Buckinghamshire stately home. He'd tired of it when he came to see that he and Julius had become other people's playthings, and it was a relief when the rich and the famous moved on. He was happy to forget everything about it except his memories of someone in films called Giles.

He'd known Giles for what he was as soon as he'd laid eyes on his paisley shirt and close-fitting hipster trousers, but Julius had thought he was just being over-friendly.

If Gerry knew Giles, then he knew himself, too.

He'd never said anything to anyone, of course, you didn't in those days. He'd gone back to Giles's flat in Knightsbridge and spent the night with him, listening to him talking about problems which weren't problems at all. In the morning, he'd said, "Cheers, mate, have a good one," and let himself out before Giles had got out of bed.

It wasn't that he felt dirty, as he had imagined he might.

He felt in some funny way that he was betraying Julius. He felt that way now, despite what Julius had caused to be done to his son.

He couldn't believe it when he heard who had done it. That wasn't Julius, not that.

But then again, weren't these special circumstances? Colin had attacked his daughter and tried to rape her, the stupid little cunt. He deserved the bash on the head she gave him for his trouble, but that should have been the end of it. If she'd come to him, he would have sorted Colin himself, one way or the other.

But Julius had got wind of what Colin had attempted, and Julius, true to form, had gone too far. Way too far. Colin was in a terrible state.

All he saw now was the world of difficulties that lay ahead for himself and Maureen and the stain upon his reputation that would remain until he had set the ledger right. And he would do that. It was only a matter of deciding how he would go about it.

43

Now there was no longer any mystery about her father's identity, and all his possible incarnations had been rubbished to that of a common criminal, Juliet's curiosity about her mother caught light and burned with a fearsome intensity.

Everyone was talking about roots these days, about knowing where you come from and being true to your origins.

Having spent the first part of her life under a cloud of uncertainty, she told Ammo that she had to know who she was before she could get on with the rest of it.

"Does that make any sense?"

"Aye, I think so. I'd want to know if I were you."

"And you can see why I have to see him again?"

Ammo had held up her palms.

"Oh, now, back up a wee bit, there. I can see why you need him to tell you about your ma. But I can also see what will happen if you do see him."

"Which is?"

"Bad stuff, Julio. In my opinion, it might go one of two

ways. Either you'll end up in trouble with him or in trouble with the law. Whatever way it goes, you lose."

"In trouble with him?"

"He's a career criminal, hen. He's a fucking crime lord, if Dad's not exaggerating the case. He'll want something from you and whatever it is, you can bet your arse it'll be dodgy."

"So, you won't help me?"

"Help you? Help you do what?"

"I want to get him out of there. Get him away from that creepy guy. Somewhere he'll have the best chance of getting better and speaking to me."

"What? That's crazy! How the fuck would you do that?"

"Give me a chance, Ammo. I don't know yet."

"For God's sake, Julio, if he's as sick as you think he is, why not just call an ambulance? Bam, job done."

"Didn't you hear what your father said? He'd be arrested. And as soon as he was fit, he'd be put on trial."

"Where he might be cleared of all charges."

"Might. And if I get him hospitalised and arrested, he'd see that as a betrayal, and I'd get nothing out of him after that."

"That's not necessarily true. You *are* his daughter?"

"He never admitted it."

"And even if you did get him out of there, where would you take him? With the polis looking for him?"

"I don't know. I don't know anything yet. All I'm asking is, if I do find a way, will you help me?"

"No way, Julio. That is a massive thing to ask."

"I know. Just think about it, please? Please?"

"I'll think about it. But I tell you, Julio, I'll probably have to pass on this one. You're warned, okay?"

"Okay."

She got off the bus on Poplar High Street and walked quickly past tatty bookmakers and crumbling Victorian pubs to the crossroads she remembered.

The six-storey block of flats was situated on the corner, where traffic noise was loudest and exhaust fumes accumulated.

Over the road was a greasy-spoon, where she ordered a mug of tea and a bacon roll before taking the last empty stool by the window. Beside her, a young man in a green shirt and blue-patterned tie tapped his teaspoon against his coffee cup and occasionally sighed.

From where she sat, she had a perfect view of the building's grubby entrance, and above it, the first-floor flat and the brown-curtained windows behind which her father must be lying.

She had come here with only the vaguest of plans. She would wait until she saw Christopher leave the building and then knock on the door and test the waters with Marjorie.

Picking up a newspaper someone had left, Juliet began reading. There was a new prime minister, a woman. Well, some good news for a change. She read a little about Margaret Thatcher, then glanced back at the street outside.

Men in Day-Glo jackets were preparing to dig a hole in the road. No one had left the building since the postman ten minutes ago. It was possible that Christopher had already exited the place on whatever business was his, but she doubted it.

The eight o'clock news rattled from the little transistor radio behind the counter. Chances were, he'd still be up there behind those brown curtains.

She turned a page of the newspaper, and then everything happened at once.

Something red and white dropped to the floor and smashed, the young man in the shirt and tie said, "Oh,

Christ!" and in trying to slide off his stool to deal with the fragmented sugar bowl and its contents, he tipped over his cup of coffee, soaking a sleeve of his lime-green shirt.

"Leave it!"

A sharp-faced woman in curlers and a soiled apron bustled out from behind the counter and began to sweep up the mess. When she had gone, the young man rolled up his wet sleeve and sighed heavily, this time.

"This is not one of my better days."

He appeared to be talking to her.

He hadn't noticed there was coffee on her skirt.

"It's really not, is it?" she said shortly.

He saw what he had done.

"Oh God, I'm so sorry. I've got a clean handkerchief. I could wet it and see if it'll rub out? I mean, of course, you could rub it."

"I'll be all right."

At least it wasn't her white skirt.

"Can I get you another tea, then?"

"No, it's okay."

"Something to eat?"

"No, I can't. I'm watching my weight."

"Are you sure?"

"What do you mean by that?"

"It's just that I saw you with a bacon roll."

"What?"

She watched the entrance across the road. An old man in workman's overalls was leaving the block, struggling with two weighty canvas bags. She saw he was watching him too.

"On your way to work?"

There was no shutting him up.

"Mm."

"Round these parts, I suppose?"

"No, I work in Chelsea."

She wasn't one for talking with strangers, but it might kill some time. There was still no sign of Christopher.

He said, "More exciting than working here, I imagine."

"I wouldn't know. I haven't worked here."

And then, because he looked a little lost as he nursed his wet sleeve and sighed one more time, she added, "Is this where you work?"

"Yes, strange as it may seem, I'm working now. Rene, there, tells people that I'm unemployed. She says I'm pretending to go to work every day."

"But you're working. In a cafe."

"Yes."

"So, what are you, a public health inspector?"

He laughed. It changed his appearance entirely.

"No, not that. I probably shouldn't tell you." He lowered his voice conspiratorially. "I'm a copper."

"You?"

He didn't look like one. He wasn't overweight like a lot of them were, and he looked too young. He was actually quite attractive when he smiled. Tousled dark hair. Nice teeth. But a copper, and here, of all places.

"You seem surprised."

"No, no, I..."

She couldn't tell him she was unnerved to find a policeman only yards from where her father was confined.

"Don't worry about it. My D.I. doesn't see me as a copper either. He said this morning he didn't like my attitude."

"I've been told that. It just means you haven't said 'Yes' enough."

"Sounds about right."

"What are you doing here?"

"I just have to keep an eye out for someone."

"A criminal?"

"Not entirely sure, to be honest. Someone who consorts with them. We haven't got anything on him yet."

"So, why are you watching him?"

"I shouldn't be telling you any of this. You'll get me sacked. That's if I don't manage it myself first."

She laughed, but she wanted an answer.

"You've started, so you'll have to finish."

"Alright. The man I'm watching might lead us to someone we want to speak to in connection with an armed robbery. In your paper, there. Page 5."

A topless blonde dangling her legs in a swimming pool, pictures of the new prime minister at the door of 10 Downing Street, and then she saw it. An old police mugshot of the man she'd last seen in the flat across the road.

"Who is it?" And hoped he didn't see her face changing colour.

"Julius Nicholson. Nasty piece of work, by all accounts."

"He did the armed robbery?"

"Looks like it. He's been due a stretch for a long time. There's lots of stuff we're pretty sure he was behind, but we never got enough evidence to nail him for any of it."

She felt a chill in the lining of her stomach. Ammo's dad had said as much, but to hear it confirmed by a policeman made it all more real and her father more of a monster.

To cover her confusion, she managed to say, "Interesting work?"

He snorted.

"Look at me. I'm sitting in a grubby cafe with my shirt drenched in coffee, watching traffic."

"And you don't do that very well."

He smiled, made a funny face. Outside, men in football shirts were gathering at a bus stop.

"I could have been something."

"A footballer?"

"A contender, I was going to say."

He laughed and asked her name.

"Juliet."

"I like that."

"What's yours?"

"Vincent. But you can call me..."

"Vince?"

"No, definitely not, Vince. Just Vincent. Like the bike."

"Okay, Vincent."

They gazed at the street.

He went to the counter and came back with a mug of tea and another coffee. When he offered her half of an iced Danish pastry, she took it.

"I don't know any girls like you."

She wondered what sort he did know.

"I mean, are you a punk or something?"

"Not really. I just like to dress a little differently."

"You look really good, if you don't mind me saying."

"Thank you."

She turned from the window and caught him looking at her.

"Your eyes are amazing," he said in a low voice. "Oh, God! Did I say that aloud?"

They laughed, but as quickly as it came, his smile vanished.

"Whoah. That's me. There's my man."

Across the road, she saw Christopher, wearing a beige raincoat and swinging a leather briefcase as he swept up the road

"See you again?" he said.

"Maybe?"

Dodging traffic as he crossed the busy road, Vincent began Following Christopher much too closely, she thought.

44

He was propped up in bed wearing a white cotton singlet, and holding a spread from a newspaper, the rest of which had slipped from the bed.

There was little colour in his cheeks, which needed a shave.

Marjorie turned to her and said, "Well, if you're not saying nothing. I'll leave you to it," and shuffled off to the bathroom.

He dropped the paper and peered at Juliet like he was searching for something lost inside her. She met his gaze and noted that his eyes were blue, quite unlike her own. Though unkempt from sleep, his dark hair had been well cut; she allowed that he must have been quite good-looking in his day.

But now, pale-skinned and enervated as he was, there was little here of whoever he once had been, or even of the man who had seemed so imposing that day at PINZ.

When he had looked enough, he spoke.

"You came, then."

He formed his words slowly, with a slight, sandpapery

rasp. The voice was softer than she remembered, but maybe that was his weakened state.

"I'm here."

"Yes. Yes, so I see."

"I came before, but you were sleeping."

"I sleep too much these days." He nodded towards the door. "Sometimes wonder if they drop a Mickey in my tea." He tried to laugh, waved his hand. "Sit down, please, sit. I've had it with people hovering like hummingbirds."

She perched on an arm, one of the boxy faux-leather chairs, just beyond what she imagined might be the extent of his reach.

After a moment in which both appeared to be awaiting the other to speak, she said, "You're better, then."

He grunted. "On the mend, I think. No thanks to Carrot's tender ministrations."

"Carrot?"

He jerked a thumb at a wall-mounted photograph of Carrot playing crazy golf with Marjorie.

"They said you collapsed."

"They said that, did they?"

His face clouded. Was he angry? Then he brightened.

"Bit of a funny turn, that was all. Nature's way of telling you to put your feet up for a bit."

"That's what you're doing here, is it?"

He grunted again. "Not exactly my choice of retreat, but needs must, as they say."

Silence. Then a soft padding along the hallway.

"So. Why are you here?"

"You asked me to come."

"And here you are."

"Yes."

"I wasn't sure you would."

"I wasn't sure either."

He put down his newspaper.

"No, I can't say I'm surprised."

A jackhammer had started up across the road. She waited for a lull.

"I see you're famous today."

The angry eyes were back.

"You've seen it?"

"It's hard to miss."

"Fucking Fleet Street. Excuse my French."

"What they say about you isn't true, then?"

"True? They're making out I'm Jack the fucking Ripper. Public Enemy Number One."

"But you're not."

His face coloured with anger.

"Of course I'm not. If I had anything to do with that job, which I'm not saying I did, it was a personal thing. A matter of settling some differences with a vicious toe-rag who's out to destroy my business."

She swallowed, out of her depth, talking to a wanted criminal who had just admitted to an armed robbery, and had to remind herself that, like it or not, he was her father.

"You have a business?"

"You ask a lot of questions, don't you? All right, yes. My business is in property, betting shops, hair salons."

"So, you're not a master criminal?"

"A what? Do I look like one?"

He saw her examining his eyes and forehead and almost laughed.

"Look, it's like this. I'm in business, so I pay taxes. I have employees on my payroll. But where I come from, you have to bend the rules once in a while just to get by. Do you understand? You have to. If you don't, you get steamrollered by the system."

"The police are after you. What are you going to do?"

Another voice, thick with cigarette smoke, said, "Yes, that's what I want to know."

She hadn't seen Marjorie entering behind her, draped in the turquoise, quilted housecoat she'd worn the last time she was here.

"I can't have him under my feet all day, no matter what Christopher says. Have you come to take him away with you?"

"I'm just visiting."

"Oh." She rummaged in a cupboard while they watched.

"Take him home," she said, and shuffled out again.

"Can I ask what you are going to do?" asked Juliet.

"Do? Go somewhere quiet and wait it out. See if anyone turns QE."

"Queen's Evidence, you mean?"

He nodded.

"There's one or two of them might give me up under pressure."

"If they do?"

"Then I might have to be on my toes. Take a foreign holiday."

"Spain?"

"You know the way it goes, then. I've got friends there. A moody passport, a change of look, flights from Dublin to Antwerp, Antwerp to Malaga—no big deal. But I'd sooner not, of course. It's a last resort. A bit like Bognor. But that's not why you're here, is it? You have questions."

"Yes."

"Let me help. Number One. I never meant for it to turn out as it did. I didn't know your mother would die."

"No, how could you?"

"Number two. Things were different then. Attitudes. I couldn't have kept you. I was married, for a start."

"So, you got rid of me."

"No. I put you with a good family. Gerry was all right back then. And it was a nice house, could have been a lot worse. It wasn't a children's home."

She looked at him. There was now some colour in his cheeks.

"Fucking hell, I don't know what you want me to say. My hands were tied. I had a wife and a little boy of my own."

As he held his palms upwards, his face reflected an expression she used herself when the occasion demanded it. The, *what was to I to do?* one.

She asked him, "What was she like?"

"Who?"

"My mother."

He slumps into his pillow, stares up at the crack in the ceiling. She waits. Is he deciding how much he wants to let go of some special memories? At last, he speaks again.

"She was like you. I can see it now. You've got her eyes, her cheeks." He turns towards her. "God's truth, it's like seeing Angelica again."

She can see his eyes shining, even in the weak light, with the bright window behind him. He says, "My God, it really is."

"Tell me more," she says.

"No. Not now. I need to sleep. Another time."

She stands up and watches as he turns his back to her and enters some private world of his own.

She goes to the door and takes one last look at the lump in the bed.

Angelica, she thinks. Angelica.

45

Gerry Hobson wiped steam from the mirror and shaved the first of the soap from his cheek.

"Don't get in too deep," he said aloud.

"What was that?"

"Nothing," he called to Maureen, who wanted to use the bathroom.

He remembered paddling in the sea at one of those places they had gone to once a year. Southend, Clacton, Margate.

His father held his hand, and they walked out into the cold water until it was waist-deep on him and knee-high on his father, Jack Hobson.

The sand had rippled under his feet.

His mother Violet called from the beach which, the tide being low, was now sixty yards or so behind them.

"Bloody Nora, what is it now?" his dad had said. "Stay where you are. I'll be back in a moment."

And off he had gone, lifting his legs and noisily splashing through the water to find out what little thing had gone wrong back on their towelled encampment.

Gerry, lost in daydreams of fishy things, had taken only a

few steps forward before the sandy ground beneath his feet disappeared and he found himself suddenly under the water, in a world of grey-green bubbles, saltwater flooding his mouth as he floundered in the deep.

Then, almost as unexpectedly, there was a burst of air, sunlight and the sound of his own screams before the water again.

His brother, who had been swimming with a friend, had hauled him out and taken him to the beach, where he, Gerry, got a thick ear for his carelessness.

"I told you not to get in too deep," his father had said.

That was the question he asked himself now. Had he got in too deep?

The first few meetings had been all right, friendly get-to-know-yous where he and Tom Adams had a couple of drinks, talked about the big money footballers were earning, the trouble on the terraces, and about paying a pound for a pint of beer.

You would hardly have noticed another conversation that was happening at the same time, weaving itself in and out of the talk about the season Spurs were having, or property prices on the Isle of Dogs.

Through this, Adams had established that Gerry was doing alright, but that he wasn't really satisfied, and yes, he might indeed be looking for a move.

Gerry himself gleaned that Adams was looking for someone with a good track record for a key position in his firm, and if that someone happened to have connections with players South of the River *and* inside knowledge of one Julius Nicholson, that person would be in pole position for the job.

Adams learned of what Nicholson had done to his Colin: "a terrible, monstrous thing," and gauged the depth of Gerry's hatred towards his old partner.

For his part, Gerry was impressed with Adams's knowledge, his sure hand, and his proven and evident success. And, like everyone else who came under his spell, he was not untouched by his charm.

Spreading himself out in the black cab driving him home from one of these meets, he concluded that he was dealing with Julius's successor, the next King of the Isle of Dogs.

Money was talked about.

He got a retainer up front; a fat brown envelope slipped across the table in a Dalston pub. The cash was in his pocket, and he was in Adams's. Not that he minded; he was going to bring Julius down and get rich doing it.

The more he came to understand Adams and his operation, the more he liked it. Adams and his associates had ways of doing things that Julius would not have considered. They were meticulous in their planning. They had useful connections, legal eagles, fences, lookouts, and coppers on the take. Adams had fish-and-chip shops, launderettes, second-hand car lots and a curious sideline in fine art and antiques.

He had a ritzy pile (swimming pool and all) somewhere near Maldon in Essex, a little place in Blackheath and a long lease on the row of converted workshops in Bethnal Green where he based his operations.

His influence was felt across East London, and he was now making inroads into the Isle of Dogs. He was doing all right, so at first, Gerry had no reason to have any qualms about his move.

Then he accepted another invitation for an evening drink with Tom Adams.

Adams regularly used a place on the river, and these days he liked to take Gerry with him. Gerry accepted his pint of lager from Adams and wondered who his drinking companion was before he came along. Probably, Derek Markham, a small, balding man wearing a pineapple-patterned shirt who joined them just as he was getting the drinks in.

Adams began by telling Gerry about the fine-art and antiques side of his business and how he needed someone he could trust to handle this for him.

Gerry shifted in his seat. "Bit of a sticking point there, I'm afraid. I'd be lying if I said I knew the first thing about any of that."

"Don't worry. I'm not looking for an expert in mid-period Rembrandts. I need a middleman who can liaise with a guy who *is* an expert."

"About what?"

"About which valuable works will be on show, what the level of security, and who he thinks would be in the market, should we decide to follow through."

"So, it's not a problem that I know sod-all about this malarkey?"

"No. But you'll know more as we go along. As I said, this guy I know is an expert. See if you can spend a few hours with him, just as an introduction."

"All right."

"Derek, go and fetch us another round. There's a good lad. And lose that shirt, it's deafening me."

Once Derek Markham had stepped into the pub, Adams said, "I've been hearing chatter about the Island."

Gerry had stubbed out his cigarette and taken a long draught of his Black Label.

"What sort of chatter?"

Below their wooden benches on the stone flags, the river

lapped against the walls of the pub. Tom Adams, silver-haired but looking young for his forty-eight years, tapped his nose.

"City chatter. Nothing definite, but there's a lot of it. Something in the wind, I can feel it."

"By development, you mean, on the Island?"

"That's what I'm thinking."

"Funny place to develop. The Island's on its last legs."

"That's what might make it interesting. That and its proximity to the City."

"So, what do we know?"

"Not much yet. There are no plans lodged with the GLC or anything like that. Could be years away. But there's still the chatter."

"What, and you can't get anything concrete from these chatterers?"

"Not on paper. These bottom-feeders trade on crumbs dropped by the guys in the corner offices. To be honest, Gerry, I don't have much more to go on than my instinct. But I tell you, it's not led me far wrong before, and my instinct now is to invest in the Isle of Dogs."

"And that's what you've been doing."

"We have a presence there. A growing presence. I see this as a game of battleships, you know, that kids' game?"

"Where you have to guess which square the other player is going to shoot at?"

"That's the one. I'm buying up cheap plots of land here and there on the off-chance someone will want to build on them."

"It's a bit of a punt, if you don't mind me saying."

"I'll turn it round, even if the chatter comes to nothing. I might build on them myself. There's a good community down there. They deserve better than they've got."

"So, onwards and upwards for the Island, then?"

"That's it. I've been making steady progress, covering my tracks with shell companies, the usual. All the stuff I hear you do so well, and which I want you to do for me. Result: no one knows how much I already own. But the thing is, Gerry?"

"Yes?"

"We'll be moving a lot faster once a certain somebody is out of the way."

"I think I know who you mean."

"He's done; he just doesn't know it. Won't admit it to himself. I gave him fair warning."

"The bookie's?"

Adams shrugged.

"But still, he won't listen. He can't see what everyone else sees. A man with failing health, a memory like a sieve and a smashed-up leg."

Gerry took a beat there.

"Was that you?"

"It may have been someone I know. He was poaching on my land at the time."

"It could have killed him, though?"

He was getting those intimations of having strayed too far from shore.

"Not a chance. The train was already slowing down. Scared the shit out of him and made him look less of the big deal, hobbling around with his stick and all. Yes, it was a little harsh, Gerry, but sometimes that's the only way. You're okay with that, I take it?"

"Yes. Of course."

"I had thought it might have sent him a message that even he would read correctly."

"He didn't even know it was you. I mean, don't get me wrong, you were in the running. But he was never certain who had set it up. Last thing I heard, he was even thinking it might have been an accident."

"Accident? I wouldn't have thought it was an accident if that happened to me."

"He's been more than happy to look for other explanations, the way I've seen it."

"Well, he seems to have changed his mind. I tell you this, Gerry, doing my club was the final straw."

"That was quite a result for you, though."

"Result? He should have been swept up with the rest of them. Safely under lock and key for a fifteen or twenty. That would have solved everything. But he slipped the net."

"Sounds like him. So, the bingo hall. Who was it?"

"My insider?"

"I can think of a couple of people it might have been."

"You can't guess? Well, just for now, I'm going to keep that little kitty in the bag, Gerry. You do understand?" said Adams.

"Of course. So, what are you going to do about him?"

"Nicholson? He's going down."

"What do you mean?"

Adams threw down his gin, the stem of his glass clattering on the tin tray. Standing, he slipped on his camel coat.

"He's finished, Gerry, that's all."

46

She was leaving the front entrance of the block of Poplar flats when she saw him looking at her, occupying the same seat in the window of the cafe across the road. He waved and beckoned to her.

To turn and walk away wouldn't look good to a policeman, she thought. So, she waited for the lights to let her cross the busy road. By the time she swung open the door and met the acrid aroma of frying food, he was carrying two teas back to the wooden stools by the window.

"There's a breakfast coming your way in half a mo," Vincent smiled

"You shouldn't have?"

"There are a lot of things I shouldn't do. In the end, though, you must plough your own field, don't you?" He frowned. "That's not quite right, is it? You have to plough your own something, anyway."

"Go your own way?"

"Amazingly better. Yes. Otherwise, you become someone you'd sooner not be."

She tried to guess what he wanted. Was he playing a clever game?

She waited for him to ask her why she had been coming out of the very same flats he was watching. He might have seen her avoiding the weirdo with red hair who was oiling himself into the front door just as she was arriving.

"There's your bacon roll, love," the woman said. "I hope he's not making a nuisance of himself. He's one for the ladies, he is."

She glanced awkwardly at Vincent and saw how he coloured at Rene's remark. It was sort of charming in a way.

"Mind you, he's not much of a catch. Sits there dreaming all day, don't you, darling? Wants to get himself a job."

When Rene had bustled off, he pointed at the block of flats.

"You live in there, do you?"

She didn't want to hear herself lie to him; instead, she raised her cup and took a sip of her tea. The action might have passed for a nod.

"I'd keep your door locked, then. And look out for anyone new or suspicious coming into the building."

"Why? Are you going to raid the place?"

"They haven't told me when."

"To arrest the man you were following?"

"Pull him in for a word. See what he knows. Search the place too, so lots of coppers coming and going. But it's nothing that you need to be concerned about. You see, I have a theory."

"What is it, then, this theory?"

"It's probably wrong, and we won't know if I'm right until we pay an official visit. But I think Julius Nicholson is in your building. Holed up in that flat I'm watching. And if he is, it might get noisy. They're saying he could be armed."

She allowed Vincent to continue while she digested that.

"Word has it, he's been ruffling feathers in these parts.

There will be people looking for him after that last job. Nasty people."

"I'll bear that in mind," she said as he switched the subject and began to talk about something he'd been watching on TV. She wound back the morning a couple of hours and hit 'play.'

Marjorie had patrolled the apartment, scattering cigarette ash as she searched for her reading specs or some other little thing she had lost.

No sooner had she left the room than she was back, on some other mumbled pretext.

Julius and Juliet talked carefully, understanding that some part of what they said must find its way back to Carrot.

At first, there was thick ice to be broken.

They talked haltingly about how he was doing (he was a good deal better, though he was tired after a bad night) and after a few minutes when she thought he had gone back to sleep, he began to talk about his past, about the hard times and scarcity of opportunities that had led him to take another route in life.

Everything he'd done, he said, he'd done for his family, his wife Kath and his son, Jimmy. All for nothing as it turned out. They were gone now, both of them.

"*I* was part of your family. Or I should have been."

"I know, I know. And I'm sorry, I really am. I was young and clueless. I didn't know what to do. Like I told you last time, I couldn't see any other way. But I was still there, in my way. I kept an eye on you and found out what you were doing. I watched you grow, from a distance, anyway. And believe me when I say I always hoped this day would come, when we could have this talk."

"Ha!"

"You don't believe me."

"How can you even dream that I would? Before I came here, I saw you once. *Once* in my whole life. And when I did see you, you weren't the father I had hoped for, not by a mile. You were this bullying, awful man scaring off kids at the shop door."

He sighed and lay back on his pillow.

"We haven't got off to a good start, have we?"

"Hardly."

"Look, in case you suddenly decide to sling your hook, there's something you need to know."

"Which is?"

"Just this. I want you to become a part of my life."

She laughed. Had she heard that right?

"What makes you think I want anything to do with you?"

He smiled. *Ruefully*, that was the word.

"I've got some front, you're thinking, after all these years?"

"Yes, you have."

"Listen, we are tied, you and me, whether we like it or not. And I for one, happen to like it. You're bright; you've got spirit. You could help me in so many ways. Most of them legal. I need you."

She ignored the wink he gave her.

"If you are really interested in talking to me, you can tell me about my mother."

"Is that all you want from me?" He sighed.

"Yes."

"Nothing else?"

"No."

"That's a shame, and I hope you'll reconsider. Because I want to know you better, see you. I want to make it up to you, if you'll give me a chance."

"My mother. She's all I want from you."

"You're a hard woman, Juliet."

She wanted to tell him about sleeping in doorways and begging for breakfast and how such a life will do that to you. But for the moment, there was only the sound of the diesel engines outside, then that of the toilet flushing.

"Look, if I tell you everything I remember about her," he said, raising himself on an elbow. "Will you do one little thing for me?"

"I don't know. What is it?"

"It's only an errand."

"What sort of an errand?"

"I just need you to go to my old drum and pick up some odds and ends."

"Will it be dangerous?"

"Of course it won't be dangerous."

"Will they be watching your house?"

"Off and on, I expect. I'm not public enemy number one, whatever *The News of the World* might say. Even if they are watching, there's a back way you can use."

"What is it you want me to get?"

"There's a bag in the attic. *Adidas* on the side. It's got a few necessities I need right now. Will you do that for me?"

"I might. But you must do something for me."

"Tell you about your mother."

"Well?"

"I'll tell you everything. Once you get back."

"Tell me some of it now, or I won't go. I mean it."

And so, he told her about Angelica and about that night when he had first seen her at the *Candy Kane*.

He told her how astonishingly beautiful she was, how classy she seemed, even in the tawdry outfit she wore for her work. He told her about all the clever stuff that she knew and the music she listened to, and the things that engaged her interest.

She watched his lips moving feverishly and saw his eyes catch a little fire as he talked and wondered what it was about him that had attracted her?

For just a moment, she allowed herself to imagine an alternative life in which this woman and this man had raised her as their daughter.

Vincent gave her a little nudge.

"Did you hear what I said?"

"Yes, yes, I was listening."

"No, you weren't. You were off dreaming somewhere." He turned his gaze from the street outside. "I nearly bottled saying it the first time."

"Saying what?"

"I was saying, did you fancy going for a drink sometime? Not here, somewhere nice. On the river, maybe."

Lost in her thoughts about this new mother, Angelica, whatever he was saying seemed like a rude intrusion. Without thinking, she said, "No, no, I couldn't do that. Sorry."

He looked disappointed.

"Boyfriend?"

"Yes. No. I just couldn't. Thanks all the same, though."

"Some other time, then?"

She picked up her bag.

"I'm late. I really have to go."

She felt him watching her as she hurried down the street to the bus stop.

47

Ammo was holding a newly-unpacked shirt up to the window light, yellow with thick black hoops. "More of Ginnie's crap," she said, over Ian Dury's croaking, "Who wants to look like a fucking bumblebee?"

Normally, Juliet would have offered her opinion. Instead, she expanded on the only thing that had been on her mind all morning.

"There must be some trace of my mother in his house. Look, he's given me the key. I have to go."

Ammo dropped the shirt and looked at her wonderingly.

"You have to know your parents before you know yourself?"

"Yes."

Ammo shook her head.

"You're *you*, Julio; you're not your parents."

"Are you sure about that? I've not had the certainties of your upbringing, *Amelia*. Can you even imagine spending your whole life with a family who never owned you as their daughter, yet having no idea who your real parents were?

How was I supposed to know who *I* was? I don't care what you say, I am not going to throw this chance away."

"You will be entering the house of a wanted man." Ammo lowered her voice. "A criminal. Will you stop for just one moment and think about that?"

"I have, and I'm going. You're not my conscience, Ammo."

"Your mind's made up, then."

"Yes, and don't you breathe a word of this to your father."

Ammo finished folding the shirt and arranged it neatly in the stacked wooden boxes that served as shelves.

"There's no chance of that just now. He's not in my good books."

"What's happened?"

"Nothing. He phoned the other night. He wanted to give me his version of something before Mum did. They'd had a bust-up, and she told him she'd tell me all about it."

"Wow. Your mum and dad always seem so solid. He's not been having an affair or something?"

"No. Not this time, anyway. This was something else. Someone had been at the house... someone she objected to. Fuck this. I don't really want to talk about it."

"Okay, I won't pry. So yes, I've made up my mind. I'll run his errand for him and have a poke around while I'm there. There must be some little thing of my mother's there."

"You've got more balls than I thought. But aren't you just a tiny bit scared? Going there on your own?"

"I was hoping I wouldn't be on my own."

"That's a joke, right?"

"Why not? It'd take your mind off whatever's bugging you. You can be my lookout."

"Just a minute, Modesty fucking Blaise. You don't know what he's asking you to fetch for him. It might be a big bag of Class A's for all you know. With the police parked, maybe just down the road. No, no, no. I don't want any part of that, thank you very much."

"And that's your last word?"

"It is."

"So, you'll let me go alone?"

"I will."

"Into the jaws of danger?"

"Yes."

Juliet pulled a funny face.

"How will you be able to live with yourself if I don't come back?"

"I'll manage somehow; Ginnie can move in. Look, there's a customer waiting. Move your ass, Julio."

The Isle was still strange to Juliet, but the rusting cranes on the docks reminded Ammo of her home on the Clyde, or so she said.

They walked into the wind, passing the house twice to be sure that no one was sitting in a parked car nearby.

On the pavement, they got a second glance from a middle-aged man in loud checks and yellow sunglasses, but they were young, and Ammo was wearing a short skirt.

Still, for good measure, Juliet followed her father's instructions and approached the property from the rear, where a gate in the fence could be accessed behind a row of lock-up garages.

Unlocking the gate, they slipped into a trim back garden.

It was still afternoon, and sunlight glinting on glass meant they could see nothing inside the house until Juliet had given Ammo a sharp tug and they had crossed the lawn to the rear door.

Ammo peered through the big plate-glass windows while Juliet pressed her ear against the door.

She turned the key in the lock.

The kitchen was tidy; everything was put away, and the dishrag was folded neatly over the tap. In the living room, there was a faint tang of lavender air freshener.

The magazines and drinks mats on the coffee table were neatly arranged, as were the ornaments in the glass case and on the mantelpiece; in the hall, the shoes and coats were in their places on a rack. She found it hard to imagine her father creating such order, but what did she know about him?

There were thick nets on the windows, but all the same, she and Ammo were careful to stay out of view from anyone on the road. Working methodically, they quietly searched cupboards and slid open drawers.

Juliet sat down in Julius's armchair and took in her father's home.

The curtains with their green and blue floral swirls must have been picked out by Julius's wife, the same as a lot of the other stuff that showed a feminine touch.

She got up and went upstairs, where Ammo was already poking about.

Looking briefly in the bathroom and toilet, she peered into the guest rooms and then into a smaller one decorated in the baby-blue and maroon colours of West Ham football club.

In his bedroom, she opened a wardrobe and found some of Kath's clothes. She pulled out a turquoise two-piece trouser suit on a hanger, gave it a sniff and detected faint traces of the perfume that Maureen always wore.

Ammo was sitting on the unmade double bed, leafing through a photo album.

"Is that him?" she said.

Juliet looked over her shoulder at a picture of a slim, bronzed man in red swimming trunks and dark sunglasses leaning against a beach bar somewhere. The little blonde girl on the stool next to him seemed to be laughing. Underneath, in white marker pen, someone had written "the Magaluf 9-5."

"That's him."

Ammo said, "Hm. Your dad was a looker."

"Well, he's not now. Turn the page."

Pictures of some men with Julius at another bar and another taken by a pool, Julius with one hand around Kath's small waist, the other clutching a drink. A blurred figure in the background looked like Gerry Hobson.

There were pictures taken in England, including professional, black-and-white shots of men at some black-tie do, bottles of champagne on the table, everyone with a big cigar.

Pictures of a serious little boy: as a baby on a rug, as an infant on Kath's knee, in his first school uniform. Juliet turned page after page.

Holidays and new cars. Christmas. People pulling faces, having fun.

"She won't be there, Julio."

"I know. But he must have a picture somewhere."

"If he's got one, it'll be somewhere his wife wouldn't have come across it."

In the attic, they quickly discovered the Adidas bag. Juliet put that aside and began to look through the clutter of lifetimes.

She considered everything she found carefully, slowly assembling a bigger picture of her father. She saw the Bullworker, the new fishing rod.

He tried things, tired of things, he had loved his boy.

She opened suitcases, turned out boxes, and checked the pockets of old clothes.

This was where all the stuff in her old wardrobe should have ended up: all of her old toys, books, and clothes. She told herself not to be so stupid, not to get emotional. She hadn't wanted to be part of this family, had she?

Downstairs again, she unzipped the bag.

On top was a black towel. An inside pocket contained his passport and a little package of prescribed tablets. She opened the passport and saw his photo. The passport was in the name of Maurice Edward Miller.

In another pocket was a folder of peseta travellers' cheques; she counted two hundred pounds in ten and twenty-pound notes.

There was underwear, socks, a pair of lightweight trousers, a toothbrush, a comb and a razor and a pair of red swimming trunks. Beneath these, she found a spectacles case containing a pair of dark *Wayfarers* and an old grey T-shirt with what looked like an oil stain.

There was a noise outside. Carefully approaching the edge of the window, she moved the nets a fraction and peered out.

Outside the low-rise flats across the way, a woman was bending to right milk bottles that had blown over on her step.

Behind the woman and the flats, the great grey river glinted in the setting sun. Looking at the water a moment longer, she was about to let drop the net when she noted a man standing on a corner who appeared to be looking at the house, the way a student might study its architecture. He turned and began to walk away in the direction of the river and perhaps the line of cars parked down there.

She started.

It must be a trick of the failing light, she thought. But

when she looked again, there was no mistaking that jacket, that hair, the shambling way he walked. She didn't think he'd seen her, but she looked about for her coat all the same.

"Well?" Ammo said as she slipped into the room and sat down. "Did you get what you came for?"

"That's the bag there. Money, passport, change of clothes."

"I meant, did you get what *you* came for? Your mum?"

"No."

Ammo gave her a quick hug.

"Then let's check the timetables. Pick up a kebab, hey? I'm starving."

They left through the back gate, and by the time they walked around to the front of the house, there was no sign of the man Juliet had seen looking so intently at the house, the man who liked her to call him Uncle Gerry.

48

"He's gone, has he?" her father said as she sat down in the chair opposite his. He looked healthier than he had last time and was half-dressed in a white vest and dark trousers.

She nodded and gave him the bag.

"Nice one. Any problems?"

"No."

She saw no reason to mention Gerry's presence outside his house.

He opened the bag, took out the passport and cheques, and counted the money. He stood up and emptied the bag on the bed.

"Was there nothing else in here?"

Like he suspected her of pocketing half the cash.

"No," she said. "Is something missing?"

"There was no one there? In the house?"

"No. Is there something wrong?"

"I don't know. There might be."

"Well, whatever it is, it's not my problem. I've satisfied my part of the bargain. Your turn now."

"What was it? You wanted me to tell you something, didn't you?"

She wondered if his memory was that bad, or was he playing her for an idiot?

"My mother. You were going to tell me everything."

"About Angelica. Right."

He sat down and slowly drew a breath. By the time the lights outside had changed three times, and three times the noise of accelerating cars and motorbikes, the straining of heavy lorries and the throbbing of diesel cabs had filled the room, she was asking him about the circumstances of her birth and her mother's death.

Why hadn't he seen that she had had a telephone installed in time? Why hadn't he answered his own phone when he hurried out the door that day? Why had he not been there for her when she needed him? He made no excuses for himself.

When Juliet had wiped away her tears and told Marjorie, who had bustled in on hearing a commotion, that there was nothing to worry about, she asked about other things.

Glad that the worst seemed over, Julius was happy to elaborate about the sort of woman she sprang from.

He told her more about the precious time they'd had together, described the clothes she had worn, and the perfume she used. He told her about everything except their lovemaking.

She learned that Angelica Casenove had come to this country to study at some stuck-up university, but when she turned up for her interview, the panel had received her indifferently. A week later, they sent her a letter telling her that she was not, after all, entitled to the funding she had been promised and could not therefore be offered a place at the university.

"It's not hard to see what happened," said Juliet quietly. "One look at the colour of her skin."

"But it wouldn't have mattered in the long run. She was razor-smart, your mum. She'd have battled until she made something of herself, poxy university or no poxy university."

She looked at the brute in the chair with his sagging blue jowls, the tattoos on his upper arms (a dog's head on one, *Millwall Till I Die* on the other), the partly exposed paunch, the thinning, peppery hair and tried to see the man her mother had seen.

"Did you love her? I mean, really love her?" she asked.

His dull grey eyes brightened, but he looked no happier.

"Believe me, Juliet. I loved Angelica more than I had loved anyone before and, God forgive me, ever since. I think about her every day."

"But you think about your wife, too?"

"Kath? Of course I do. But I tell you this; it's the memories of Angelica that cut me like broken bottles. I still think she's here, somewhere."

He paused as if uncertain whether or not to continue. After a moment, he fished in his pocket, pulled out a handkerchief and coughed into it. "Angelica's why you're here now."

"What do you mean?"

He was looking at her intently, causing her to shift in her chair.

"It's just that a while ago it occurred to me that she wasn't gone, or not totally. I realised there was still a little bit of Angelica left in this world."

"You mean me?"

"Listen, did I tell you I cried when I parted with you? After I took you to Gerry and Maureen's? In the car driving back, I cried. I couldn't stop myself. But like I say, there was no way I could keep you. I was married."

"But even if you hadn't been..."

"Things were different then."

"Not much different."

"But it wasn't all my fault; you must see that much."

"Everyone tells me I should stay right away from you."

"Look, I'm not suggesting we live together in a bungalow by the sea. All I want is to see you." He looked around at the decaying interior of Carrot's mum's flat. "In slightly more congenial surroundings. Couple of months, I'll be in Spain. You'd like it there. The thing is, I think you could be good for me. Help me make sense of some things. I could be good for you, too."

"I don't believe this."

"I understand. But think about it. That's all I'm asking of you."

"There's something I should tell you," She said when she heard Marjorie using the Bakelite telephone in the hall.

"Yes?"

"The police are watching the flat."

"How do you know that?"

"I saw one of them. In the cafe across the road."

"Watching this place? You sure?"

"I'm certain of it."

"Okay. We'll have to move things up a gear. Get down to Kent. I can lie low at Frank's place in Margate 'til we can sort out a safe passage to Spain."

"Frank?"

"My cousin. If they're watching the front. When we go, we'll use the service door around the back. We'll need to make our move tomorrow. Day after at the latest. You won't be able to get me out of here on your own. Can you trust anyone to help?"

"Not so fast," she said. "I need to think about this."

But she already had.

She wanted more from him, to understand him better, to find out what had attracted her mother to him.

Whatever that was, it was buried deep, she thought.

Most of all, she wanted him to release his every buried memory of her, so she could build her up in her mind and see her like he would have seen her, a beautiful, clever, fallible human being, with desires and disappointments, hopes and memories.

Because of these needs, she wasn't ready to cut the flimsy bonds that had grown between them, not just yet. She could do that at a time of her choosing. Right now, she would try to get him down to Margate.

49

Seated at his usual table on the stone-flagged terrace behind the pub, Tom Adams was hidden behind the first edition of the *Evening News.* Above the river, buccaneering seagulls wheeled and screeched. Gerry pulled out a chair and dropped into it.

"Sorry, the traffic was unbelievable. What's the problem?"

Adams closed his paper, ran an eye over Gerry's new suit.

"It's our friend. He's gone AWOL."

"What?"

"Nicholson. He's done a bunk."

"From where? We don't know where he is. Or was. Do we?"

Adams tipped back the last of his scotch and turned his chair towards him.

"Thing is, Gerry, I've not been entirely straight with you. Sometimes you must take precautions. You understand?"

"Of course."

"I knew where he was. I've known for some time. One of his soldiers came to me about him."

"Who?"

"About time you knew. Christopher Kibble."

"Carrot? That figures. I often wondered about him."

"It was a few days before they did the *Fat Fortune*. Not a happy man. Said he could run Nicholson's operation for me, if Nicholson wasn't in the way. Spilt his guts."

"Little fuck."

"That's what I thought. If he sells out Nicholson, he'll sell us out too. But I thought we could use him against Nicholson."

"To take the fall? If something were to happen to Nicholson?"

"I wasn't thinking of anything so final. But good to know you're on side for all eventualities."

"That's not what I said."

"If things had gone as planned, the Old Bill would have done our job for us. And to an extent, they did. What we didn't foresee was Kibble's absence on the job, allowing Nicholson to slip the net. I told Kibble to keep an eye on him until I decided on our next move."

"I'm not sure I'd have done the same. Kibble makes the Grand National look predictable."

"Even so, you can reasonably assume he will take one of a limited number of options. In this case, I had a feeling that he might take things into his own hands if I waited long enough."

"Why?"

"Nicholson would suspect him for not showing up that morning, no question. Kibble knew he'd put himself in a ticklish position, and from what he let slip, I think he was planning to do something about it. Which would have suited us fine. With Nicholson out of the way and his looney-tune friend under lock and key."

"But it's not worked out?"

"Nicholson must have got wind of what was in the offing. Kibble told me he wouldn't get far, the state he was in. But who knows? He may have been putting it on for Kibble's benefit."

"No, he was right there. A sick man with a stick wouldn't have a chance without help."

"Can he get help? Is there someone he could call on?"

"All his boys are banged up or working for you. I can't think of anyone."

"I can't afford to have him loose like this, Gerry. If he clears off, all well and good. If he's got any sense, he'll get himself over the water, soon as the heat's off."

"So, what's to be done?"

"We need to cut off his places of retreat. There's his house, first of all."

"He's hardly going to go back there. The filth will be all over it."

"I've been thinking about this. It would send out the appropriate signal if that house were no longer there."

Gerry blew smoke through his nostrils and waved out the match.

"I think I'm catching your drift."

"Hold on. Hello, Derek. How long you been lurking there?"

"I was just waiting to ask you if you wanted a drink."

"Of course you were. Usual, and a lager for Gerry. Off you pop, now. Where was I?"

"Notting Hill."

"Yes. You proved yourself to me on that job. So, can you do it?"

"I don't see a problem."

Gerry thought about what Julius had done to Colin. Would this balance the books?

He said, "As it happens, I've already done a recce of the house."

"You have? Why?"

"I was down the Dogs seeing a client, thought I'd take a look at the place. Nicholson may not be coming back, and I'm a little concerned there may be papers left there, stuff I'd quite like to retrieve."

"I can understand that. This way will kill two birds with one stone: his house, your papers. I'll see this one makes the news. He'll get the message. Julius Nicholson is finished on the Isle of Dogs."

50

The day before Gerry met Tom Adams, the subject of their conversation had been looking like death.

"What's happened to you?" asked Juliet, shocked at her father's appearance.

Julius Nicholson groaned.

"I think I've been poisoned by fucking Quasimodo. Cramps, headache."

"And vomiting. You'll need to take that shirt off. Where is he now?"

"No idea. Him and that old crone cleared off this morning and left me to it. Feel like I've swallowed battery acid."

"Can you move?"

"I'll be all right if you can help. It's not so bad. He fucked up on the dosage I think."

"What did he give you?"

"A mug of Bovril. Probably laced with weedkiller."

"What makes you think that Mr Nicholson?" Ammo said.

"What's it matter? He wants to kill me; I fucking know it. And by the way, he may have my gun. We need to go."

"Give me a hand here, Ammo. He's heavy."

Juliet found his jacket and draped it over his shoulders and vest.

Together, they stumbled along the passageway, edged through a doorway and then almost fell headlong down the two flights of concrete steps.

Julius walked like a drunk. They turned a corner of the ground-floor hallway and discovered the rear door was blocked by the janitor, who was unpacking bottles of disinfectant from cardboard boxes. He didn't bother to look up.

They moved slowly towards the outer doors. Leaning heavily on his stick, Julius brushed off the girls and tried to walk unaided as they left the building, but no sooner had they stepped down onto the pavement than he swayed dangerously.

"Help me," Juliet hissed, but Ammo already had his other arm and was righting him even while she scanned the high street for the amber light of a vacant black cab.

Juliet tried to hide her face behind her father and prayed Vincent was not already in his regular place.

"Where are we?" Julius asked. He seemed to be losing his clarity.

"There's a taxi," Ammo said and waved madly.

As the vehicle stopped by the kerb, Ammo swung open the door. Juliet could not resist a maverick impulse and snatched a glance into the window of the café across the road. He was there.

She couldn't be certain, it happened much too fast, but it seemed that as she looked up, he had looked down, probably at the newspaper he always had with him.

If that was what had happened, then she had been lucky.

"Had a skinful last night, did he, love?" The taxi driver asked, eyes on his mirror as they bundled him onto the seat.

In the kitchen in the flat, Juliet had told Ammo where they would take him.

"Are you sure about this?" Ammo had said, "Because I'm not."

"It's somewhere they won't necessarily be expecting us to go. And it will only be for one or maybe two nights, while we sort things out with his brother in Margate. It's a risk, but what choice do we have?"

"I can think of a few. Take him to hospital. Turn him in. Leave him to sink or swim. Pretend you'd never met him."

"He'll be alright. I don't think it's serious. But short of moving him into our place, there's nothing else we can do."

"But do we have to do anything?" Ammo said. "What's he ever done for you?"

"He's family, I can't change that. Are you with me or not?"

Ammo folded her arms, shook her head and then allowed a little smile.

"Ah, fuck it. I'm not going to leave you this deep in your own shit, am I?"

Their destination was not distant and after a few minutes the taxi turned into Preston's Road and onto the Isle of Dogs.

The driver had given no sign of having recognised their charge as the 'gang lord' in the newspaper.

Now, as they pulled up on the overgrown track before the row of lock-up garages, Julius seemed to know where he was and managed to get out of the cab and stand upright, wobbling heavily on his stick.

Ammo opened the back gate and bolted it behind her.

In the nick of time, too, because Juliet thought she heard a diesel engine throbbing as a vehicle drove down the track and come to a stop.

Inside that house, her father seemed to be getting

heavier as they rolled him through the kitchen and into the living room, where he toppled onto the sofa like a felled tree.

The room was exactly as they had left it.

"Knew I could count on you," he breathed.

"We're not done yet," Juliet said.

She found a blanket and made him comfortable while Ammo looked out at the street from behind the net curtains.

"Now what?" Ammo asked.

When Julius had rested for an hour, Juliet asked him how he was feeling.

"Not so sharp," he said.

"Where does it hurt?"

"Stomach...dizzy...muzzy. Not fucking right."

"I'm going to call an ambulance."

"Take my chances. Not going back inside. Too many fuckers want a piece of me in there."

"You don't look good to me."

"Milk of magnesia. Bathroom cupboard."

"You weren't well before this. You need proper treatment. Let me call them."

"No! You do, I'll tell you nothing. Just let me sleep."

"Your funeral," she said, because his stupidity and bull-headedness angered her.

Downstairs, Ammo was getting her things together.

"What's going on?" Juliet asked.

"I'm off. I've done my bit. I've got the phone number; I'll call you tomorrow."

"What are you talking about? I need you. Ammo, I don't know what to do."

"What you should do is come back to Peckham with me. Poison. Guns. This is all so sick."

"I thought you would never leave me in the shit?"

"That was before I joined you in it. They call it aiding

and abetting. I don't want a criminal record. I'm not wired for this kind of thing."

"Ammo, please. I can't do this without you."

"For God's sake, Julio. Don't you feel that what you're doing is wrong? As well as fucking dangerous?"

"It's not a matter of right and wrong."

"Oh, spoken like the crime-lord's daughter."

It was like she had been slapped.

"Is that what you're saying? I'm my father's daughter?"

"No, not that. Not that at all. Look, my own father is..."

"Your father is what?"

"Listen, I understand where you're coming from. But I have a choice. If I stay with you now, the rest of my life will go one way. If I leave, it goes another way. Julio, I've made that choice."

"Well, fuck you, Ammo."

But Ammo was already turning the key in the back door.

"I'll see you when you've come to your senses," she said.

51

The morning's exertions seemed to have taken it out of him; he slept fitfully.

When his eyes opened, she encouraged him to talk.

He spoke as if he had only to reach Margate and all his troubles would be over.

"We used to go on holiday there," he said. "Just me and Mum. Lovely."

In the late afternoon, he slept for an hour or more without complaint. When he awoke, Juliet asked, "Are you sure your cousin will take you in?"

He appeared much brighter; a little sleep had done him good, she thought.

"Frank's as good as gold. He can get me treated on the QT, too. You've got the number, give him a bell. Listen now, there are some plates in the garage under the workbench. Make sure we're wearing them when we go."

She made the call to Margate, and gave the three-word message her father had told her. *Seaside break tomorrow.* There was silence at the other end. Then the voice said, *Can't do tomorrow, day after* and rang off.

She cursed—that would mean a whole day of doing nothing but looking after her father.

Opening a door to the cool spacious garage, Juliet pulled a bundle wrapped in paint sheets from under the workbench. Looking in a heavy canvas sack, Juliet found a confusing array of tools. Selecting a few at random, she took them up to Julius.

He shook his head, laughed and then explained which ones she'd need to change the plates.

When she returned to the garage and had finished that job, she approached the big, grey garage doors. They were locked and appeared to be motorised. She was going upstairs to ask him how they worked when the phone began ringing. It had to be Ammo, she'd changed her mind. She could always rely on Ammo. She returned to the hall and picked up the receiver.

When no one spoke, she said, "Hello?"

"It's me," said a voice. "Your friend from the cafe."

Swallowing, she was suddenly conscious of the accelerated beating of her heart.

"We need to talk. Please stay on the line."

He spoke in a low voice, as if careful of being overheard.

"How did you know I was here?"

"I followed you. In another taxi."

"As in, follow *that cab*?"

She could hear him smile as he agreed. Now she waited to discover how much he knew.

"It's safe to talk," he said. "The line is not bugged."

"How do you know? And how did you get this number?"

"Cop stuff."

"Oh, have you reported seeing us?"

"I said I saw Nicholson take a mini-cab but I couldn't make out the company name. I said that it disappeared up Chrisp Street, heading North."

"That's the wrong direction. Won't you get into trouble?"

"That's my specialty. And this call never happened, right?"

"Right."

"Do you mind if I ask who Nicholson is to you?"

"He's my father. But I've only just found that out."

"Okay. Well, your father didn't look in great shape when I saw you with him."

"He's not. He's raving about being poisoned by the man you were watching."

"Poisoned? Why's he not in A&E?"

"He refuses to let me call an ambulance. He won't go back to prison." She added, "Are you going to arrest us?"

"Not me. But your dad's top of our shopping list now. One of his associates has agreed to testify against him in court. He's finished."

"I see."

"But what I am going to do is offer you some advice. If you will let me."

"Go on."

"You need to call this in. You can keep yourself out of it and get him the help he sounds like he needs."

"I can't do that to him."

"Why not? If someone has tried to kill him, they'll probably try again." He paused, she waited, then he added, "I don't want you caught up in this. I'm going to see if I can get Kibble picked up before he does anything else. You need to get out of that house before my lot finds out where your dad is and do something silly, like sending in DII."

"Who?"

"The guys with guns."

He paused. There was another voice, muffled. "I have to go," he said.

"Okay, thanks. I won't forget this."

"I'll make sure you don't. Good luck."

52

Not quite awake, she thought the insistent buzzing was a helicopter overhead.

Then she thought it was someone flying one of those petrol-driven model airplanes, like Colin was supposed to have built, but Gerry had ended up flying by himself on the Common.

She lay on the sofa, slowly accustoming her eyes to the bright morning light seeping through thin, yellow curtains, and listened.

The buzzing was sometimes softer, at other times louder, as if the source of the noise was coming close to the house.

She jumped up.

Now the noise was very loud, and whatever it was seemed like it might be on the other side of the French doors.

She slipped off the couch and went softly upstairs. In the little bedroom at the back, the one painted in the colours of West Ham, was a small window. Approaching it cautiously, she peered out.

In the garden below was Christopher Kibble; he was mowing the lawn.

The police hadn't picked him up then.

Grimly fascinated, she watched as he guided the machine up and down the lawn, keeping his stripes as straight as he could, sometimes stopping to empty a box of cuttings onto a pile by the fence behind the shed.

Oh, God, she thought.

If Kibble has keys to the side gate, he could have a key to the house, too.

If he had really tried to kill Julius, then there was no saying what he would do to him if he found him here, or what he might try to do to her.

With her hand placed over his mouth, she tried to wake Julius, but he was dead to the world. A bottle of scotch, three parts empty, lay by the bed.

She swallowed her panic and made a plan. She would slip out the front door and phone Vincent from the call-box down the street. With luck, they would have cars there before Kibble had even looked upstairs, if that was what he was going to do.

She watched as he completed the lawn and unplugged the lead from a rubber-clad socket in the wall. She wouldn't go until she was sure he was not intending to enter the house.

He took his time as he wound up the cable, opened the door of the garden shed and hung the machine on a hook inside.

Seemingly satisfied, he now took a pair of secateurs and addressed himself to plantings in the border, humming softly as he snipped off unproductive stems and added these to the pile of clippings. When he had finished, he went into the shed again and came out minus the secateurs, but gripping what looked like a catalogue of some kind.

He closed the shed door, snapped shut the padlock and gave it a sharp tug. For a moment, he seemed at a loss. Then he delved into a pocket, found a set of keys and walked towards the back gate. She heard a car start, and after a moment or two, drive away.

There was no point now in calling Vincent, she decided. Kibble probably came to cut the lawn once a fortnight, something like that. It was just unlucky that she happened to be there today.

She told herself she shouldn't be surprised by his odd behaviour, acting as if he still worked for Julius was just the way he was.

Even so, she would make damn sure that they left for Margate first thing the next morning.

The rest of the afternoon was spent finishing Julius's packing and wiping fingerprints from every surface. He wasn't well again and seemed weaker, though that might be the effect of his hangover.

The sun was disappearing behind the old sugar mill across the waste ground that backed onto the house when she heard the noisy click of the side-gate latch.

From the upstairs window, she saw Kibble again.

He was dragging a large plastic bin across the garden to the flagstones outside the shed. Positioning it to his liking, he opened the shed door and took out a fork and began to pitch the pile of cuttings into the bin.

When he had finished, he tipped his head at the dusky sky, checked his watch and then looked about the garden, as if satisfying himself that he could do no more until daylight. His hand on the side-gate latch, he was looking like he was about to leave again, when he stopped, turned and walked up the path towards the kitchen window.

Juliet was struck by a chilling thought. Her dirty dishes were on the side and her pan had been left unwashed in the sink. She thought she might be sick.

For a moment, there was no sound.

Then the latch on the side-gate clicked again, and she heard footsteps walking away from the house.

She exhaled quietly, hearing the tinny sound of a car-door opening and then closing again. She heard no noise of an engine starting.

Another imponderable silence.

Now she registered his shoes retracing their steps up the path and the kitchen door opening and softly closing again.

She could hear him moving about below her, perhaps looking for signs that might tell him who had entered the place and whether they were still under that roof.

Then he started to mount the stairs, slowly, one by one.

She hid behind the door in the little bedroom at the end of the landing and waited. Now, she could hear him breathing, close by, on the landing.

A door opened, the second bedroom. The bathroom. The door she was crouching behind inched open.

She closed her eyes and froze.

All she was aware of was the beating of her heart.

Silence.

And then she heard his distinctive nasal tones emanating from the direction of Julius's room. She got up and silently made her way down the landing.

At the door of Julius's bedroom, she stopped and listened.

"You're awake, are you? How are you this evening? You look a little peaky, if you don't mind me saying. Something you ate, I shouldn't wonder. You're a cheeky one, hiding here, aren't you? To tell the truth, had positions been reversed, it might not have been the place I should have chosen. What am I saying? Our positions *are* reversed, you see that, don't you?"

"What do you want, Carrot?" She heard Julius's voice, weakened, punch-drunk.

"Ah, there you have it. You should have turned your mind to that a long time ago, if you don't mind me saying so. You should have trusted me, looked after me. I would have repaid that trust. You never knew where you were with Gerry Hobson, did you? Too clever by half, that was his trouble. And all the time, he was sliding himself slowly into your shoes. I was there, ready to support you as he should have supported you. We'd have been unstoppable, you and I. But you passed me over, time and again. And now look where it's got you."

Julius sat up in bed, pulled aside the bedclothes, and put on his glasses.

"What are you wearing? Have I interrupted your washing up?"

"Rubber gloves are a good choice when you don't want to leave fingerprints."

"And what's that? Is that my fucking gun?"

"I'm surprised at how heavy it is. You see them waved about in the films and you never think they might be heavy, do you?"

"What you going to do with it? Start a race?"

"Dry. That's your kind of humour. If ever I tell anyone about this, I will say that you were game to the last."

"So, you're going to kill me."

"We both know that one of us must go the way of all flesh. You're only annoyed it won't be me, as I'm sure you intended."

"I'd have taught you some fucking manners, Carrot. Not killed you."

"Ah, you say that now, don't you? When I have the upper hand, when I hold all the aces. When I hold the gun."

"Fuck off, Carrot. That's a starting pistol."

"La! That's a good one, a very sharp one. But you're

having me on, I think. Shall I fire it, and we can both find out?"

"You'll just wake the neighbours. Take a butchers at the ammunition. You'll see."

"I think I should just shoot you now."

"Don't be stupid. Next doors know who I am. They hear a bang; this place will be overrun with Old Bill."

"I'll have vanished before they get here. And it's not me they'll be blaming for this."

"What do you mean?"

"You can come in now, Miss. Don't be shy."

For a second, she could see herself flying down the stairs, tearing out into the street, screaming for help. But then she saw the bullet ripping into her back as it threw her down the staircase, and slowly, she opened the bedroom door.

"Juliet, there you are. Most fortunate you being here, I must say. Propitious, that's the word. What will they make of it, I wonder? Let's see; finding her father drunk and waving a gun, daughter tries to wrest it from him, the gun goes off, overcome with guilt and grief, daughter puts an end to her own life. Or something cut from that cloth."

"That's not going to happen, Carrot."

"Why not?"

"I'm telling you, look at the ammo."

"I'll humour you then. Stay there while I take a peek. How do I open this thing?"

"Give it here."

"You're a sly one, aren't you? I've got it. Here it is."

"Now, how do I tell if this one is a blank?"

He moved a bullet into the stripe of light that fell across the bed and illuminated Juliet.

In that moment, Julius made a violent lunge for the

weapon, but his starting position had doomed the attempt from the start.

Carrot shook him off and struck him in the face with the butt of the gun, bloodying his forehead and cracking a spectacle lens.

As Julius fell back against the headboard, he snapped shut the barrel of the revolver.

Backing away, he levelled the weapon at Julius and pulled back the hammer, which clicked into the firing position.

Julius said, "I'm not going to be killed by some cunt wearing a pair of Marigolds."

He was looking at something over Carrot's shoulder.

The man with the gun turned, but too late to stop the heavy wrench that was already describing an arc as it flashed in the streetlight and made violent, crushing contact with his left temple.

He moaned, staggered, reeled, then collapsed, dragging Juliet down with him.

53

"I can't breathe."

But Julius was already there, dragging the lumpen weight from her. She got to her feet, shaking. Julius was on his knees, rolling the man onto his back. He lit a match and pulled open his eyelids.

"Fuck this," he said.

"We should tie him up."

Julius stared into unseeing pupils.

"There won't be any need for that."

"What? Oh, no, no..."

"It's all right."

"What have I done?"

"You've saved a life."

"What?"

"You saved my life."

"I didn't mean to kill him. But he...Oh, God."

"You saved my life. He was going to kill me."

She stood up and looked at what she had done.

"It was real? The gun?" she breathed.

"If you hadn't whacked him, I'd be lying there with a hole in my head the size of a golf ball."

"I killed him."

The shaking became worse.

"You did what anyone else would have done. Any right-thinking person."

"I just wanted to stop him." She began gulping for air.

"You don't know your own strength, do you?"

She was vaguely aware of Julius bending, taking hold of the man by his heels and beginning to drag him from the room.

She heard his body smoothing the carpet, his head bumping against the doorframe. She found it difficult to breathe and barely noticed Julius re-entering the room.

"They should bottle adrenaline," he said. "I've shoved him under the bed in the spare room. We'll wrap him in bin bags and hump him into the boot of the car in the morning. I've bent his legs in case he's too stiff by then. Keep the faith; I need to do something about my head."

He went to the bathroom.

Still gulping her breaths, she began to cry, softly at first, but soon the crying became louder. Julius returned and told her to hush, remember the neighbours. When she wouldn't or couldn't stop the streaming tears, he lifted her quivering form from the chair and carried her to the bed, where he sat himself up against the headboard and pulled her close into him.

She didn't try to stop him; there was nothing left in her to do that.

He stroked her hair. "There," he said. "Everything's going to be all right. I promise you."

She didn't know what she was doing when she slipped her arms around his neck. She cried until she had no more tears left and exhausted, she fell asleep.

It was still dark when she awoke with a start.

Something was wrong; her whole body was alive to it. And then the awful events of however long ago crowded in on her.

The man in whose arms she was entangled slept soundly. She shook him off and sat up, sickened as she tried to distract herself from the dreadful realisation which towered above her like a breaking tsunami.

She was familiar with it. It had been there when she left Colin on the floor of her room. *I have killed someone.*

But though she hadn't recognised it at the time, there had then been a small, fluttering sylph of doubt. Now, there was none.

Weaving through her tangle of terrible thoughts was something else, the awareness of a pungent smell. Was someone burning toast? A sudden brilliance beyond the window made her sit up.

It flashed upon her that the house was on fire.

Now she could hear crackling and an occasional whooshing sound like air being released.

The smell of smoke grew stronger.

Leaping up, she crossed quickly to the window, peered out.

The larch cladding around the living-room windows was blazing fiercely.

Someone ran out from the house across the road.

She tried to wake her father, who moaned softly.

Shouting at him, beating on his chest, she slapped his face until he came round and opened his eyes, saying slowly, "You half killed me..."

"The house is on fire," she said. "We have to get out."

She grabbed his car keys and peered below.

"How bad is it?" he said.

Bad, she thought. At the bottom of the stairs she could

see thick, black smoke seeping out from under the living room door and beginning to well up the staircase.

"Now!" she screamed at him.

She pulled, dragged, coaxed and manoeuvred him towards the head of the stairs.

"Don't breathe," she said.

She leaned him against the stair rail and they went down into what was fast becoming a boiling hell below.

The heat in the hallway was intense, but the living-room door was still holding back the flames gorging on whatever was in there with a ferocious appetite.

The curtains and the nets would have gone up, the sofa too; the air would be lethal.

Faces covered, they felt their way to the kitchen just as a blast of coral flame burst through the breached living-room door.

The back door was already burning as they opened the other door and fell into the garage, as yet untouched by the fire. Gulping air, she pushed him towards the car.

They got in and closed the doors.

He started the car and turned on the headlights.

"That box on the wall. Operates the door."

She got out and toggled a switch.

"It's not working."

"Powers gone. Try and open it manually."

"Help me, then."

They took one end each and tried to raise the door.

"It's fucked," Julius said.

"What are we going to do?"

"Get in the car and close that window. Fucking Gerry Hobson."

"What do you mean?"

"I mean, this has got his dabs all over it."

She got in, wondering how long the flimsy frame of the car would postpone their incineration or suffocation. She could hear the fire rampaging through the rooms above, and smell the smoke. The distant two-tone sirens sounded like heralds of disaster.

54

It had been so much easier than he'd imagined.

He saw no one as he approached the house in dark clothes and deftly prised open a side window. Slipping silently into the house, he opened the first can of fuel and emptied it over the carpet and the curtains, before dousing the furniture.

The second can of petrol can he applied to the exterior wooden cladding at the back, and then, afforded concealment by tall hedging, he threw the last of it upon the woodwork beneath the windows and around the door at the front.

Laying a drip-trail across the dry lawn to the house, he opened the back gate and laid the empty cans in the boot of his car. Setting light to a fuel-soaked rag, he dropped it on the lawn, where it zipped towards the back of the house.

Starting his car as flames licked their way up the clapboard, they would be around the front and through the window by the time he'd reached the bottom of the track. He had no doubt the place would be effectively destroyed before the fire engines got there.

Result.

Notting Hill had been so much more difficult. It takes a real expert to burn a house without killing a lot of people living inside it, he thought.

That's for Colin, he said aloud as he directed the Capri through Tower Hamlets in the direction of Victoria Park.

At Stratford, Gerry stopped under a tower of crushed cars and lobbed the three empty jerry-cans over a fence and into a scrapyard, setting its dogs barking. He took a moment to light a cigarette before getting back in the car and driving at an unimpeachable speed towards the A12.

Glancing in the rear-view mirror, the anger trapped inside came out.

"Fuck you, Julius Nicholson, you're history, mate."

Fumbling a cassette into the player, he twisted the volume and slapped the wheel in time to *Satisfaction*.

He could see a rosy future with Tom Adams. Yes, there were flies in the ointment; there always were. Take Derek Markham. Markham plainly saw Gerry as a threat to his relationship with Adams. Well, he would just have to be dealt with, firmly but fairly, the same way Julius thought he had dealt with him.

The business he was getting into with Adams was too specialised, too delicate, and hell yes, too damn lucrative for some clod like Markham.

Meeting with the art expert at his plush gaff had left him with the feeling that this was a new world he wanted to get into, one in which a man could get rich very quickly.

He parked the Capri on the road outside his house and opened the front door in time to see Maureen tripping down the stairs to answer the phone.

"Who's that at this time?" she asked. "And where have you been? It's six-thirty in the morning."

She listened and then handed the receiver to Gerry. "It's for you."

Taking the phone, he turned his head away, wanting privacy.

"Fleming. Have you seen my daughter?"

"Who?"

"Amelia. She lived with your daughter."

"What? I don't have a daughter."

"The girl you raised and brought up for nineteen years."

"Juliet? I don't know where she is. She left us months ago. You didn't say you knew her?"

"Okay, okay. Sorry if I got you up. It's just that Amelia stayed with us last night, after some sort of blow-up with Juliet. I must have said the wrong thing because the next thing I knew, she was out of the door. I've called her flat, had some very annoyed people banging on her door for me, but she's not there. I thought there was an outside chance she was with you."

"I'm sorry I can't help you. But while you're here, I'd like to speak to you about that picture you got us a line on. You're sure the alarms will be down before we go in?"

"Not on the phone, man! What are you thinking of? That can wait. I'm worried about my daughter. You have absolutely no idea at all where she may be? Don't you care?"

"Of course I do. But like I say, I just can't help you."

"Are you certain of that? From what I gathered lately, she and Juliet were seeing a bit of our friend Julius Nicholson. Her real father, as I understand?"

"Yes."

"I can't get hold of Nicholson, though I was approached by someone called Leslie Shipham who tried to sell me information about him. I've heard that Nicholson is lying low in his house on the Isle of Dogs, of all places. Shipham told me that he saw two girls outside the place and thought he recognised Amelia."

"How does he know her?"

"He'd been watching that place on the King's Road for our mutual friend."

"Are you telling me that Juliet was at Nicholson's house? When?"

"I can't precisely say."

"Try, please."

"Very recently."

"I have to go," he said.

Gerry paled, found himself gulping for air as he snatched up his car keys.

"What's going on?" Maureen called from the kitchen, but the car was already pulling out into the light morning traffic, accelerating away and heading towards the A12 for London.

55

"Belt up and hang on."

"What are you going to do?" Juliet looked at her father.

He revved the car, filling the closed space with carbon dioxide. Reaching down, he selected Drive.

"Ready?"

"Do it," she said.

He let go of the handbrake; she saw the garage doors fly towards them, felt the brutal shock of the impact throwing her against her seat belt.

The car was still trying to take itself forward, straining against the grey metal doors, which were badly crushed but held.

Julius swore, reversed as far as the garage allowed, and rammed the stick into Drive again. Once more, he released the handbrake.

The impact this time was more violent; the seatbelt cut into her, only just saving her from connecting forcibly with the windscreen.

"It's going," he said.

Again, he threw the car into reverse. Shooting back, it smashed its taillights against the rear wall. Julius was breathing hard. The garage now filled with smoke from the exhaust.

"This time," he gasped just before he released the brakes. Juliet heard the sirens again, now much louder.

The doors were hanging off their rails at an unusual angle. Through the gap between the obstructing metal and the outside world, she could see the small crowd gathering by the road, and the drawing sky over the river.

"Get your head down," her father said.

Once more, the car reversed, stopped, and then suddenly leapt noisily towards the doors and the gap which might or might not be large enough to allow it through.

There was another jarring impact, which came with a long, noisy scraping and screeching of rending metal as the Jaguar threw aside the last of the doors and with one last effort emerged into the early morning.

He didn't stop.

People scattered as he slung the car onto the road, his sweating face lit blue by the fire engine he almost collided with.

Glancing behind her, Juliet saw the house, which was fast becoming a bonfire of larch and brick.

"Road map."

"In the house."

"Fuck's sake."

"Blackwall Tunnel, A2 all the way to Margate."

"Good girl. First stop, a scrapyard I know at Stratford. We'll need to swap motors. There's a man there who'll sort us out. We can do this."

But rounding the corner at the bottom of the incline, the Jaguar almost ploughed into one of two squad-cars parked across the road.

Dropping the selector into neutral, Julius activated the handbrake and wrenched the wheel full circle, spinning the car in the direction of the house and knocking Juliet's head hard against the doorframe.

"Where are we going?"

"You'll see."

Almost immediately, he turned the car sharply onto the track beside the house.

Bumping over an unmade road, he drove rapidly past the lockups at the rear of his house, which now looked like the dockside warehouses he'd seen ablaze in the war.

At the end of the track was a flimsy wire gate, marking another plot of land for sale.

He stopped, revved the engine and stamped on the accelerator. Juliet was thrown back as the gate flew open and the car leapt onto a large patch of wasteland, jolting over hardcore and swerving to avoid great lengths of rust-eaten piping and brick foundations.

Behind them the police cars, sirens blaring, remained in pursuit.

"Don't let them see your face," he said.

Blue lights flashed in her vanity mirror.

"We're not going to lose them here, are we?"

"Once we get to the road on the other side, I can lead them a dance through the streets I knew as a kid. But you're not coming with me."

"What?"

"Not a chance. When we turn this corner, I want you out. Fast, and keep your head down 'til they're gone."

"You won't get to Margate without me."

"We'll see. Go home. And don't worry. There won't be enough left of Carrot for a murder charge. And if there is, it's me they'll want. Just go home, get on with your life."

Through the cracked windscreen, she saw spoiled land which must have been home to some docklands industry, but now only crumbling walls, some roofless shells and foundations remained. The Jaguar struggled to make headway on a road of broken bricks.

Between two abandoned buildings was a narrow, concrete section which allowed Julius to increase his speed and put some distance between the car and its pursuer. Juliet turned to her father, who looked as broken and abandoned as the world around him.

"I can't leave you here."

"I'll throw you out if I have to. Take off your seat belt."

She did as she was told. He slowed the car, turned between the remnants of two more old buildings.

"Open the door. Do it!"

She pulled the catch, and the door opened.

"Now, go!"

A big hand shoved her forcefully. She fell from the car, hit the ground hard and rolled.

She just had time to pick herself up and take cover behind a great pile of masonry before the police car flashed past her.

Through broken brickwork, she watched the damaged Jaguar, all but lost in a cloud of red dust, reaching the far side of the wasteland.

Her shoulder hurt, and her head was bruised.

She was about to get up when she heard another car approaching, fast. She waited until that too had flown by, this one close enough to deafen her with the noise of its sirens. Now she rose and saw Julius turning onto the road, saw the Jag speeding down the street, the two police cars not far behind.

He seemed to be going impossibly fast for such a narrow road. Then he turned noisily onto another road and was lost to sight.

She heard the car accelerate and then there was a

sudden loud noise, not quite an explosion, more like a heavy, violent impact.

She saw the police cars slow down as they turned onto the road and they too were lost to view. Their sirens went on a little longer and then stopped.

She was aware of a strange silence.

Struggling to her feet, she dusted off the worst of the debris that covered her and found a path leading her off the wasteland.

56

Gerry made good time until he got to Brentwood, where traffic was gridlocked. Police and ambulance crews were dealing with a collision between an articulated lorry and a hatchback.

By the time he smoked a cigarette, the traffic had begun to move again.

He didn't bother craning to peer at the small car crumpled like a Coke tin; he was thinking of Juliet. He'd thought of nothing but her all the way. It was unthinkable that she'd been in that house when he'd torched it, or that her friend had probably been in there with her.

Why hadn't he made bloody *sure* the place was unoccupied, as he'd believed it to be?

He sifted through his memories of her and almost laughed when he recalled her smiling at him while he pushed an unsmiling Colin on a swing.

He'd always thought she was a good kid. He had liked her, even if he never showed it.

Perhaps, he *had* loved her in his way. He remembered the packet of fags she bought him wrapped up with a birthday ribbon while she was still at school. She'd stood there, half-expecting him to smile or thank her, but he'd just grunted. She was a good, sweet and funny little girl. Why couldn't he have been nice to her?

Yes, she'd had her little upsets, but they all did when they got to their teens. He pondered all this as the A12 overleapt the M25. Could they actually have been closer than he liked to admit to himself?

Vaughan had been on the money when he called her his daughter, because Julius Nicholson had not earned that right.

But sweet Jesus, neither had he, that much was starkly clear now. She might be safe in her room now, had he taken the interest in her that a father should.

When had it all gone wrong? When he was still sour about Julius's repudiation of him as a partner, a friend, a declared lover? When to even think of Julius left a repugnant, filthy taste in his mouth, and he wanted nothing to do with him or the child he had left on his doorstep?

Too late now to realise you were her father, he thought bitterly. You stupid, stupid prick.

Parking down the road, he approached on foot, a criminal returning to the scene of the crime. Turning the corner, what he saw smacked him in the face.

The smouldering ruin looked like the houses he'd played in after the Blitz. Three of the walls were still standing, but the roof had gone. Through blackened window-frames, he could see charred uprights and fallen roof beams. Black smoke was rising from the ashes, and the smell of whatever had burned there lingered in the air.

Dear God, he prayed, let no one have been in that house, not even Julius Nicholson.

As a casual onlooker, he tried to watch dispassionately while firemen cleared up and policemen talked to neighbours.

"Here, mate," he said to a man staring at an open notebook. "What's going on? Anyone hurt?"

The man turned to him, pleased to be able to relay what he'd seen.

"They found a body. In Julius Nicholson's house. In a bit of a state, as you might imagine." He extended his hand. "Ian Gale, *Island Argus*. Are you acquainted with the people here?"

For a moment, he thought he might fall.

"You alright?" the man said.

He forced himself to respond. "Bit of a night. Whose was it, do you think—the body?"

"Anyone's guess. Not the owner's, though. Julius Nicholson scarpered and smashed his motor into a concrete wall. Went off in an ambulance. Did you know him, Nicholson?"

Gerry shook his head and turned away.

With every difficult step towards his car, he told himself that Juliet was dead, that *his daughter* was dead, and he had murdered her.

Some eight miles south of where Gerry was fumbling with his keys, Juliet was paying off a taxi driver outside her flat in Peckham.

She had walked off the Island, found a cashpoint and flagged down a black cab. The cabbie had looked at her like she was from Mars and demanded to see her money before he switched off his light.

When the cab stopped outside their house, Juliet glanced up and saw Ammo in the upstairs window and wondered at the alarmed expression shaping her face.

Ammo disappeared, presumably was on her way down the stairs.

In front of the house, everything looked normal, as if she had never gone away and experienced everything that she had. The Australians who shared the ground floor, all tanned bodies and beads, were laughing and joking as they tried to fix the campervan that had stood where it was for weeks.

Nearby, some boys from across the street had set down a huge ghetto-blaster and had begun performing acrobatics on the pavement. One of the boys saw Juliet coming towards the house. He ceased his gyrating and looked.

The Australians looked, too.

She was too tired to wonder why she might suddenly be so fascinating. The boys stood aside to let her pass. The Australians were silent for once. Now she saw Ammo at the door, and she was frowning.

Ammo was saying something about having gone to look for her. She followed her mutely up the stairs, down the hallway and into the flat. The unwieldy cheese plant, the second-hand records, the colourful spines of Ammo's tatty books and the cheap cane blinds seemed like artefacts from someone else's life. She stood in silence for a moment, trying to make sense of a world in which no one was pointing a gun or setting a house aflame or falling dead at her feet.

"Why were they staring at me?"

"Take a look in the mirror."

When she turned and looked in the glass, a stranger stared back.

Her matted hair was now white with chalk or plaster dust. She had grazed her face when she rolled out of the car. Blood had run down her white shirt, and there were large spots of it on her grubby skirt—that too had once been white. Her cheeks were bruised, her eyes were red, her stockings were torn, her boots were scuffed and filthy.

Ammo exhaled loudly.

"Do you want to tell me about it?"

She looked at herself a moment longer, then fell back into the armchair they'd found outside a pub one night. For a moment, she could say nothing.

"No. I don't think so," she said at last. "Not just yet. Maybe not at all. I need a bath and some sleep. We can talk later."

For an hour or more, she was kept from sleep by Christopher Kibble, the man whose life she had taken. Feeling again the cold, hard wrench in her hand, she thought she was going to be sick.

She succumbed to sleep only after she had repeatedly reminded herself that killing him had saved her father's life and her own. She slept patchily through the remains of day and into the night and woke at the same time she had smelled the fire.

Her father, Julius, she saw him driving off alone across the dusty landscape, heard again the heart-stopping *wham* and the police cars braking and turning off their sirens.

The questions piled up.

Was it possible that he had survived, despite the speed of the collision and his failing health? She was vaguely surprised to find herself hoping he had.

What would have happened if he had gotten safely to Margate and then to Spain? Would she have continued to see him and help him as he'd said he wanted her to? Could she have lived that different life?

She heard Ammo getting up from her bed in the other

room. She padded into her room in her Daffy Duck nightshirt and slippers.

"Hard to sleep with you groaning away in there."

Juliet clicked on her bedside light, bringing into being her messy dressing table, overspilling chest of drawers and the teddy bear she had bought in a junk shop to replace Marvin. She had the strangest feeling of wanting to ask if this was where she lived.

"Do you have a cigarette?" she asked.

"I've given up."

"Again?"

Ammo was now sitting on her bed and put her hand on Juliet's forehead.

"Are you okay?"

"Not sure. I'll have to think about that one."

"You need to rest. I told Chas you had been struck down by a vicious fever."

"It feels like it."

"Look, I have to go in today; we're short-staffed. But there's half a chicken I nicked from home in the fridge, and I won't be late. Will you be alright?"

"Of course I will."

"That's good."

"Don't worry. I'm fine."

Ammo looked at her doubtfully.

"So," she said, "did you find out who you are, at last?"

Juliet took a moment.

"I know more than I did."

"Well, that's something. Is it over now?"

"I don't know."

"It needs to be, hen," Ammo said.

While Ammo put the kettle on, Juliet tried to formulate an answer to that question. Was it over? Even assuming she wasn't implicated in the death of Christopher Kibble, she would still have to find out what had happened to her father.

And then there was the man who had played her father's part, though very badly, all these years. She'd have no peace until she found out why Gerry Hobson had set the fire that had so nearly killed her. Julius had been certain it was him.

Above all, perhaps, she needed to know if she was the same person she had been before she left Colin for dead, before she hardened herself on the streets, before she had killed a man.

They drank tea and talked, Ammo avoiding anything to do with Juliet's father. Instead, she talked about the unrest at PINZ, following Chas's announcement that he was looking for someone to buy the shop as a going concern, but failing that, he'd be selling up.

She needed time to think—lots of time.

One thing she could do this morning was to buy a newspaper and see if there was anything in it about Julius Nicholson.

If by some miracle he was alive, she would see him, she decided, in hospital, in prison, it didn't matter. She wasn't ready to give up on her mother just yet. Closing her eyes, she drifted off.

Fragments of her experiences floated before her: Colin bleeding out on the floor; freezing nights on hard ground; Arthur, the drunks battering that poor old man and, of course, her father. She tried to bring Gerry into focus as well. The fire, and then Larry Hughes—what had happened to him?

She must have slept again because it was fully light when she opened her eyes. Someone was rattling a key in the lock. She thought she had heard Ammo leaving for work, calling from the hallway, "I'll see youse tonight, then," and the sound of her heavy boots on the stairs but now here she was, bursting back in, dressed to provoke in ripped black jeans and her *Stonewall* tee-shirt.

"There's a guy downstairs who says he wants to see you?"

"Who is it?"

Ammo shrugged.

"I've never seen him before. Dresses like a twat but quite nice-looking, I suppose. He told me to tell you, it's Vincent."

She sat up, hearing his footsteps on the stairs.

ALSO BY ROSS GILFILLAN:

In Leicester Fields

The Snake Oil Dickens Man

The Edge of the Crowd

Losing It

Crime and Punishment in Victorian London

Printed in Dunstable, United Kingdom

67256943R00201